The Silver Collar

His face was so close now it was going out of focus. Still dazed, Iris closed her eyes.

And Alfie kissed her.

His lips were hot and familiar, slightly urgent. His mouth opened up wider and he tasted like the sating of a craving she hadn't previously been aware of. He shifted his body so he was covering her. Big, long, borne on his thick arms. 'Iris,' he said. He said it right into her open mouth and his voice was heavy with desire. God, it was all so familiar. It felt like a dream. But then his mouth was suddenly harder, firmer on hers. Greedy. He'd got a hand in her hair, holding her head so he could force his tongue deeper into her mouth. She couldn't help herself. She took it. She wanted it. She wanted Alfie more than she could believe. These weren't the sweet youthful kisses they had shared eleven years ago. This was different. Spiked by pain and loss and longing. Viscous and bruising, Alfie was biting her bottom lip, forcing her mouth to open wider. She could feel his chest through her shirt. He was so hard, hot and smooth. Iris was light-headed with it.

The Silver Collar
Mathilde Madden

BLACK LACE

First published in 2007 by
Black Lace
Thames Wharf Studios
Rainville Rd
London W6 9HA

Copyright © Mathilde Madden 2007

The right of Mathilde Madden to be identified as the Author of the
Work has been asserted in accordance with the Copyright, Designs
and Patents Act 1988.

A catalogue record for this book is available from the British Library.

www.black-lace-books.com

http://lustbites.blogspot.com/

Typeset by SetSystems Ltd, Saffron Walden, Essex

Printed and bound in Great Britain by CPI Bookmarque,
Croydon, CR0 4TD

The paper used in this book is a natural, recyclable product made
from wood grown in sustainable forests. The manufacturing process
conforms to the regulations of the country of origin.

ISBN 978 0 352 34141 9

Distributed in the USA by Holtzbrinck Publishers, LLC, 175 Fifth Avenue,
New York, NY 10010, USA

1

Saturday 1 June 1996

'Iris, when you asked if I'd help out on a saucy photo shoot involving you and your twin this wasn't what I had in mind.'

Iris smirked. 'Yeah, yeah, stop complaining and get your clothes off.'

Smiling, Alfie took off his jacket – brown leather, nicely beaten up – and held it out. Iris took it and watched while he started to unbutton his shirt. He wore that particular shirt – or one like it – a lot. It was pale blue. The material was a kind of textured cotton, which Iris knew was unbelievably soft and delicious to touch. All her memories were woven into that fabric. Usually this shade of blue against his skin made it look beautiful – sweet as caramel. But tonight, he was more than just beautiful. Beyond. It was dark, the moon was out, and the skin Alfie was revealing – as he popped button after button – shimmered. Like magic.

Alfie shivered. 'Why am I doing this, again?'

''Cause you're a nice guy.'

'Oh, am I now. Seriously, it's cold out here. Why am I doing this? Why am I stripping off in a park in the middle of the night?' He'd got all the buttons undone now and he let the shirt fall off his shoulders and bunch at his elbows. Iris glanced away for a moment and when she looked back, he was smirking. 'Well?'

'"Well" what?'

'Aren't you listening to me? What could be distracting you? Could it possibly be my half-naked self? I said, "why am I doing this?"'

'You're doing this because I asked you nicely. And Matt's my twin, which did funny stuff to your perverted brain.'

'When you told me that I did think you meant, like, a girl twin.'

'I know.' Iris smiled, looking at him. She couldn't stop looking at him. 'Well, you have the right kind of look for his photographs. I mean, your arms, for example, you have nice arms.' Iris reached out and nearly touched his bicep, but stopped before her fingers made contact. She noticed Alfie looking at her hand hovering in mid-air. Iris pulled it away.

'You're wrong,' Alfie said quietly. 'Those are all reasons, but they aren't the real reason why I'm doing this. And you know that.'

Iris held his gaze.

From beyond the trees, Matt shouted, 'Are you done yet? I'm all set up here.'

Alfie shouted back, 'Is it just shirtless? You don't want me to take my jeans off?' He looked Iris right in the eye as he spoke, so it felt as if he was asking her how naked he should be.

Matt shouted back, 'Nah. Keep them on for now.'

'OK, I'll just be a minute.'

Alfie always wore a silver ring on the little finger of his left hand. It used to be his grandmother's eternity ring. When he brought his hand up and touched Iris's cheek, the ring glittered in the moonlight. 'I'm doing this for you, Iris, because you wanted me to.'

Iris nodded.

'And I'm doing it because it means I get to spend time with you. I wanted to talk to you. Alone.'

When he said that, Iris pulled away from his hand, 'Alfie . . .'

'Iris, I'm sorry, please, can't we give it another go? You and me, we were really something together. I know I messed up. I know I messed up really, really badly. I wish I could say that I didn't know what I was doing or that it was a moment of madness. But it wasn't. It was a moment of stupidity. But, Iris, I am so, so sorry and if I could turn back time or something, God, but ... Please, Iris, give me one more chance and I promise I will never, ever do anything to hurt you again. I'll do whatever you want. I'll make it up to you every single day.'

Iris dropped her gaze and looked down at the ground. It was wetland out here – a flood plain. The ground was really boggy and her shoes were filthy.

'Please, Iris. You did say you liked my arms.'

Iris swallowed. 'OK,' she said, quietly.

'Yes! God. Thank you.' Alfie darted forwards – a sudden hurricane of desire. He whirled Iris around so she was pressed up against a tree, the bark patterning her skin through her thin coat. His mouth was so tight, so hard on hers. His big bare chest was hot and smooth even through her clothes. Her feet were off the ground.

Her answering passion was every bit as strong, every bit as relieved. She ran her hands over the back of his head and twisted her fingers in his hair in a way that always used to make him gasp and cry out in bed.

Then – too soon – a voice right beside them said, 'For goodness sake, are the model and the costume girl making out already? Put her down, Alfie.'

Iris opened one eye. Matt was all head cocked, arms crossed, foot a tapping.

She really didn't care.

A little later Matt had Alfie posed sprawled across a fallen tree trunk. He was on his back. He'd got his eyes closed and one hand resting on his flat stomach. Matt was trying to persuade him to undo the first couple of buttons of his jeans so he could slip his hand inside and touch himself a little.

Alfie opened one eye. 'What sort of photos are these?'

'It's art, darling,' said Matt. 'Classy. Black and white.'

'Oh, go on, Alfie,' Iris called. She'd climbed up a tree a little way away and was nestled in its branches, watching.

Basking in her own happy little glow. She caught Alfie's eye. 'Just touch it, model boy,' she shouted.

'Not you too,' Alfie called, tipping his head back to look up at her. 'Is this a perversion that runs in the family, then?'

Iris shouted back an affirmative and Alfie laughed. She and Matt had talked about the plans for this shoot. She knew a few things that Alfie didn't yet. Such as Matt's prop bag containing oil and ropes and a blindfold. Matt had shown her a picture of a beautiful half-naked man tied to a tree in the moonlight, which he referred to as 'inspiration'. As she thought about Matt recreating that image with Alfie, she squirmed a little against the bark. God, he looked amazing down there. The fallen tree, his skin, the moonlight on him. Alfie. His eyes were still on hers. They were both still laughing.

And then she looked over at Matt. And she saw it. A dark shape in the trees. Huge. Moving. Prowling through the long grass and bushes behind him. Some kind of animal.

She screamed. Then they all screamed.

There was a noise as it attacked. A growl. A snarl. A roar. The place where Matt had been standing was shadowy. Too dark. Hidden by trees. Iris couldn't see. But she could hear. And all she could hear was Matt screaming.

Then there was a flash. Matt's camera. Suddenly Iris saw everything. A frozen image. Jaws. Claws. Fur. Blood and bone. Matt's face hardly a face at all.

And then the light was gone and Iris couldn't see anything at all.

Noises. The creature was running away through the park, startled, dragging something: Matt.

'Stay there. Don't come down. Stay up there.' It was Alfie shouting.

'Alfie! No!' Iris's voice sounded strange.

Alfie was already running away from her in the direction the creature had taken Matt. 'Stay there,' he shouted again.

'What are you going to do?'

Alfie didn't respond and didn't look back. Iris had no intention of staying in the tree and started to climb down. As she climbed, she peered into the dark, trying to see what was happening. But Alfie had disappeared into darkness. She could hear him shouting though. And some screaming. Matt screaming. And then Alfie. And then nothing.

As soon as she got both feet on the ground, she saw Alfie running back towards her.

He grabbed her wrist as he ran, pulling her along behind him, heading out of the park and away from where the creature had gone with Matt. She only just managed to keep her footing as he yanked her over the pitted ground.

'What about Matt?'

Alfie didn't stop moving, but he sort of half turned so he was running sideways and part-way looking at her. 'It's just ... He's ...'

Iris tried to look in the direction the animal had dragged Matt. 'Don't,' Alfie shouted, 'don't look back.'

Iris turned. Alfie had his back to her, running and dragging her with him. It was then that Iris saw that his naked left shoulder was covered in blood.

With Alfie's big hand tight on her wrist, Iris ran with him through the park. Eventually they hit the quiet little residential street that led from the park up to Marston Road. It was late evening. The street was quiet. Alfie leant up against a street light for support, bent double, breathing hard. 'Iris ...'

In the circle of orange light, Iris could see him properly.

The wound on his shoulder was more than a tear. There was a gap there. A missing hunk of his flesh. The raw meat of his shoulder was glinting orange and red under the street lamp. His back was covered in blood now.

A huge chunk of his flesh was actually gone. Bitten away.

Alfie fell right down onto the sodium-lit pavement, half unconscious.

Eleven Years Later

2

It was nearly dark. Sitting in the car park was an old army truck – the sort with a khaki canvas roof arching over it. Sat inside were three lean, mean, werewolf-killing machines. Iris's team – the Reds, named for their dark-red fatigues – ready for the off.

Iris was shouting as she ran over. 'OK, guys, you're all ready, good, good . . .' She pounded to a halt in front of the truck's open back and looked at three excited faces staring at her, as she paused to catch her breath.

'Yes, ma'am.' It was 'Pure' White giving the affirmative. He was standing up, moving forwards so he could stretch up to his full, and not inconsiderable, height without his shiny, shaven pate brushing the canvas roof of the truck.

'OK. Blake's, just, uh, Blake's just coming.' Iris looked back at the door she'd just run through. No sign. She turned back to her team. 'OK, this is a training session but we are going to play it completely as real. Here's the lowdown. Strange animal activity reported at the University Parks. Full moon. All the signs. We need to investigate.'

New girl Pepper stood up next to Pure, her sturdy five foot four looking almost comical next to his six-and-counting. 'Ma'am, do you have a description of the lycs, ma'am?'

Iris sucked in her bottom lip. Little Ella Pepper had already exhibited a tendency to make her feel nervous and wrong footed. 'A description?' Iris began. 'Um. Big. Grey. Golden eyes. Pretty much your standard lycs. Um, classification W1XY, male. Actually, does it matter? If you see anything that is even wolf shaped, fill it with silver first and we'll do an ID parade later.'

Iris paused, waiting.

'Ma'am,' said Aurelia, not standing up but sliding forwards along the bench inside the truck, 'so aren't we going to get going, then?' The classical beauty and cut-glass vowels combined to make Aurelia the most intimidating of them all.

'Yes. Just as soon as –'

Before Iris could finish, the emergency exit doors flew open and Blake – his usual whirlwind of crazy dark hair and crazy dark everything else – hurtled across the yard, practically vaulted in through the open driver's door and seemed to be revving the engine before he was actually in contact with the seat. Iris jumped up into the back of the truck just as Blake started to pull away.

Three hours later, Iris stood in the dark watching her Reds load dummy hounds into the back of the van. Blake sidled up to her. 'Those dummies are too small, really,' she said, not looking at him.

'They're all right for training. They're just meant to be strays. You don't get proper pack hounds out here any more. Mostly thanks to you, you super-powered lyc-killing bitch.' He winked. 'Besides, you just think every lyc you see is some kind of toy breed because you cut your teeth on Mr Big. The Beast.' Blake arched his eyebrows. 'Nothing is ever big enough for you, Iris.'

Blake was holding a ripped-up cygnet's body in a clear plastic evidence bag. Iris looked at it. 'That was a particularly horrible touch. You didn't kill that thing yourself when you were setting up, did you?'

'Nah,' said Blake, 'I found it. A fox or a dog must have got it.'

Iris looked closer. 'You sure. The head's been ripped off and the claws that split it open were pretty big. It looks just like . . .'

'Yeah, I know what it looks like, that's why I bagged it.'

'Taking it back to your creepy lab?'

Blake shrugged, putting the bag on the ground, and took out some cigarette papers and tobacco. Blake rolled the thinnest cigarettes Iris had ever seen. She watched while he finished, put the tiny paper tube in his mouth and lit it, the flare of the lighter making his tight ratlike face glow. He took a deep drag and then tipped his head back and exhaled. 'This is the place, right?'

Iris knew just what he meant. 'Yeah,' she said very quietly, hoping Blake would drop that subject as quickly as he had brought it up.

'Brother killed. Boyfriend turned into a monster. Where's the tree you were in when it happened? Is it round here?'

Iris shook her head. 'No,' she said, 'other side of the river.'

'Yeah? Maybe you should pay it a visit. You need to respect what happened to you here, Iris.' Blake took a step closer, his face lit by the glowing end of his cigarette.

Iris stepped back. There was a tree right behind her and she ended up tight against it. A flash of Alfie pressing her up against a tree in this same park rushed through her. All she could think of was how young she had been then. How young and simple to think that Alfie kissing another girl at a drunken party was the worst thing he could ever do to her.

She was so busy thinking about that kiss, that she didn't notice the kiss that was nearly happening in the here and now. Blake suddenly had his hands on her upper arms, was pushing her against the tree trunk, had his lips almost on hers. 'Blake!' She pushed him away.

'What? So my wife looks sexy. I can't kiss my own wife? Isn't there some law that says you *have* to kiss me if I want you to?'

'Yeah, maybe, if this was the Middle Ages!' Iris was slightly breathless. She rounded on Blake, still close enough that she could see him in the dark. 'And I'm not your wife, Blake. Not any more.'

'Yeah, yeah, babe. You keep telling me I'll be hearing something from some lawyers but I never do.'

'Don't go making out that's some kind of sign I still want you. I've been busy.'

Blake moved nearer again, his body almost touching hers. Iris could have stepped away but she didn't. 'Who was the best fuck then, me or the werewolf?'

'I wasn't with him when he was a werewolf. We split up. That was kind of the point.'

'Yes, you were, though. After he was bitten. There was a whole month before full moon and his first change. Virgo, it's called. Virgin wolf. He hasn't changed yet but it's in his blood. Throbbing with it. They're ravenous, Virgos. Crazy for sex. Used to be sought after for it, in fact. Prized, once upon a time. Was he too much for you then? Is that why you split?'

'You know why we split, Blake.'

'And then you traded in Mr Monster for Mr Monster Killer.' Blake smiled. 'That's what I like about you, Iris.' His voice was full of some kind of fucked-up Blake version of love. 'You are so warped.'

'Just leave me alone, Blake.' Iris turned away from him and headed across the park – first walking fast, then running. He shouted something after her, but she didn't look back.

She crossed the river and ran up the hill, ending up by the exact clutch of trees where it happened. She found the one she had climbed that night and stood with her back against it. The fallen tree where Alfie had been posing wasn't there any more.

They'd found Matt's camera equipment and developed the photographs for the inquest. Alfie had been embarrassed when he saw how overtly sexual the images were.

The perfect semicircle of moon in the sky was waxing now. A week to go until the big one.

It was then – with her night vision gone from looking up at the moon – that Iris thought she saw something. A flicker in the darkness.

Here? Again? It couldn't be? But she knew the way werewolves moved now, the slightly unearthly way their pelts seemed to shimmer. She squinted at the familiar shape. It certainly looked like a werewolf. Exactly like a werewolf. Except for the part where it wasn't full moon and so it couldn't be . . .

It couldn't be.

In that moment, that tiny questioning second, the animal leapt out from the tree cover, making straight for her.

Black and grey and shimmering. Fast and loud and sickening. Iris wasn't wearing her coms headset; wasn't even holding her gun. It was too late to pull anything out of her pack. She closed her fingers tight around the one thing she did have – her silver blade – feeling light headed at the thought of close combat.

She was only starting to turn around – to try and run – when the creature smashed into her, rearing up, knocking her down, flipping her easily onto her back. She closed her eyes, dazed, stunned by the way she had smacked into the ground.

The blade wasn't in her hand any more. She didn't even know when she had dropped it. The last few moments were nothing but a blur of wet fur and wet ground and wet pain.

Except there wasn't enough pain. The wolf that she could hear and feel and smell standing over her, pinning her down, wasn't attacking.

She opened her eyes and saw nothing but wolf. Silent, slavering wolf.

Her first thought was *teeth*.

My, my, what big teeth you have.

Above those teeth, golden eyes. The air was cold. The damp grass was colder. *Yes, much better, focus on the eyes. Not the teeth, the eyes.*

My, my, what big eyes you have.

This wasn't the Beast. Not the huge creature that had killed Matt and bitten Alfie. This was a big wolf – but not that particular monster. Iris looked deeper into the wolf's eyes . . .

It was like a flash of an image. Subliminal. She saw – or thought she saw – just for a fraction of a second, not a wolf over her, pinning her, but a man. A man whose warm breath was sweet on her cheek – not stinking of her own mortality. Whose body was toned and shaped like a secret fantasy. Whose face was flushed, rakish, handsome. Who was holding himself over her, supporting himself on big pumped up forearms. Beautiful and shimmering with monstrousness.

A man she knew, recognised.

'Alfie?' She felt stupid even saying it.

The wolf just stared at her. There was no sign of the man she had seen.

'Alfie,' she said again. 'Is that you?'

You really think that's Alfie? Iris turned her head, slightly. Matthew was squatting right beside her.

'Not *now*, Matthew. Can't you see I'm busy?'

What, you don't want me here for your death, Iris? I'm hurt.

'Matthew, as you actually died yourself eleven years ago I don't want you here at all. Ever.'

Not even for this. But this is the big one. You're going to die right where I died. The same way. That'll be one for the weird twin phenomena books. And you're lying on your blade, by the way.

'What?'

You can feel it. It's that pain in your shoulder. It's sticking right in you. Get it out and kill him. Isn't that your job?

'But it isn't full moon?'

Think about that later. After you've finished fighting for your life.

Iris closed her eyes, reminding herself that Matthew was a figment of her imagination – if she couldn't see him he didn't exist. She concentrated on the deadly smell of the wolf all around her – much more real than imaginary Matthew.

Focus.

Her mind raced. Clicking into gear. She was trained. In this situation she ought to react like a machine. All at once she remembered everything she knew about how the wolf wasn't the man. How a lyc could become a wolf and kill his parents, his lover, his child. If this wolf *was* Alfie, then he could still attack her at any moment. The Alfie she knew wasn't in control.

The blade.

She could feel it. She twisted, trying to move without really moving. She got her left hand up under her left shoulder and pulled it out. Solid silver.

The wolf's paws were on her shoulders but she reckoned she could get a good thrust in. It was so close.

Aim for the heart. Aim for the head.

The wolf snarled.

Do it, Iris.

She thrust as hard as she could into the wolf.

Right into its left eye.

3

When he woke up, Alfie slowly became aware of several things. All of them bad.

1. He was outdoors and naked
2. His left eye really, really hurt
3. Someone was coming

Voices. 'I found him.'

'Really? You sure, Zac?'

'Sure, I'm sure, doll.' *An American accent. Zac. That was familiar.*

'How is he? Still hairy? I've got the gun.' *Zac and a woman.*

'No, Misty, honey. He's smooth. Naked as a babe. Two hundred pounds of butched-up alpha dick, right here.' *There was something lazy and lilting about his accent. Southern? Some kind of Southern American accent. Yes this was Zac. And the woman was Misty.*

'What? His cock weighs two hundred pounds?' *That was someone else again. Another man. British. He sounded like Ozzy Osborne. So that must be, what, a Birmingham accent? A Brummie? Leon. It was Leon.*

'Alfie?' said Misty. Alfie knew he ought to answer her. But he couldn't seem to speak. The grass underneath him was damp. He still didn't move.

'Man, he looks like shit,' said Zac.

'What the hell happened? Did he flip? Weren't you marking him?' said Leon.

'He was in the attic,' said Misty, 'I was down in the kitchen. He said he wanted to be on his own and he'd fitted the reinforced panels and all the locks up there. We both thought he'd be contained, but I think he must have gone out of the skylight from the way the glass was broken. Oh, Alfie, babe, I'm sorry. I thought it would be OK.'

'So what made him flip? If you were down in the kitchen I assume you weren't screwing him,' said Leon.

'He was on his own. In his bedroom. You work it out, Leon,' said the woman, a little hard edge in her voice. Alfie could smell her now. He felt a hand on his bare shoulder and heard a voice very close to him say, 'Alfie? Alfie, babe?' That smell. So Misty. *Misty*. Misty, who was saying, 'Zac, take off your pants.'

'He won't fit into my pants.'

'Not your *American* pants, your British pants. Your underpants. He can have Leon's jeans.'

'He is not having my jeans.'

'Oh, yes, he is, babe. He's the alpha and he is not going to hospital naked. He's having Zac's underpants, your trousers and my T-shirt.'

'Your T-shirt. Yeah, right, because he really looks like a Powerpuff Girls fan.'

'You know, you'd be surprised what the average Powerpuff Girls fan looks like.'

'Anyway,' said Zac, 'why is he going to hospital?'

'Because,' said Misty, 'he is bleeding out of his eye.'

'Ew! Motherfuck!'

Alfie didn't really want to be dressed in an assortment of inappropriate clothes, but somehow he didn't feel able to do too much about it either. He grunted and rolled as he felt Misty's familiar hands tug on a pair of satin-smooth underpants, a pair of horribly tight trousers and a T-shirt so snug it really wasn't worth him wearing it. Misty had only just finished trying to pull it down over his nipples when he opened his good eye.

He saw Misty first – standing over him – a pretty, bird-boned Japanese woman, wearing her black hair in pigtails and fastening up her military-style jacket over her naked torso. Zac was behind her – a tall skinny black guy wearing tall skinny black clothes. And Leon, as ever about 40 per cent flowing blond hair to 60 per cent tight denim.

His pack. Oh, God help him.

Misty saw Alfie's eye open and crouched back down. 'Alfie. Thank God. Are you OK, babe?'

'Can't go to hospital,' Alfie said.

Misty shook her head. 'Don't be butch about this, Alfie. You've got to.'

Alfie pulled himself up on his elbows and gave her a look. Even in the dark that look made her stiffen a little. 'I'm not safe, Misty. Look at what just happened. I don't even know what I did. I killed – something – I can taste it in my mouth. You need to lock me up before I flip back again.'

Misty knew Alfie was in no state to walk. And she knew that dealing with getting him home would be down to her.

Now Alfie was unstable it was always down to Misty.

She ducked into the all-night chemist for gauze and surgical tape. She dressed Alfie's eye as best she could. She hailed the taxi. She spun the driver a line about Alfie having had a drink too many and fallen down. ('On his eye? Poor bugger!')

It had been Misty who had chosen the house that the pack were renting for their stay in Oxford. She had chosen very carefully. The house wasn't in a particularly nice area. There was litter on the streets and in the unkempt front gardens. Kerbs and front windows were broken. The whole place was simply worn out from the lack of care and investment typical of a transient population. But for a group of werewolves who'd really rather not be noticed – especially arriving home dragging a bleeding semi-clothed man – it was perfect.

In the hall, Misty said, 'The cellar's secure. If you're still feeling unstable, babe, do you want to be shut down there for a while?'

Alfie nodded. 'In my cage.'

'You don't need your cage, babe, the cellar is enough.'

Alfie looked at her. His left eye was bleeding behind the gauze. The look in his right made the hairs on the back of her neck stand up. 'OK, OK, Zac and Leon will have to shift it down, though.'

The cages were still in the front room where the removal men had left them. Alfie's was especially heavy as it bore all the extra reinforcement required by his build, his time as a werewolf and his neuroses. Zac and Leon grunted as they hefted it down the narrow steps.

Misty followed them down. 'You might as well get the other ones down here too,' she said, 'then we will be able to invite people round without them wondering why our front room is done out like a gothic dungeon.'

Alfie, who had followed Misty down the stairs shouted to their retreating backs, 'Get my chains too.'

'Alfie, no. This isn't about being secure now, is it, babe? This is about punishing yourself.'

Alfie looked at her. 'I got out, Misty. I should have nailed a panel over the skylight.'

'You're hurt, babe. You've changed once today already. The cage is enough.'

There was a clatter and scuffle on the stairs and Leon and Zac appeared back in the small space. Zac was carrying Misty's small cage by himself. Leon had Alfie's chains.

Misty eyed the bundle of metal and manacles. 'I'm not putting those on you now, babe,' she said.

'Yes you are,' Alfie said, turning away from her and pulling off the T-shirt.

Misty swallowed.

'I'll do it,' Leon said.

Alfie turned back around. He was shirtless now and something about that made him more terrifying. More animal. 'Misty does it. Get out.'

Leon gave Alfie a petulant look, then turned and walked up the stairs with Zac trailing behind.

Alfie said, 'Misty. I need the extra security. I'm too dangerous. I could have ... I don't know what I did.'

Misty looked at the dressing on his eye. It was already coming loose. He needed stitches, possibly an operation. If he did change again the dressing wouldn't survive it. He'd probably start worrying at the wound when he was hairy – maybe even give himself an infection. Perhaps the chains wouldn't be such a bad idea.

Alfie's chains weren't meant for his changes, though. They were so he could have sex.

The first time Alfie had changed form without the moon, his orgasm had been the stimulus that flipped him. And Misty had been in his bed. The wolf's jaws had replaced Alfie's tongue inside her and in that one terrifying confusing moment Alfie had become Misty's sire, Misty's greatest love and Misty's darkest nightmare.

Even now, Misty thought of nothing but Alfie at night. Touching herself right where his jaws had been. Screaming in the dark and twisting her fear into arousal.

And every time he'd climaxed from that moment onwards, Alfie had changed into a wolf.

There were other stimuli too – high emotion: anger, stress, distress. But it was orgasm that made him change more than half the time.

After that there wasn't a lot of choice – Alfie had stopped having sex. He couldn't have anyone in the same room with him when he came. Sex just wasn't possible.

Not unless he was chained down.

4

By the time Iris got back to where they had been parked the truck had gone. She walked back to Summertown, shaken up, keeping to the main roads even though it would have been much quicker to take the fields.

Back at home, she spent a long and frustrating time trying to get a dressing on the wound on her left shoulder blade. It was a hard spot to reach and her hands were still shaking. She cursed several times as she tried to stick the skin back together with little sticky strips.

After she'd made a mess of that, she found a bottle of wine, opened it and drank half of the contents before she started to look for a glass.

She took her drink into the living room, planning on unwinding in front of a flickering screen one way or another. Matthew was perched on the arm of her sofa waiting for her.

Iris stopped in the doorway. Matthew appeared in her home far less often than he did at the office or when she was out on sweeps. It was nearly always a bad sign. 'Oh no. No. I've told you. I really don't like you being here.'

I live here. Matthew slipped his slender non-corporeal body off the sofa and gestured around.

Iris shook her head. 'You're dead? You can't *live* anywhere.'

Well, thanks very much. I just thought you could use some company.

'You're not company. You're imaginary.'

So you keep telling me. Haven't you ever heard of psychic twin phenomena? Anyway, I just thought you might like to talk about it.

'About what?'

About what? About what just happened! About Alfie.

'It wasn't Alfie. Alfie's gone'

You saw him.

'I just got attacked by a lyc on a night that wasn't full moon. That is freaky enough without you adding Alfie to the mix.' Iris turned away from Matthew and picked up the remote control for the TV.

She jabbed the on button. It was tuned to a channel that showed reruns of old sci-fi shows, and there was Matthew, right on the deck of the Starship *Enterprise. You could have killed him with that blade out at the park. Why didn't you? You could have hit him in the heart or the brain. You went for the eye. Why not a killing blow?*

'I don't know. It was my best chance to get away. Do we have to talk about this?'

Matthew rolled his eyes. He walked forwards until he was climbing out of the television like that scary thing in *The Ring.* Gently, he said, *Didn't you tell him that you'd kill him if he ever came back to Oxford? Have you changed your mind?*

'I said drop it, Matthew. Can we talk about something else?'

Matthew started. His face was suddenly wary, scared. *What was that?*

'What was what?' Iris said. But then she could hear it too.

Someone was moving around in the hallway outside her flat. He or she was trying to be stealthy, but one of the reasons Iris liked this place was that its creaking floorboards were like an early warning system. Iris set her glass down on the coffee table. She looked over at Matthew again. He'd already vanished.

But she wasn't alone.

Iris stood up and crept into her tiny entrance lobby. She peered through the spyhole. There was no one visible out in the hall, but she knew there were several blind spots. She pressed her ear to the door instead and listened. She strained to hear anything. Then, yes, she could hear breathing. The person must be close to the door, probably flat against the wall next to it. A split second of calculation was all Iris needed to decide to attack and attack now.

She snicked the latch as quietly as possible. Then dived.

She had someone by the throat, then shoved them sideways, kicked out their legs and sent them crashing to the floor through her open doorway, with her on top of them.

She pinned them down on the floor of the hallway. She got the man's arms – it was a man – up over his head and used her entire body weight to hold him. Panting, she looked down at him.

'The thing I just don't get,' he said, 'is why you say our marriage isn't working?'

'Blake! What the fuck are you doing?' Blake was splayed underneath her, his hair everywhere, his filthy lab coat spread open like butterfly wings on the floor.

'I was passing.'

'Passing! You live in Rose Hill. It's in the opposite direction.'

'Yeah, well, I used to live here. I just forgot . . .'

'You only lived here for three months. If you want to start pretending you still live here, there's actually a queue for that.'

'What?' Blake wasn't fighting her, but she knew if he did she wouldn't be able to hold him for long.

Iris let go of his wrists and sat back. She was straddling his groin. 'Blake,' she said, 'actually I do need to talk to you about something.'

'I know, I know, you want me back. You can't live without me. I'll think about it. I have a few offers on the table.'

Iris ignored this, because sometimes you had to let Blake be Blake. And right now she needed him. He would be able to explain it all. Blake was like that. He could explain practically anything. In fact, he liked to say that

Iris was the only thing that had ever got the better of his incisive brain powers, but Iris really didn't think that was true.

Iris climbed off him and he followed her into the living room. She started explaining on the way.

'Something happened in the park after I left you.'

'A Damascene conversion?'

Iris sat on the sofa and picked up her glass. She didn't bother offering Blake a drink; if he thought he still lived here he could get his own. 'I got attacked by a lyc.'

Blake didn't sit down. He stood with one elbow up on the mantelpiece. 'Okay, you just got my attention.'

'You're not going to say I've lost my edge and I imagined it.'

'No. I'm going to say I ran the tests back at the Institute just now and that cygnet was killed by a lyc.'

'Oh. That's sort of weird.'

Blake raised his eyebrows at her, weird happenings – as a rule – did not faze him much. Weird was actually Blake's preferred state of things.

'It nearly got me, Blake. I wasn't prepped. It knocked me to the ground. I wounded it and got away, but there was a moment there when I thought I might be going the same way as Jude.'

Blake narrowed his eyes. 'Are you sure you're OK?'

'I didn't get bitten, if that's what you mean.'

'I didn't just mean that. Damn, a moonless wolf, that is really rare.'

'But you have heard of it? I'm not going nuts?'

'Lycs changing in response to other triggers? Yeah. It's talked about, speculated on. I mean all the covert military stuff, that was what they were trying to do – can't fight all your wars on full moon nights. As for whether it really ever happens ... I don't know. God, Iris, you said you didn't kill it?'

Iris shook her head.

'We really ought to try and bring it in alive. We could learn so much from ... I need my books really. Hang on, where's that box I left?' Blake vanished into the bedroom and returned a moment later carrying an armful of books and with his glasses perched on his nose.

'Blake –?'

He talked right over her. 'There's stuff written about it being possible for a strong wolf, first or second generation from ancient ones; after seven years the changes can get unstable ... Something like that, I think.' He set the books down on the mantelpiece and picked up the top one, flicking through it. 'OK, here we are.'

'What?'

'Well, these older books can be a bit melodramatic. They're all about how after seven years the wolf gets stronger and more restless and starts to try and break out at other times. But it's probably something more like, I don't know, the transformations get less stable after that long. Maybe the body actually starts fighting it off and the curse breaks down. We know that the curse can work a bit like an infection.'

'Yeah. OK. Um, Blake?'

'What?'

'There's something else. It doesn't really make any sense, but when the attack happened ... I don't know. I sort of thought the wolf was Alfie.'

'Alfie! Your ex-werewolf fuck-monster Alfie? The amazing man who was bitten by the Beast and survived?' Blake closed his book and took off his glasses to emphasise his already quite emphatic point.

'Yeah. Except I know Alfie would be dead by now. It was eleven years ago.'

'But that would be the whole thing. That's why this breaking down thing is so rare. We know that lycs don't usually live more than five years give or take. But if Alfie has, for whatever reason, that would be why this is happening to him. And he was bitten by the Beast. So he's first or second generation from the ancient ones, like it says.'

Blake's eyes were wild. Dancing with excitement. Iris

couldn't help feeling the electricity in the air. The fact Iris had been attacked was already nothing more than a note in the margin. The way Blake would see it, she was attacked, she was OK, end of discussion. Especially when the next thing on the agenda was discovering more about werewolves. That was Blake's thing.

They had all had a thing. Back in the day. The original lyc-fighting trio. Iris's thing had been killing the Beast who had killed her twin brother and bitten Alfie. Jude's thing had been, well, Iris thought she was probably the only person who knew that Jude's real thing had been all about the fact that werewolves killed her mother. Jude used to change her story a lot, but Iris had been the only other person there when Jude had been bleeding to death and then it had been all about how she was dying like her mother had.

And then there was Blake – no retribution in particular, just in it for the weird science.

Iris watched him. Still buried in his book. But she was also thinking of Alfie. So it had been him. Blake had practically confirmed it. Was he really back in Oxford? Why? She thought of the wolf's eyes and she knew exactly how Alfie would look now. Lycanthropy changed the physique, worked on the metabolism. Blake would be able to explain it all with equations and graphs. All Iris knew was how it made the werewolf look when they were in human form. Alfie wasn't bad looking before. He'd be spectacular now.

She looked at Blake again, but thought of Alfie. She thought of pinning Blake to the carpet in her hall. She thought of Alfie on top of her.

Blake looked up at her and he must have caught something in her eye that gave her away, because he said, 'Wolfie's left you a bit tense, huh?'

Ever the pragmatist, Blake approached sex and romance rather like it was yet another scientific experiment. Certainly, he had made it pretty clear in recent months that he didn't think the fact that Iris didn't want to be married to him any more meant that they shouldn't have sex any more. Iris smiled a non-committal smile, but Blake clearly wasn't tuned in to such subtleties. A smile was a smile was a yes. Grinning, he set down the book and came over to where Iris was sitting. He climbed onto her lap.

Blake kissed her and she was just so shaken up from nearly dying it was impossible to resist. Blake's mouth, so soft on hers, exploring, somehow convincing her that this wasn't the same mouth she had felt a hundred times before. But in her mind this was Alfie's mouth, Alfie's hands, Alfie's hard cock nudging against her.

But really, Alfie and Blake couldn't have been more different. Blake was strung tight, hard and tense. Alfie was big, a sprawling a hulk of a man. And Blake was right about that first month after Alfie had been bitten. Iris had been crazy with grief over Matthew. Alfie had been constantly horny. All Iris had wanted that month, before either of them really knew the truth of what had happened, was for Alfie's much bigger body to overwhelm her, to hold her down, to fuck her into oblivion.

Blake's hand moved under her shirt. His fingers grazed the edge of the dressing on her shoulder. 'Iris?'

'It's not a bite, Blake. It was my blade. I fell on it.'

Blake had pulled back from Iris and was watching her closely, his head on one side. 'You sure about that, Iris? You know the oath. If I think you've been infected I'm meant to shoot you.'

Iris pulled him back down into an embrace by the collar of his stained lab coat. 'Sure, Blake, sure,' she cooed, 'because you make it your business to put hounds down, don't you? If you think I might secretly be a lyc how about you do what you really want and interrogate me, huh?' She poked out her tongue and licked his sharp nose.

Blake smiled, then pulled away and sat back. He reached into the inside pocket of his lab coat and pulled out a pair of handcuffs. Standard Institute of Paraphysiology issue. Just one rigid piece of metal with two holes. Uncomfortable. Inescapable. He held them up so they sparkled like treasure. 'So,' he said, his voice instantly in the dark place, 'you're going to be wanting these tonight then?'

Iris felt her breath catch. She thought of the wolf on top of her and felt the hairs on the back of her neck stand up and her nipples stiffen. Wolves. Alfie. Matthew. Only Blake could make this all go away. She held out her wrists.

5

It took an hour for Alfie to feel he was out of the danger zone. This had started happening a lot. He'd flip, but after he turned back, he wouldn't feel stable again for a long time afterwards. He knew the only way to calm down was to lock himself up and zone out until the feelings receded.

He looked up when he heard footsteps coming down the cellar steps. He saw the slim black-clad legs first. Zac.

'Hey, man,' Zac said in his musical American drawl. 'I know you'd prefer Misty but she's awful tired. I've come to unhitch you, if you're ready.'

'Yeah, yeah that's fine.'

Zac started working the padlock on the cage. 'This is fucked up, man,' he said softly.

'I know.'

After Zac had unlocked all the manacles, Alfie climbed out of the cage. As Alfie began to dress, Zac turned to leave. 'Zac,' Alfie said, slipping on his jeans, 'wait a minute.'

'Yeah?'

'Keep your eye on me, mate. It's dangerous for me here.'

'In Oxford, yeah, I know. They hunt werewolves here.'

'It's not just the Vix. Oxford's where I was bitten. There's a lot to stir up. We need to be quick. Get the collar, do Misty's thing and get out. We can't hang around here. It's not a good place for me.'

'Because of Iris, right?'

Alfie bit his lip. Misty knew about Iris. Therefore Leon knew. Therefore Zac knew. No secrets in the pack. 'Yeah.'

'But doesn't she work for the Vix?'

'Yeah.'

'And aren't they the ones who have the collar?'

'Yeah.'

'So, it's not like you can avoid seeing her?'

'No,' said Alfie pulling on his shirt. 'I can't. The best I can hope for is that we can avoid killing each other.'

Blake and Iris had moved to the bed. Iris's wrists were in the cuffs. Blake had let them slide a notch too tight before he'd put on the safety. She'd gasped as the metal bit at her wrists and he'd laughed and ground his hard cock into her groin. 'Lyc-killer bitch,' he whispered. 'I know what you need.'

Now Blake had one hand on the cuffs, holding them down onto the bed, pinning Iris's arms above her head as he leant in and bit her on the jawline. Then he let his mouth move over to her ear. 'So, you want me to fuck you?' he said softly, before biting the sensitive spot at the top of her ear.

Iris nodded.

'Oh come on, baby. After ten years you need to do better than that.'

Iris ran her tongue over her lips. 'Fine,' she said softly, 'fuck me.'

'And how you want to be fucked, baby?'

'Hard,' Iris said, her voice fading in and out of a whisper. 'Very hard.'

'You want me to tie you down properly first?'

Iris nodded, turning her head a little.

Blake reached out and caught her chin, bringing her eyes back level with his. 'Say it, Iris.'

'Sure. Fine. Tie me down. Tie me down and fucking fuck me, Blake.'

Blake smiled. He let go of the cuffs and sat back, then rummaged in his pocket. Somehow he was still wearing his lab coat, although he wasn't wearing anything else. He'd put that back on. He produced some rope – Blake had very deep pockets – and used it to fasten the cuffs to the headboard.

Then Blake's hands were tight on her arms as he fucked

her. He was teasing her, kissing her and then pulling his mouth out of her reach, rolling his hips so his cock danced inside her.

One of Blake's hands snaked down between her legs. His thumb touched her clit. It was a light tease but she was so close. He looked into her eyes, holding his body weight on one arm. Blake wasn't a big man, but he was so damn strong. He chased all her demons away. He smelt grubby-familiar: tobacco and old paper. The wolf – Alfie – had smelt like blood and her own fear.

She shouldn't be doing this. Not just thinking of Alfie but all of it. She was meant to be divorcing Blake. And Blake had always been every kind of mistake.

'Good girl,' Blake muttered. 'Come for me now. Stop thinking about the wolf and come for *me*.'

But Iris barely heard him. She was thinking of Alfie. Alfie's big body on top of her. Alfie a foot taller than her and so full of power. Blake's fingertips rolled over her clit again, but she was still thinking of the wolf. Blake started to thrust into her harder, as if he was trying to get her attention. Iris bucked up and cried out as she came.

'Alfie.'

Up in his attic bedroom, Alfie eyed the broken window. The room wasn't secure. If he wanted to get off tonight without setting his wolf loose, there was only one way. As he fixed his chains to his bedposts, he was already half hard.

Once that was done, he stripped off his clothes and climbed onto the bed. Sitting up he fixed each metal cuff around his ankle. The chains were magical, spelled so they would hold the wolf as well as the man. He felt the subtle movements as the spell caused them to contract and adjust to hold him perfectly. Then he lay back and attached a cuff to his left wrist. Obviously he'd need to keep his right hand free but it should be secure enough. He taped the keys to the inside of his wrist.

With a long sigh he took his cock in his right hand and

stroked gently. It was instant fire. He'd always had a high sex drive but once he'd become a werewolf it had moved to another level. This was a pure animal thing. God, he wished he had someone else here. Not for much. Just someone to kiss him while he did this. Kissing was the thing he missed most of all. He never got to do enough kissing. He was good at kissing.

Iris, kissing Iris. One time he'd taken her out in a punt. Pure Oxford tourist nonsense. But she'd looked so beautiful sitting there, while he powered the boat by dipping the long pole into the water.

She'd said it had turned her on. Seeing him do that. Something about the pole. They'd found a place to moor the boat and had just lain together kissing for hours. He missed kissing for hours. *Kissing Iris for hours.*

Oxford. Vix. He'd have to see her. He could sense her right now. Out there in the city. He'd been able to sense her since they got off the train at Oxford station.

He moved his palm against his cock a couple more times then forced himself to break off and take it a little slower. Iris. The punt. Pushing her T-shirt up to her neck and biting her nipples. He ran his palm over his own hard chest once or twice. His hips thrust up into empty air and then the tease was almost too much. Fuck. Fuck! The wolf always did this to him.

Pinning Iris down in the bottom of the boat. Some water had splashed in from somewhere and they were both getting wet. He'd touched her through her jeans, made her buck just from that. They were so young then. Early twenties. Not a care.

He'd gone to fuck her and she'd said, 'No. I want to see it. On me, not in me.' And she'd touched herself while he did the same, coming over her little tits and making her moan – a little of it splattering over the side of the punt into the Thames.

In his bedroom, Alfie fisted his cock again. Moving fast. Too aching and needy to draw this out much longer. His body fought against the chains that held him down hard and fast. Unconsciously, his left hand tried to move towards his body. To touch something. Anything. But the chain was secure and it clanked loudly as he reached the limit of the restriction. He fought against the chains on his legs too, trying to draw his knees up, to roll, to move with his pleasure. But he was held down. Helpless.

But close now. So near . . .

Werewolves don't always remember everything that happens when they're in their wolf form. Alfie thinks the simplest comparison is with dreams. Although Leon once said it was more like a night of heavy drinking.

Sometimes the memories are all there. Orderly in your head when you change back. Perfectly normal. Sometimes you never remember. (Those were the nights Alfie always wondered about, even if he started and finished in his cage.) And sometimes, most times in fact, the memories come a little later than usual. Like déjà vu.

It was the way the light from his table lamp caught the empty metal cuff that lay on his pillow. Just that sparkle and suddenly he saw a dagger coming up to his eye. He felt a faint pain. An echo of pain. But spooling back, he saw who was lying on the ground underneath him. Who it was thrusting the dagger into his eye.

Iris.

Alfie moved his hand against his cock again. *Iris. Kissing Iris. Iris pinned under him. Iris scared of him. Scared of the wolf. Iris!*

And he was coming. His mind full of her as his body spasmed and he moaned and the wolf took his body back.

'Blake, don't mess around.'

'I'm not messing around.' Blake was standing, fastening his shirt. He reached for his lab coat.

'Blake!' Iris was still on the bed. Still wearing the handcuffs that were tied to the headboard.

'What?'

'Don't, Blake. Look. Fuck. I'm sorry, OK. Can you take them off me now? You know you ratcheted them too tight.'

'Did I? Well that's a shame.' Blake turned and began to walk towards the door.

'Blake!' Iris shouted. 'You wouldn't fucking dare! Blake!'

Blake turned in the bedroom doorway. 'Bye, Iris,' he said before he vanished through it.

6

It had been nearly an hour since Alfie had woken up, still chained to his bed with every muscle aching. Now, he sat at the kitchen table drinking a mug of coffee, watching Misty cooking.

Alfie drained his mug. Misty was waiting for his response to her latest plea that he go to hospital. He swallowed. 'I can heal this.'

'I looked it up this morning, babe. You can't. Your eyeball'll need stitches at the very least. Do you want to lose the eye?' As she spoke Misty cruised over on her four-inch heels, took Alfie's empty cup out of his hands and replaced it with a full one. Along with the sky-scraper shoes, Misty was, for some typical Misty-type reason, wearing a nurse's uniform. Not a normal one. A full-on Victoriana one with puffy sleeves and a frilly headpiece. Alfie wasn't sure if this was supposed to help her argument. He had already decided not to comment.

He took the mug from her gratefully. His mouth was still dry from the change. 'I can heal this. I've healed worse. Misty, I trained for three years. I was nearly a doctor. I'd have been a doctor if I hadn't got bitten. I know what I'm talking about. No one understands this stuff as well as me. I heal. I'm a werewolf. Before I got stabbed I jumped off the roof of this house.'

'Yeah, Alfie, I get that. You're a tough guy. But, look, just go to hospital. For me.'

Alfie looked at her. 'I can't, Misty. A building full of ill people. Kiddies, newborn babies. What if I flip?'

Misty's face turned pale. 'I'll come. I'll mark you.'

'What? And not sleep? Who marks me then? Do I take the whole pack? Look, I don't want to get alpha on you, Misty, but no. There isn't time. I have stuff I need to do. I want to be out of Oxford as soon as possible. Find the collar today. Then full moon – you do your thing, we grab the money and go.'

Misty went back to the stove. She was poaching eggs. Two pans were bubbling and an empty egg box lay on the counter. Alfie had taught Misty how to make perfect poached eggs. He had been something of an expert.

'If you do lose your eye then Leon will be pleased,' Misty said with her back to him.

'I'm not going to lose ... What? Why?' Anything that pleased denim-boy Leon was not good news.

Misty looked over her shoulder and smiled a twisted sort of smile. 'He thinks if you lose the eye you won't be able to be alpha any more. He was saying so in the taxi home yesterday. He thinks his time has come. You're getting unstable. You're getting too old.'

Alfie made a dismissive noise. 'Well, that's just it. Wolves don't get old. Aren't meant to get old. Wolves are meant to die. Alphas are meant to be killed by their cubs. If Leon wants to be alpha he has to kill me and he can't. My thrall is still too strong. Whether or not *I* should be alpha is one thing. Whether or not *he* should be is a separate question. He's hardly a natural alpha.'

'You should hear him on that subject. Anyway, if not him, then who?'

'You.'

'Me?'

'You practically are already. Since I've been getting more unstable you've been running this pack. You are the alpha. You arranged this house. You sort out the money. Get jobs for Leon and Zac, jobs for me ...'

Misty rolled her over made-up eyes. 'I nag you about your eye. I make the coffee. I poach the eggs. I'm the mum is what I am.' She began fishing the eggs out of the water with a slotted spoon. 'Anyway, I've got to go. I have other patients you know. But we'll talk about this later, Alfie. You do need to see a doctor.'

She plonked a plate of poached eggs in front of Alfie, then turned and loaded up a tray with two steaming mugs and a plate of toast piled cartoonishly high.

As she turned back around, Alfie stood up. That foot and a half he had on Misty had never seemed such a big distance. He towered over her. 'Misty, no. I don't need a doctor. I did three years at medical school for God's sake and even if that was a long time ago, one thing I distinctly remember is that conventional medicine doesn't know shit about how a werewolf heals . . .'

'You can't leave me with Leon,' Misty said. She said it quietly, but it stopped Alfie in his tracks. 'If you lose the eye, Leon will challenge you for the pack and I can't have him as my alpha.'

'Fine, then, fine,' said Alfie, bristling with anger. He walked across the kitchen and pulled a silver-bladed dagger out of a drawer. 'You do it then.' He held the dagger out to Misty, hilt first, his fingers stinging where he gripped the blade.

'Don't, Alfie.'

'No, Misty, here's how it works. Werewolves aren't supposed to live this long. That's why I'm flipping. That's why I need to get the collar. One of my cubs needs to take me out and become alpha. That's you or Leon. So if you don't want it to be him, you'd better step up.'

'You know I can't,' Misty said. She still hadn't taken the dagger and the silver blade hurt so much that Alfie dropped it on the floor, then pulled his hand back and blew on it. 'And you know what happens to female werewolves without decent protection. Without you I end up dead or in some pervert's collection of paranormal women. You know it.' She picked up the tray with the toast, turned on her heel and stalked out of the room.

*　*　*

Iris had screamed herself hoarse after Blake the night before. Mixing threats and pleading long after she knew he really had left her.

In the morning, things had seemed simpler. She could actually twist her hands around to get her fingers into the knots in the piece of rope that secured the cuffs to the headboard. She'd found the key on her kitchen table with a note that just said, 'Catch you in the office, Blake xxx'. Once she had the cuffs off, she'd stuffed the note in the toaster and turned it on – almost burning the house down in the process and ending up having to chuck the whole thing in the bath.

Now Iris was cycling into work as fast as her wheels would carry her. And even though she knew her main focus should be what she was going to do to Blake, she couldn't stop thinking about Alfie. About the wolf.

Why didn't I kill him? She freewheeled down Cowley Road, dodging traffic, until the Institute of Paraphysiology loomed out of a block of derelict and soon-to-be-derelict buildings. Not that you'd know that that particular building was the Institute of Anything, unless you knew what you were looking for.

The Institute of Paraphysiology was so secretive that it couldn't be more inconspicuous if it didn't actually exist. It was, what it liked to call, deniable. As for who was doing the denying, and to whom, Iris wasn't exactly sure. All she knew was that even her mum didn't know what she did for a living and the building her office was housed in still looked like the ramshackle disused bingo hall it once was. They'd even left the TO LET sign fixed to the outside of the building when they'd moved in over a year ago. You had to be on the doorstep to see the one clue: the tiny plaque by the entryphone which said THE INSTITUTE OF PARAPHYSIOLOGY. Iris's boss – the werewolf-destroying legend Dr Tobias – had come up with that impressive-sounding title.

I could've killed him. I should've killed him? Iris jogged up the steps outside the bingo hall, tapped her code into the security pad and the door auto-unlocked. As she shoved it open she bumped right into Dr Tobias on his way out.

'Iris,' he said with a bright smile, 'you look a little flushed, are you feeling alright?' Dr Tobias had been the scourge of werewolves in Oxford since forever, and yet with his dainty, spry little walk, slight frame and mild manner it was more than impossible to believe.

'Er,' said Iris, feeling the realisation of what had just happened break over her like a wave. 'Yes. Um. But. Oh God, sir, I . . . was . . . attacked . . . by . . . a . . . lyc. Last night! A werewolf! Not even full moon!' *And I could have killed it. And I didn't.*

'Oh. Really.' Dr Tobias didn't sound shocked. More intrigued. He cocked his head at her, catlike.

Iris didn't say anything. They were both stuck. Jammed in the doorway. She couldn't get in, he couldn't get out.

Dr Tobias took a deep breath. 'Well. Now, Iris, this is very interesting. I would love to talk to you in more detail about it, but unfortunately your timing could not be worse. I am needed elsewhere.' He paused. 'Talk to Blake about it. He's upstairs now. He knows as much about lycs as I do.'

'Yes. I did mention it to him.'

'Well, that's good. I'm glad the two of you are managing to keep your private difficulties and your professional lives separate. So important.' Tobias gave Iris a brightly inappropriate smile and she moved back to allow him out of the door.

Iris forced herself not to stare after him; there was something about Dr Tobias sometimes that drew the eye. Something a little freaky. She put her hand out to stop the door before it closed fully again and hefted her bike inside. She threw it onto the carpet and then darted through a little archway to the stairs and galloped up to the second floor.

* * *

When Misty and Zac appeared in the kitchen a while later, Alfie was still sitting in the same spot at the table with an empty plate in front of him.

'Don't stress about it, babe,' Misty was saying. 'We're only going to be here a few days. Then we can go someplace else.'

Zac crossed the kitchen and stood in front of the window. Backlit, with his dark skin and dark clothes, he looked slightly iconic. Zac always seemed to know where to stand to look a bit like a movie-poster. 'Yeah, well, I don't like it. Everyone knows Oxford is goddamn Vix Central.'

Alfie said, 'You don't need to worry about Vix. There are plenty of lycs in Oxford. They know how to handle them.'

'I don't?' Zac said. 'Look at what they did to you, man.'

Instinctively, Alfie reached up and touched the dressing over his eye. 'What I mean is *you* don't have to worry. You're a stable wolf. You only change at full moon and you can do proper lock down then. Vix won't touch you unless you're off the leash. And you won't be, will you?'

'I guess not.'

'Yep,' Leon said, striding in through the kitchen door with an armful of chocolate bars, 'we're all going to be good little weredogs. For Daddy.'

'Where've you been, man?' Zac said.

'Sire,' Leon growled. 'C'mon, Zac, you've got to do it properly. Where have you been, sire?'

Alfie rolled his eyes as Zac parroted back, '"Where have you been, sire?"'

'Newsagent's up the road. I got these. Need the calories, don't I. Lycan metabolism.' He tipped the chocolates onto the table. 'Also, I think daddy dearest is going to have to make me cub of the year.'

Alfie made a face. 'What?'

'Guess who I met while I was out? Only a cute nurse. Pearl, her name is. I told her all about you, well, all about your mangled eyeball, anyway; I'd have been there all day if I'd gone into full details about what a prize tit you are.'

Alfie snarled low, but didn't react any more than that.

'Anyway,' Leon went on, 'she told me to get you some of this here ointment.' Leon pulled out a scrap of paper and read aloud from the scrawled note, '"AntiBactro". She says I'll need a prescription, but if our brave soldier still won't go and see a proper doctor I'll just have to pop out and see if I can't come by some.' Leon said all this, seeming to swagger with his *voice*.

'Dammit, Leon, I do *know* these things. I did three years of a medical degree, for fuck's sake. Will you all stop fussing.'

'What cute nurse, man – uh – sire?' Zac looked at Leon as if he might have a cute nurse on his person at that moment. 'How come I don't meet none of these cute nurses?'

Leon grinned and plopped himself down at the kitchen table opposite Alfie, skinned a chocolate bar and took a large bite. 'Well, some of us have just got it,' he said, barely intelligible through the clod of chocolate in his mouth.

Misty was standing behind Alfie. She often did that after they'd argued: moved close to him for reassurance. She leant over and picked up the prescriptive chocolate bar Leon had tossed onto the table, simultaneously twining her fingers in Alfie's hair. Alfie concentrated on the sensation, feeling faintly buzzy and out of it, like he wasn't really there.

Zac and Leon's conversation continued, fading in and out of Alfie's mind. Zac was still letting Leon lead him on. 'So where is she now? Is she coming over?'

'Yep. She just had to pop home first.'

Zac moved away from the window to sit next to Leon at the table. Leon and Zac kept on blathering about nurses.

Alfie concentrated harder on the sensations of Misty's slender little fingers twining in his hair. God, he was horny. This was the wolf's doing. The wolf used up all your body's resources; the body you got back was racked with fatigue, thirst, hunger and horniness. Especially horniness – that always seemed to hit Alfie like a runaway train. Werewolves were supposed to have sex after they changed back. Cement themselves back into their bodies.

On another day, in another place, he'd have given Misty a look. Met her eye with something she'd understand and she'd have responded by twining her fingers tighter in his hair. Pulling until he gasped. He'd have growled as he stood up and thrown her over his shoulder, carried her upstairs and fucked her until she was practically levitating.

But not now. Now he sometimes felt like he might flip if he stood up too quickly. He was like a stick of dynamite. For all his strength and overt power he was a delicate thing. Unstable. Coming apart. And after what he had done to Misty that one time, she wasn't getting willingly into his bed again – no matter how securely he was chained down. She had made that very clear. Neither of them really understood how she'd survived it.

He took a deep breath and tried to think about something other than his dick. 'Look,' he said, 'I'm going to get the collar. Today. I need you to all understand something –'

Misty interrupted. 'First, we need to get this nurse to look at your eye. Then we'll talk about you going to get the Silver Collar. I mean it, Alfie.'

Alfie looked at Misty and made a low noise with his throat. He didn't like pulling alpha on Misty. With Leon or Zac he didn't care, but with Misty everything was different.

She put up her hands, showing him her palms. 'OK,' she said. 'Fine. Be maimed, see if I care.'

Still chewing, Leon said, 'How are you even going to find them? Don't the Vix have cloaking spells to stop werewolves finding them and turning the tables?'

'Yeah,' said Alfie. 'I can't trace the Vix, but I can trace Iris and since last night I'm pretty certain she's still working for them.'

''Cause she's his life mate,' said Zac casually. 'Werewolves can scent them anywhere. There isn't a cloaking spell on earth –'

'She is not my life mate. I don't believe in that super-stitious lyc crap,' Alfie growled.

Misty said, 'Then how can you trace her?'

'I don't know,' Alfie said. 'That's not important. What is important is that I need you all to understand that when I go to the Vix I might not come back.'

Misty said, 'What! Don't joke, babe.'

'This is serious. The collar is my last chance. If the Vix don't have it, or if I can't take it from them, I won't be coming back. They can decide what to do with me.' Alfie stood up. 'Now excuse me. I'm going to my room. I need to be alone to concentrate and get a fix on exactly where she is.'

Zac and Misty looked like they were in shock. Leon was clearly hiding a smirk.

As Alfie left the room he heard Leon mutter, 'Oh, nice one, Daddy. Well handled.'

7

Iris didn't knock on Blake's door, but she paused in the doorway, a little surprised by how tired he looked. His eyes were red-rimmed behind his glasses, his small body hunched over and cramped with fatigue.

Matthew was also in the office, standing behind Blake. Iris didn't find that at all surprising. When she was alone with Blake she tended to see her favourite imaginary dead brother a lot. Weirdly, they looked quite similar – small compact bodies, too much dark unruly hair.

'Hey,' Blake said. 'How are your wrists?'

'OK. A lot better than you look.' Iris wandered across the room. 'You been here all night? You look rough.'

'You don't like me looking rough?' Blake said.

Iris just raised her eyebrows.

Blake pulled a face and rolled his shoulders. 'I came back here and pulled an all-nighter; the doc wanted some translations doing. And I've been thinking about your wolf. Possibly even more than you have.'

'Alfie?'

'Yeah. Well, if it is him. But if there's an unstable wolf out there we need to bring him in.'

Iris nodded.

'And I have something that I'd like to try.'

'You do?'

Blake was already up from his desk, heading to the door to his lab. 'Yeah, come and see.'

Iris followed Blake into the bright white space of his laboratory. Everything glistened in here, sparkled with cleanliness. Walking in in front of Iris, Blake said, 'I have this thing. Cate gave it to me.' He started rummaging through cupboards as he spoke. Iris caught glimpses of Blake's supplies, guns and chemicals and strange metal devices. 'Aha!' he said after a moment, straightening up. 'Look.'

Blake was holding a thick ring of metal about the size of a tea plate.

'And what's that?' asked Iris.

'It's a collar. The Silver Collar. It's a werewolf collar. It's meant to stop them changing.'

'Wow.'

'Wow indeed. Could be interesting for your wolf, no? Stop him changing at the wrong times.'

Iris bit her lip. The collar was such a simple object, and yet, looking at it made her hold her breath. 'And you want to find out?'

'Yeah, I do. So I need that wolf. Which is kind of your area.'

Iris shifted. Her sore shoulder ached. Blake was looking at her, waiting for her to say something. 'Well, I do have one idea.'

Blake grinned – all animal. 'I knew you'd have something.'

'Hospitals. I stabbed him in the eye out at the parks. He'll need to get it checked out.'

Blake winced. 'Really. You didn't say you'd injured his *eye*. Ew. What were you aiming for exactly?'

'*Now* you're squeamish? But what choice did I have? It was on top of me, I didn't have much reach. But, anyway, if I go to the hospital I'll need Cate to give me some cover and she needs Tobias to sign it off. Except, oh damn, he's gone out hasn't he?'

Blake said, 'I can do that for you.'

'You can?' Iris was a little surprised. She didn't know Blake had that sort of clearance.

'Um, yeah. I can sign off on Cate's stuff. So, why don't you get going and I'll talk to her – she can do it by remote – and I'll text you when you're good to go?'

'OK. I'll take one of the Reds with me – whoever is unlucky enough to cross my path first – so make sure Cate sends enough of her freaky mojo to cover us both.'

As Iris turned to leave the lab, Blake came up behind her and put his hand on her shoulder. He pulled it away again. 'Iris, you're bleeding.'

'God, am I?' Iris craned to try and see. 'The dressing must have come off. The strain you put on it last night didn't help either.'

Blake looked wary. 'Yeah, er, Iris, I can't help noticing you haven't done anything violent to me for that. Are you feeling OK?'

Iris shrugged, then winced as the movement hurt. 'Yeah, well, I had a few things to sort out. But thanks for reminding me.'

Iris turned around fast. Her knee came up and hit him hard in the groin and, as he doubled over, she smashed him in the chin with her right fist. He went over backwards, missing the island workbench and crashing onto the floor.

Iris dropped to her knees and straddled him as he submitted, lifting his head with a fist tangled in his hair. She made him kiss her. Made him give it up and let her own him. She felt his mouth open up for her even as he was still moaning in pain.

She licked the side of his face – so turned on – then she said, 'And that's way less than you deserve. Now come on and help me redo this dressing on my shoulder.'

8

A little later, Alfie was still in his room in the attic thinking about Iris when he heard the front door open and close. Then voices in the hall. Zac and Misty.

The chatter downstairs got louder. He figured he should go down. Time to do the right thing. Make nice with Misty. Promise to take better care of himself. Maybe she'd tracked down that antibiotic ointment he was meant to be using. But before he could begin, he heard light footsteps on the stairs, footsteps coming all the way up to the attic. He turned, ready to tell Misty he was sorry. But it wasn't Misty coming upstairs at all.

He knew who she was straight away. Leon's nurse. Had to be. Wearing a lilac-coloured uniform; a sort of wiggly squiggly blonde. Just the type Leon would be following around with his tongue hanging out. Very, very pretty.

Alfie had never had much of a thing for nurses, despite his lost ambitions to be a doctor. But right now, looking at this nurse in particular, he thought he might try to start to develop one.

'Hey,' she said, holding out a dainty arm. 'I'm Pearl. I'm a nurse. Your friend Leon asked me to come and take a look at your eye. He said you wouldn't go to hospital.'

Alfie shook his head. 'It's fine really.'

'He said you'd say that. Come on, I don't do house calls for just anybody. I really think you should let me take a look.'

Alfie nodded. Resigned. 'OK, OK.' He sat down on the bed and let Pearl remove the dressing.

Pearl looked at the wound and gave a low sort of whistle. 'Weird.'

'What?'

47

'Well. OK. It's deep. Nasty. There's also some blistering. Are you allergic to anything?'

'Yes. Silver. It was a silver blade.'

'Oh. OK. Well, maybe that would explain ... I don't know, allergies aren't really my specialism. You should go and get it stitched. And you might need an op. You ought to see a specialist.'

'Can't,' Alfie grunted. 'Just patch it up as best you can and I'll take my chances.'

'You know, he said you'd say that too. Your friend downstairs really does know you pretty well.'

Alfie shrugged. 'I guess he does.'

Pearl got out a little kit from her bag and smeared some stinging cream into Alfie's eye before redoing his dressing. 'Interesting bunch, your friends,' Pearl said conversationally as she worked. 'I mean, they're kind of eclectic. That tall black guy and the Japanese girl. Is she your girlfriend?' The question was just not quite casual enough.

'No. She's a friend.'

'She's very pretty.' Pearl had finished with the dressing now. She stood back. 'And the guy I met earlier in the shop ... What's his ... ?'

'Leon.'

Pearl nodded and bent down beside the bed to put her kit back in her bag. Alfie looked at her arse while she was bent over, because he couldn't not, the way it was presented tight and cotton-covered right next to his good eye. He really ought to start working on that nurse fetish. He wondered, then, if he was only interested in her because he knew Leon was.

'So do you like to get tied up, or to tie people up?' said Pearl as she stood up again.

'Uh. What?'

'The chains on the bed.' She raised her eyebrows. 'I know I'm a nurse but I'm not an angel.'

'Oh, them. Actually, it's not really like that.'

'Really? Because you have a whole load of heavy-duty

chains there, so you being kinky is probably one of the least disturbing explanations.'

Alfie raised his eyebrows.

'So? Which is it? You like to be tied or do the tying?'

'Guess.'

Pearl quirked a smile. 'Well, you do seem pretty bossy, but, I don't know. They're big.' Pearl reached down and lifted up one of the heavy wrist cuffs. The chain attached to it clanked. 'So either you tie up people who are just as big and built as you, or, you're something of a pussy cat underneath all that snark and snarl.'

Alfie smiled slowly.

Pearl gave him a look right back that made him squirm. 'You know, the thing about nursing, Mr . . .' Pearl stopped.

'Friday,' said Alfie, 'Alfie Friday.'

'The thing about nursing, Mr Alfie Friday, is that most of the people who I deal with are unhealthy, unfit, unwell. For all the sexiness that nursing is supposed to embody, there really is nothing sexy about my job.' She paused. 'Most of the time.'

She was looking at him. Alfie looked back at her. Looked at her softly parted lips.

Like life mates, Lure was another one of those werewolf stories that Alfie didn't believe in. Some packs thought that after the change, when a werewolf was at his most horny he could persuade human women to sleep with him just by looking at them. Alfie thought that was nonsense. But despite that fact he knew he used Lure all the time. He was using it now. He knew he only had to wait.

Pearl bent at the waist and kissed him. Slow and delicate. After a few little explorations she pulled back, quite flushed. It was so good. And not enough. *Never enough kissing.* He had only had the very tip of her tongue, but Alfie was panting and half hard. *This wasn't safe.* He reached out and put one big hand on Pearl's flushed cheek. 'You need to chain me down before you kiss me again.'

Pearl smiled as if she understood. 'OK.'

Alfie lay back on the bed, stretching out his arms and legs. As Pearl fixed the cuffs in place she didn't seem to notice the way the magic made the chains subtly adjust themselves, shortening, tightening, pulling taut, making Alfie's breath catch in his throat as his body was drawn rigid, just over the edge of what would have been comfortable.

'You have the keys for these, right?' Pearl said, half joking.

Alfie managed to say, 'In the bedside cabinet.' But he was already half lost to the restriction. His hips were rocking gently – the only bit of movement he really had. Sex had been like this for so long now – over three years – that his cock seemed to jump up in a Pavlovian response as soon as he was held fast.

Pearl climbed onto the bed and straddled Alfie's waist. Alfie caught his breath as he felt hot bare skin between her legs. 'Do you usually work without any underwear?'

'Only for very special patients,' Pearl said, laughing as she unbuttoned his shirt and opened it up, before leaning down to kiss him again. Even more slowly this time. But again she pulled back before he had taken all he wanted. 'OK?' said Pearl, teasing. 'You want me to kiss you again, big boy?'

Alfie was panting. He'd strained at his bonds chasing her mouth. He wanted it back on his so desperately. He twisted against the restraints, feeling his arousal and frustration both increase, both feeding off each other. He could feel his nipples tightening. In fact, his whole body felt super sensitised. Kissing. Damn. He never got to do enough kissing. Kissing was always curtailed too early, because of the muzzle.

He swallowed. He couldn't help staring at her mouth. 'No. I can't. There's something else I need,' he said scratchily, 'but I need you to not freak out, OK?'

'OK.' Pearl's voice seemed a little bit husky as she looked at him. 'I'm not squeamish you know. I was just looking at your mangled-up eye.'

'Yeah, I know. OK, in the cabinet there's, uh, something. I need you to take it out and put it on.'

'Put it on? What is it? A French maid's outfit? Because I'm already wearing a top-ten male fantasy uniform.'

'On me. Put it on me.'

Pearl didn't say anything else. She reached over. Her cotton-covered breasts grazed his chest. *God, he was so close already. She'd only have to breathe on his dick . . .*

When she sat back up, she was holding an arrangement of leather straps and buckles. 'This?'

Alfie nodded.

'Right, so which part of you is this going on?'

'My face. It's a muzzle. Look, Pearl, it's very important that I don't bite you. That I can't.'

Pearl frowned. 'Maybe this is a little too . . .'

Alfie inhaled. This was the point where he often lost them. The chaining him down part seemed to fly with most girls, except the ones that were disappointed that they weren't the ones getting to writhe in bondage – and in actual fact sometimes Alfie was pretty disappointed about that too – but the muzzle, well, the muzzle could be a little bit hardcore.

Alfie caught Pearl's eye and gave it his best shot. The spiel he had honed and refined over the years for just this situation. Was it part of Lure? He wasn't even sure. Not that he believed in Lure. 'Look, baby, don't you like this?' He held her gaze and then struggled against the chains, straining and flexing his body, showing how much of a prisoner he was. He was so horny already it really wasn't much of an act to seem frustrated and aroused. 'Don't you like seeing me like this? They're real, you know. It's no trick. I really can't get free from these things. You can do what you want with me. You can use me to make yourself come over and over if you like. Use my face, my chest, my cock. Any part of me. You can make *me* wait for hours if you want to. Don't tell me you don't want to strap that thing over my mouth so I can't even beg. Look at me, I'm

51

so big and I'm so strong – much stronger than you – but I'll be totally helpless. At your mercy.'

He could see Pearl running her tongue around the inside of one cheek. 'Well,' she said, 'when you put it like that . . .'

Alfie pulled at the chains holding his wrists. 'You know, if you were to force that thing into my mouth, right now, I wouldn't even be able to stop you.'

Pearl's breathing was coming a little more heavily now. There was a scent in the air. A scent Alfie knew very well. 'OK,' she said, 'I would actually really like to find out whether or not that's true.'

Pearl turned the muzzle over in her hands until she figured out how it worked. 'So, this plug goes in your mouth and then this piece covers it, and the straps go . . . uh?'

'One goes round the back and the other under my chin.'

'Right, right. Not a fan of the simple life, then. Well let's see how this works.'

Alfie made a muffled sound as Pearl shoved the big leather plug into his mouth. Another wide piece of leather sealed it shut and buckled around the back of his head. Extra straps stopped the whole thing from moving up or down. It was, by necessity, very secure.

When she was done, Pearl scooted down Alfie's body a little, letting her naked crotch rest on his denim-covered one. Alfie's cock seemed to move involuntarily, rocking against her.

'You know,' said Pearl, 'this kinky stuff of yours really is kind of pretty.' She touched the leather straps on Alfie's face then stroked his hair. Alfie pulled against her fingers so her grip tightened and gasped into the muzzle, bucking his hips harder, when the tension reached the point of pain.

'Oh,' said Pearl, 'you like that do you? You really are a kinky boy.' She stroked his hair gently for a moment more and then, suddenly, tugged hard. Alfie hissed. It was so good.

Keeping her grip on his hair tight, Pearl started unbuttoning Alfie's jeans with her other hand. His cock was straining through the opening in moments, but still covered in the white cotton of his underpants. With one-handed expertise, Pearl liberated it. Alfie moaned through the muzzle and thrust up into her hands, uncontrolled.

Pearl let go of Alfie's hair and shifted slightly, adjusting herself so she could slide herself down onto his cock. She paused for a second, making Alfie shudder as he was marooned not quite in and not quite out.

'F-uck,' she said, still not moving, looking at him. 'You are so hot. And the patch over your eye really doesn't hurt any.'

Then Pearl jumped in surprise as, below them, the front door slammed. There were voices. Footsteps on the stairs.

From somewhere on the landing came a noise like a growl. But a human growl. Rough and nasty. Alfie knew exactly what it was.

Pearl turned slightly as Leon appeared up the stairs into the attic. He was already shouting before he was properly in the room. 'You sick fuck, Alfie! What the fuck are you doing that shit with her for, you sick fucking bastard?' He was in human form, of course, but he actually looked surprisingly inhuman as he raged.

As he reached the bed, Leon put one big hand on Pearl's shoulder and Alfie met his eyes.

Alfie knew that if he wasn't muzzled he could have made Leon leave right now. He could have used the voice. The voice of Leon's sire. A voice that would hit him in the guts and make him think his god was angry with him. If Alfie even had both his eyes, maybe a look, a glare, could do it.

But as Leon climbed up on the bed there was nothing Alfie could do except close his good eye and turn his head away.

Pearl was looking from one man to the other as if desperate for some kind of explanation for what was going on. Leon grinned. He leant forwards and he kissed Pearl in the crook of her neck.

Pearl turned. 'Leon, right?'

'Sweetheart! You remembered.'

'Um. Is this . . . ? Um.'

Leon put a finger to her lips. 'Shush,' he said. 'Alfie has, uh, different tastes. This is how he wants it. If you're up for it of course.'

'Up for what?'

'For me to fuck you while he watches. Chained down underneath like that. That's what I came up here for. That's what he wants. He asked me to.'

Alfie shook his head violently. 'No!' he said into the muzzle.

'Then why is he saying no?'

'Because.' Leon leant over Pearl and pinched Alfie's cheek. Hard. Alfie stopped shaking his head and looked at Leon. Giving him the most terrible and fear-inspiring look he could. On other occasions he'd made Leon drop to his knees with a look like this. But not today. Leon flinched slightly, but that was all. 'Because,' Leon said again, his throat sounding a little drier, 'that's all part of the fantasy for him. That's why he has these chains. He gets off on this really twisted stuff.'

'And you just happen to oblige?'

'Who's saying I'm not a little twisted too?' Leon smirked.

Alfie wasn't trying to communicate any more. He knew Leon could just manipulate anything he did, but he was desperately hoping Pearl might read his thoughts. *How can Leon be telling the truth? How could I have planned this? How could I have known you were even coming by, let alone that you were going to make a pass at me? Think, Pearl, he's got to be lying.*

Pearl either didn't pick up Alfie's psychic messages or didn't want to. She was kissing Leon now, turning her head as he held her from behind.

Watching them, Alfie's cock burnt. He twisted his hips from side to side, desperate for some friction. *Aching.*

Leon's long dirty-blond hair was all flyaway frizz from being outside. It was down to his mid-back now. About the length he let it get to before he cut it to just above his shoulders. That was a lot of hair. It was covering most of his face as he kissed Pearl. He was still in his street clothes. His denim jacket was spotted with raindrops. His boots were making dirty marks on Alfie's bedclothes. Pearl slid a hand up under Leon's black T-shirt, exposing a flash of his lean abdomen.

Leon had unbuttoned Pearl's uniform halfway down the front. The lace trim of her bra was visible. Leon put his hands inside it as he kissed her. He cupped Pearl's breasts and worked his fingers inside the lace until she broke his kiss to throw her head back and moan out loud. Her neck was so white.

Alfie moaned too, tortured by the sight of Pearl's delicate breasts, her kiss-swollen lips, her dizzying arousal. Leon caught Alfie's eye as he licked at Pearl's swan neck and his expression was nasty.

Still holding Alfie's gaze, Leon pushed Pearl forwards. She fell onto all fours, caging Alfie with her body. Her uniform was bunched right up around her waist now. Behind Pearl, Leon started to unbuckle. Pearl was looking at Alfie with an expression that was half quizzical, half overwhelmed by lust.

She gasped as Leon pushed a finger inside her. He withdrew and grinned at Alfie over her shoulder. The scent was everywhere all at once. Alfie could barely stand it. Leon brought a glistening finger to his lips and licked once, delicately. Then he reached over and ran it across Alfie's chin below the muzzle. 'So you don't forget this, sire,' Leon said. His voice sounded even but Alfie could hear the rough nastiness underneath. He was loving this. This was Leon's version of sticking a silver dagger in Alfie's heart. It was every bit as debilitating.

Pearl didn't seem to have noticed this mini soap opera, she was too busy quivering in anticipation as Leon finished liberating his cock and thrust into her from behind, driving her forwards. Her face ended up inches from Alfie's. Kiss close – if it weren't for the muzzle.

A moment later, a hand touched Alfie's cock. He arched into the touch. Desperate. Desperately close. He yanked hard at the chains and twisted his body. He was biting down so hard on the leather in his mouth his jaw ached. His mouth was full of its strange salt-musk taste. The urge to bite got stronger and stronger. The hand on his cock felt amazing. Leon and the weirdness of everything that was happening seemed to recede. His approaching orgasm became the most, the only, important thing in the world.

Leather felt something like flesh in his mouth. He pulled at the chains again, harder, bursting with the need to get free. To flex himself. To run and rip and bite and fight. He was coming and he was changing. He heard himself roar and at the same time saw the speed of Leon's reflexes as he sprang backwards off the bed, pulling Pearl with him.

9

As Pure and Iris parked their bikes outside the John Radcliffe Hospital, Iris wondered idly if anyone might mistake the two of them for a couple. A sporty couple, riding their bikes together through Oxford in the drizzle.

Although, she thought Pure might actually be gay. Or maybe bi, it was hard to tell these days. He did seem to talk about male actors quite a lot. Then again, he talked about a lot of actresses too. And he did seem rather fond of Aurelia. He had a shaved head – but that didn't necessarily mean anything. Was there something in the way he walked? That long lean gait? Something in the way he was so devastatingly beautiful? Iris hoped not. Not because she coveted Pure for herself, but just because she liked to think that a passer-by might see the two of them and think that she – a scruffy little brunette in dark-red army fatigues and a lop-sided ponytail – might be the apple of Pure's beautiful eye.

'Have you ever used Cate's spell cover before?' she said.

Pure finished chaining up both bikes and stood up. He shook his perfectly shaped head. 'Well, only the kind of cloaking she puts on us when we go out on the sweeps, but not this stuff.'

'OK.' Iris tried to think of a way to explain it. She settled for what Blake said to her that first time, back in the bad old days when they'd had to mix the magic themselves. 'It can be weird at first, but just act as if you have every right to do what you're doing.'

Pure frowned. 'OK. I still don't get why we need it though. Couldn't we just ask them the stuff we need to know about?' He started to trot after Iris as she headed for the hospital front gates.

'Not really,' she said, as he reached her and dropped into step. 'Why would they tell us? We're a couple of nobodies. We have no jurisdiction. Claiming to be from the Institute of Paraphysiology would just get us laughed out of there. But if Cate's got us covered, we can just go up and ask to look through their records and it'll seem perfectly OK. It's easier to do that to explain.'

'But is that really ethical? I mean, should we be doing this? If we have no real right.'

'Here's the thing, Pure.' Iris stopped in the entrance way and turned to him. 'Werewolves are mythical, magical, not real. Except, of course, that they *are* real. Along with all the other stuff that we know is real and other people don't seem to be able to believe. But because no one else really believes in them, we don't really have any proper status. We're not like the police; we can't go in there and demand information. Even though we're working in the public interest.' Iris stopped and shrugged. 'So we use Cate. Or, at least, we use magic.'

Pure was looking at Iris with his pretty head cocked to one side.

'Look, if you don't like it, take it up with Dr Tobias, but believe me, we couldn't work without it.' She turned away from Pure and began walking in through the doors. Pure was back at her shoulder in moments.

'Sorry, I –'

'Shush.'

The foyer was busy. Depressingly grey chairs containing depressingly grey people. Iris strode over to the reception and walked straight to the front of the queue.

'Excuse me,' she said calmly as the people at the front of the queue stepped aside to let her through. 'I'm Iris Instasi-Fox and this is my colleague William White.' As she glanced at Pure, a confused expression flashed over his face, almost as if he was wondering who William White might be. But introducing her companion as 'Pure' might have been a stretch – even for one of Cate's powerful spells.

The receptionist on the other side of the glass screen smiled broadly and said, 'Oh, yes, do come around,' indicating a door marked STAFF ONLY. Iris flashed a quick grin at Pure and slipped through the door.

'Um,' said the receptionist, confused for a moment. Then, 'Iris Instasi-Fox and William White. Uh . . .'

'We need to look at your admission records for today,' Iris said, coolly. 'Oh, actually, and yesterday evening too.'

'Oh. Uh, Sally, could you?' The receptionist said over her shoulder.

Another woman, who had been typing into a computer and ignoring Pure and Iris, turned around, looking a little bit weirded out, but she quickly smiled as she caught Iris's eye then stood up smiling. 'Sure. They're all on computer. Shall I show you how to access them?'

'Please,' Iris said. 'Actually, if you could show my colleague. I'd like to talk to as many staff as you can spare.'

'Certainly,' said Sally.

Iris looked at Pure, who still seemed a little confused. She urged him to go over to Sally's computer with a jerk of her head. He gave her one last wary look, before walking over and sitting down on the swivel chair Sally had vacated. Sally herself remained standing, leaning over Pure, with a lusty gleam in her eye. Iris hoped for her sake that Pure didn't start singing the praises of various Hollywood actors too soon.

Leon stood in the hall listening to the noises coming from upstairs. Alfie. Wolf Alfie. Angry wolf Alfie. Suddenly he felt very scared. Very, very scared.

Misty came out of the living room, demanding to know what had happened.

Leon pointed at Pearl, who was white and shaking. 'She needs a memory wipe,' he said. Misty would know what that meant.

'No, I don't,' said Pearl. 'I'm fine.'

Misty looked from Pearl to Leon. 'What did you do?'

'He nearly killed her,' Leon said. 'He's too unstable to be

alpha. I've had it with him.' He lifted his head and called up the stairs. 'Zac, Zac, get down here.'

'He's your alpha,' Misty said quietly, 'and your sire.'

'Not like this,' Leon said as Zac appeared and started down the stairs. 'We have to leave. All of us. You too, Misty.'

'Leave? Leave him?' Misty shook her head and looked horrified. 'I'll never leave him.'

'Fine. You stay. We'll go.' Leon turned to Pearl who was still standing by the door looking ... shocked? No, not shocked. Intrigued. In fact Pearl looked downright fascinated by the conversation. 'So,' Leon said, 'you want to come with us, babe. In fact, could me and my pal Zac, here, stop at your place for a bit.'

'Uh ...' Pearl looked over at Zac. And then she swallowed very distinctly. 'I don't know. I have to go to work right now.'

'No problem, babe. We'll go and have a drink. Meet you later. Where do you work?'

'The hospital,' Pearl said. 'The John Radcliffe Hospital.'

While Pure was looking at the computerised records, Iris spent a frustrating couple of hours tracking down and interviewing a selection of doctors, nurses, care assistants and receptionists. But no one seemed to remember seeing. 'A tall guy; muscly; dark hair; eyes a kind of gold colour; nice smile; good looking,' with a weirdly fast-healing eye injury.

'Well, he sounds like something I might have remembered, even on a busy shift,' one of the doctors had said, running a hand through her cropped blonde hair.

When Iris rejoined Pure back in the office behind reception, he was equally frustrated. 'Nothing,' he said. 'There was one eye injury yesterday. But more like a person who'd been punched in the eye. And anyway that was a woman.'

Iris's shoulders sagged.

As they were walking dejectedly back through the waiting room, past all the waiting ill people, who didn't seem to have moved in the last couple of hours, Pure suddenly shouted, 'Hey,' and broke into a familiar loping trot.

'Pure,' Iris called after him. But Pure was running towards a blonde woman in a lilac-coloured nurse's uniform who was just walking in. He caught her by the shoulder and she turned, looked at him and smiled. She was really exceptionally beautiful in a rather familiar way and her dazzling smile was exactly the same as his.

Iris caught them up and Pure said, still grinning, 'Hey, Iris, meet my cousin, Pearl.'

10

Iris was as polite as she could be to Pure's cousin, but she knew she was acting distracted. Over Pearl's shoulder, she could suddenly see Matthew out in the car park, trying to attract her attention.

Woo-hoo. Iris. I've found something you ought to see. You need to come with me.

Pure said to Pearl, 'So, girl, I've not caught up with you in forever. You want to grab a coffee? That OK, Iris?'

'Mmm, sure,' Iris said, as Matthew kept on waving at her from outside.

Pearl said, 'Can't right now. Maybe later? My shift's about to start.'

'Oh, don't worry about that, doll. I can get them to give you the afternoon off. I'm on a special project.' Iris saw him waggle his eyebrows at Pearl. 'It's called, uh, Operation Red Hood. I've got special jurisdiction.'

'You have? What's your project? Operation . . . ? My dad said your dad said you'd left the army and were renovating that old bingo hall off Cowley Road.'

'Well, you shouldn't believe any of that rubbish. I had to tell them something. Now, why don't you come along with me and we'll have a chat with your boss about giving you the rest of the afternoon off?' Pure held out an elbow to Pearl.

Iris barely noticed them go. She was already wandering towards the exit door through which she had seen Matthew, wondering where he would lead her.

By the time Iris got out of the building, an ambulance was pulling up outside, blocking Matthew from view. She skittered out of the way – light and bouncy in her running shoes. Matthew was heading out of the car park down a long ramp. Iris followed.

Down at street level, Matthew was on the other side of the road. Iris had to wait to cross and then started to sprint after him as he darted into a nearby pub.

Iris followed.

It was a pretty quiet little place. It looked like a few of the hospital staff drank in here. Among the doctors and orderlies and a thin black guy sitting incongruously with a long-haired denim-clad headbanger, Matthew was sitting at a table in the corner. Iris walked over and joined him.

Hi, sis.

'Hi,' she said.

Matthew nodded. He had a pint of lager in front of him, which he took a long draw from before he spoke again. *Aren't you drinking? The landlord'll wonder what you're up to if you don't.*

'I'm working.'

Get a drink.

'I thought you said you had something to show me.'

I do. Get a drink.

In the hospital canteen, Pearl White and Pure White faced each other over predictably bad coffee. 'I'm actually really glad I ran into you,' Pearl said, 'because last time I saw you, you had such outrageous stories about people you'd been with, but now I can top them all.'

Pure set down the polystyrene cup he was drinking from. 'You think so, doll? Hit me.'

'OK.' Pearl smirked. 'You are going to love this. OK, this morning I met this guy in the newsagent's by the bus stop at St Clement's. He was quite nice looking but could have done with a haircut. He was bit of a metal head, bandana, all the denim, but, you know, I kind of like that when I'm in the mood, and you could tell that under all that eighties clobber he had a fantastic body.' She stopped and took a tiny sip of coffee. 'Well, he clearly clocked the uniform and, at first, I thought he was just one of the usual perverts, but actually when he started talking to me he was all concerned about this guy he lived with who'd hurt his eye. It was quite sweet.'

'He lived with another guy?'

Pearl rolled her eyes. 'Yeah, but don't get your hopes up, more like a shared house kind of thing. He lived with these two other guys and this girl. He seemed really concerned so I said I'd pop over.'

'You're such an angel,' Pure said sarcastically.

Pearl hit his arm. 'Shut up! OK, he was fit. Anyway, I ended up seeing the guy who'd hurt his eye and, man, was he gorgeous too. Like, all the time I was looking at his gross gouged eyeball, I was still practically drooling on his duvet. And he was kind of flirty, so I was kind of flirty back. And he'd got these chains fixed to his bed. Really heavy nasty chains, right, so he asked me to chain him up.'

''Kin' hell, Pearly, strike the angel remark.'

'That's not all. Oh my God, listen, I chained him up. He even asked me to put this weird contraption on his mouth.'

'What like a gag? A ball gag or something?'

'More like a muzzle. A great tangle of leather and chains and stuff.'

Pure ran his teeth over his bottom lip. 'Did you say, "a muzzle"?'

'Yeah. Like dogs wear.'

'I know what one is.' Pure stopped. *And didn't she say he'd hurt his eye? Gouged his eye? Oh fuck.* He was ignoring his drink now, half-hoping this conversation was going where he thought it might be, half hoping it wasn't.

'So he put it on – the muzzle thing – OK, actually I put it on him because he was tied up. Chained up. It was hot. He was a really hot guy, though, so anything that involved him on a bed would have been incredibly, well, hot. He was built, you know, kind of pumped up. And kind of, this might sound weird, but kind of animal like.'

Pure nodded and swallowed, thinking, Oh God, oh God, oh God . . .

'OK, so we were like going for it and then out of nowhere this other guy appeared. The first guy, the one I met in the shop. I didn't know what on earth was going on. At first I thought this other guy – Leon – was upset because he'd seen me first, or something, but then it turned out that this was some kind of kinky thing they do and what the super-hot guy really wanted was for Leon and me to fuck while he was tied up underneath! And then Leon reached around me and started wanking the hot guy off. He was moaning and stuff, because he'd still got his mouth strapped up, totally out of it. And he looked so fucking hot, totally hot. I was on top of him, getting fucked so good and hard and this tied-up guy underneath me, God, he was just like a piece of live porn or something. I came so strong. Not even touching my clit.'

'Woah, Pearl. TMI,' Pure said. He bit his lip and looked away. He took another nervous drink of his coffee. It was really bad coffee.

'That's not all,' said Pearl, stopping Pure's relief in its coffee-assessing tracks. 'After I'd come, Leon was still inside me and still wanking the big guy off. I was a bit, you know, on the ceiling, but then, oh God, it was weird. At first I thought something was wrong with my eyes, because the hot guy started to kind of go out of focus, but then I realised it wasn't my eyes; he was changing, twisting in the chains and actually morphing into something else. Leon yanked me off the bed and sort of covered me with his body so I couldn't really see. He bundled me down the stairs pretty fast, telling me the hot guy had had some kind of fit; he wouldn't let me back up to check on him. I don't know what happened to that guy, but I have really never seen anything like that in my life, have you?'

Pure's hands were shaking so much that he knocked his half-cup of coffee all over the table.

11

Across the sticky pub table, Zac watched the way Leon drank his pint, licked his lips, smiled with his teeth. He had never been able to get over the way his sire managed to look so damn feral. Was it something about the kind of werewolf he was? Was Leon more of a wolf than he was? Maybe he was just like that before. Zac didn't know. Leon had two or three wolf years on him.

Leon had his own theories on Alfie's flipping problem, which he hadn't stopped outlining since they'd left the pack house. 'We shouldn't be in Oxford. Not looking for that collar. It's wrong, cub. It's not right. A werewolf in a collar? Don't tell me that isn't all kinds of fucked up. And Alfie thinks flipping is a bad thing, right. Instead of trying to cure that, he should change the way he thinks. I've done my own research. Changing like that – having the wolf close to the skin, it's called – it'll happen to any wolf that lives long enough. It's a great achievement. To be more wolf than man. Isn't that what we all want?'

'Woah! Man, you think flipping's good?'

'Yeah, of course. Don't you?'

Zac gasped and looked warily around the pub. It was pretty empty apart from medical types and a woman with dark hair who was sitting at a corner table talking to herself. He nodded cautiously and took a drink while Leon got back to his favourite subject.

'It all went wrong for Alfie because his sire rejected him. Now, I know how that feels. Alfie didn't come for me when I first changed. You know why? Because of his stupid ideas about lock down. Sire's supposed to come to you on your first change right? Explain the rules. Yeah, except not if he's some prize tit who gets off on locking himself in a cage at full moon when he should be running his wildest. He didn't even know he'd bitten me until that night. He did himself some damage trying to get out of that cage when the wolf realised what had happened.' Leon stopped and laughed. 'If you look, he still has some scars on his hands from trying to get to me.'

'But you have to do lock down here in Oxford because of Vix. You can't be out in wolf form, dude. It's far too dangerous.'

'Yeah, right? That's what Alfie says. But how come he makes us do lock down wherever we are? I'll tell you why. Because *he* never ran with a pack properly. A real pack, not his own twisted idea of one. He never learnt how to be a real wolf. Because his sire was this lone beast thing, he never got to find out how it's meant to work. We shouldn't be shutting ourselves away. It isn't natural.'

'But someone might get hurt if we're running wild.'

Leon ignored Zac's caution. 'I have this theory – you'll like this – about the kind of wolf you are. It has to do with three things: the kind of man you were before; the kind of wolf that bit you; and, the state you were in when you got bit. Now, before I was bit I was a pretty tough guy, even if I do say so myself. Doorman, security guard, construction worker, all that. Plus I got bit by Alfie. Now he's a bloody strong wolf.'

'I thought you thought Alfie was weak.'

'Nah. I don't like his attitude, I don't like the way he thinks turning into a wolf is a bad thing. His attitude is weak. Being a werewolf is a good thing. He acts like it's a curse. I think it's more like a super power. We're superior: stronger, better looking, harder to kill. But, fact is, bad attitude or not, Alfie is a pretty strong wolf. Probably down to the ancient beast stuff. Therefore, with me, the combination of what I was and what bit me makes me something else in the wolf world.'

'Right.' Zac was Leon's only cub. He thought that might be the problem. Leon got so hung up on werewolf protocol and respecting your sire. Zac was the only cub Leon had to lecture at. Zac often wondered why Leon had never bitten anyone else, seeing as how he seemed to think it was some kind of werewolf prime directive.

Maybe he was worried what Alfie would think.

So, you're looking for Alfie?

'You know I am. You're inside my head.' Iris rolled her eyes. She was really rather more interested in the two men sitting a couple of tables away. On the way back from the bar she was sure she had heard one of then say something about 'the kind of wolf you are'. Still half listening to them, she turned back to Matthew, and downed most of her glass of whiskey in one shivery mouthful. 'Look, Matthew, I'm very busy. What have you got to show me?'

Matthew sighed. *Oh, sorry, I forgot you were so important.*

'Not important, just busy. Busy, avenging your death, Matthew.'

And who ever asked you to do that?

'Don't start that one, Matthew, please. Look, do you really have something for me? Because if it's just to annoy me . . .'

You noticed those guys, right?

Iris nodded.

They are what you think they are.

'What? What are they?' Iris frowned at him. 'What are you talking about?'

You know what I'm talking about, Iris. Those two guys over there. You've been looking at them. Listening in. You think they might be werewolves. You're right. They are. They're very important. Matthew grinned. Iris looked at the two guys again. *Oh,* Matthew said, *and you've got a missed call on your phone too. It's gone straight to your voicemail. You probably can't get a signal in here.*

Iris glanced at her phone, which was resting on the table. It did indeed have a missed call. Pure's number. She turned back to Matthew to apologise for having to go and return the call, but he wasn't there. Iris picked up her phone and went outside.

She had to take her phone out of the pub and across the street to get a signal. She didn't bother to listen to the voicemail, she just called Pure.

It took a while to understand what he was saying. He was talking really fast. Iris managed to make out: 'She was with him. Pearl was with him.'

'With who?'

'With a man with an eye injury who turned into a wolf.'

Iris went hot and cold at once. 'Seriously? Pearl? Your cousin Pearl? Where? Where did she see him?'

Pure said, 'I don't know. She wouldn't say. But she said she was going to meet up with some of his friends. She was really pleased I'd got her out of doing her shift. They're waiting for her in a pub called the Golden Hind. You know where that is?'

Iris looked up at the sign above the door of the pub across the road. *Good old Matthew.*

'Oh, don't worry about finding her, Pure-boy. I've got it covered,' Iris said as a familiar wiggle came around the corner. Pearl White, heading straight for the pub she'd just left.

12

Zac was sure he'd seen her first, but Leon hissed, 'Well, look who it is?' and jerked his head in the direction of the door. 'She must have skipped work, after all. What a little tart.'

Zac took a long pull of his pint, set it down and wiped the lager foam from his top lip. 'Wow, dude, I'd forgotten how smokin' she is,' he said, letting his voice trail away as she got near to them and took a seat.

Zac glanced at her. He couldn't help noticing her swooping curves as she sat down; her lilac uniform tight over her spectacularly plumptious arse.

'Hey,' she said to Leon, 'I, er, didn't have to work today after all. So, er, do you think your friend's OK?'

'My friend?' Leon looked lost.

Zac nudged him. 'Alfie.'

'Oh, Alfie, oh yeah. He'll be fine. Happens to him all the time. But let's not talk about that now, baby, eh?' Leon said, sliding across his seat towards Pearl and putting an arm casually around her waist.

'OK,' said Pearl. 'Why don't you introduce me properly to your other good-looking friend?'

Leon grinned. 'This is Zac.'

Pearl swivelled around in Leon's arms so she was facing Zac square on. 'Pearl,' she said, extending a long pale arm. 'Pearl White.'

'Pearl White?' Zac raised his eyebrows. 'Great name. I like it.'

'Yeah,' Leon drawled. 'Pearl *White*, are you a porn star on your days off?'

'No,' said Pearl smoothly. 'On my days off I'm a dancer, a choreographer, a poet and a dramaturge.'

'You what?' said Leon.

Zac said, 'A dramaturge, dude. It's a bit like a play-wright, isn't that right?'

'OK, sure, now you're telling me that *you* know what a drama-whatnot is,' Leon said, smiling slyly at Zac.

'I'm right.' Zac turned to Pearl. 'I'm right, ain't I?'

'He's right,' Pearl said, sweetly, nodding at Leon.

'OK. Fine. Whatever. I get it. That means you're an arty chick, right? Happens I like arty chicks. And by my reckoning we've got a little bit of unfinished business. So how about we go somewhere a bit quieter and get *creative*? All three of us?'

Zac's mouth fell open. 'Leon!'

But Pearl looked hard at Zac and said, 'Well, actually *that* might be interesting.'

'Great,' said Leon, quickly.

'Uh, I haven't got any, um, equipment, though. I mean, I'm not into all that kinky stuff, normally.'

Leon grinned, 'Forget that, we don't need that shit without Alfie here. But, just before we go, baby, how about a taste first. Call it a refresher.'

Pearl bit her lip and caught Zac's eye. Leon was already moving in.

Iris was still loitering outside, across the road from the pub, when Pure appeared. 'What's going on? Why are you still out here?'

'I'm watching.' Iris nodded at the big grease-smeared windows of the pub through which Pearl could clearly be seen sat at the bar, talking to the two men Iris had noticed earlier.

'Why? Don't you want to talk to her? She saw Alfie? She might know where he lives or . . .'

'Yeah. I know. But she's talking to a couple of guys in there that set off my wolf-dar. The pub's only got one entrance. She's not going anywhere while we're out here. And I just want to see what happens next.'

Pure squinted across the street. 'The long-haired guy

and the black dude? I don't see anything special about them?'

'Well, I do. And if you're right and she does know Alfie, that could be the rest of his pack right there.'

'So you're going to leave my little cousin Pearly in there talking to a couple of suspect lycs?' Pure twitched.

'Look, she's in no danger. They won't flip. They're stable. Well, we have no reason to believe that they're unstable.' Iris grazed the inside of her bottom lip with her teeth. 'We can't lose this chance to bring them all in, and then Pearl can give us the location of the pack house.' *God, that sounds like Blake talking.* 'We just need to find the right moment. That is all. I am not having you rush in there. You won't be able to hold them both. At least one'll bolt.'

Then, at just the wrong moment, the blond suspect-lyc put a big hand on Pearl's shoulder and leant in to kiss her.

Pure's reactions were fast: he pulled his silver blade, held it ready, tight in his fist, and made to move across the road. But Iris's reactions were fast too. As Pure tensed, ready to spring, Iris lunged and forced him back, slamming him into the wall behind them – a closed-up Methodist hall. She knew there was no way in the world she could be stronger than him, but something made her hold him. Maybe it was her anger, her need to bring in Alfie's pack, or maybe Pure's army training really did count for something – Iris was technically his superior officer.

Iris pressed herself hard against his taut muscle. 'Stand down, White, you're compromised,' she growled.

Pure tried to say something, but Iris talked over him. 'Listen to me, White. Listen to me –'

'Car! Dammit, Iris, look!' Pure shouted.

Iris looked round. Too late. Pearl and the two suspect lycs were climbing into a tiny black Mini parked on the street outside the pub and, with Pearl in the driving seat, they screeched away.

'Fuck!' Iris said. 'Have you got her number? Phone her, phone her, quickly.'

'She doesn't *have* a phone,' Pure said. 'Oh God.'

'OK, Pure, keep calm. She's in no imminent danger. OK, do you know where she lives?'

'Flat in Marston. Near the University Parks where we did that training exercise yesterday.'

'OK, good. Breathe. That's less than five minutes from here. Get your bike, go there, stake it out. Remember, she's in no danger, we just want to bring them in.'

Iris's shoulder felt hot and damp. The wound there was bleeding again.

13

'Alfie. I brought you some tea.'

Alfie opened his good eye. He was lying on his bed. He'd been sleeping. The restraints were off. His limbs ached.

Misty was standing over him. With tea and a concerned expression. He sat up, took the tea and forced a sort-of smile. He looked through the broken skylight. Short days. It'd be getting dark soon.

'How are you feeling?'

'Pretty rough. And I really need to speak to Leon. Right now.'

'Leon's gone.' Misty looked worried – quite upset. 'Hours ago, while you were still hairy. He said that you were too unstable to be his alpha any more. He took Zac and he went off with that nurse. He told me I could come, but, well, I said no.'

Alfie swallowed a mouthful of tea. He thought about what Leon had done. It made him feel weird. Not angry so much as dirty with humiliation. 'Oh,' he said. 'Maybe you should have gone with him.'

Misty shook her head.

'You say there's a cure for your problem here in Oxford. I believe you.'

'There is, Misty. The Silver Collar. It'll work. I know it.'

'Except that the Vix have it.'

'Which means Iris has it.'

'Iris? Oh.' Misty's face was unreadable. 'Is that a problem?'

'No. Well, apart from the fact I can scent her, it does mean I might need something of a plan.' Alfie sat up and started rooting through the top drawer of his bedside cabinet.

'What are you looking for?'

'The silver ring.'

'What, your grandmother's ring?'

'Yeah. Uh, got it.' Alfie pulled a small black velvet bag out of the drawer. 'It was my grandmother's, originally, but it's Iris's really. I gave it to her. And then she gave it back. Gave it back rather forcefully actually. But maybe she regrets that now.'

Misty frowned. 'OK.' Alfie knew she didn't want him going to the Vix. Walking straight into the firing line. And he knew she wasn't saying anything. He knew she also wasn't saying anything about his taking the ring. He sometimes wondered if Misty felt thrall stronger than any of them.

'Thanks. Are we friends again then?'

Misty nodded. A small enough nod that there was no need to say anything else on the subject.

Alfie drank a little more tea, then said, 'Did anyone give Pearl a memory wipe before she left?'

Misty shook her head. 'Sorry, babe. We're completely out.'

'Seriously? I'm sure there were four last time I looked.'

'Well then, I'm betting that the last time you looked was before that final night in Miami before we flew back here.'

Alfie bit his lip, trying to mask the slight smirk. 'Oh. Oh yes. Were there really four of them that night?'

'Yes there were. You had them lined up outside, wore them out one after the other,' Misty said slightly coldly. 'I'd have thought you would have remembered. That was the hotel where they charged us two hundred dollars extra for the marks your chains made on their antique four-poster.'

Alfie couldn't hide the smirk now. 'Ah yes, you know, when you put it like that it was kind of memorable.'

'Yeah. Not for those four girls after they'd had their memories wiped, though,' said Misty and both of them laughed a little bit.

Then Misty caught Alfie's eye. 'Um, Alfie, what did Leon do? I mean if Pearl saw you change and you and her were . . .'

'He fucked her. I didn't. I was going to, but . . . But, uh, Leon wanked me off while he was inside her. Made me come watching him fuck my woman. I think it was Leon's idea of asserting himself over me. Stupid cub-sire-hierarchical-werewolf bollocks.' Alfie spat those last words. Then he shook himself, as if he was trying to shake off the memory. 'He can't sink a blade into me, so he's letting his frustration out with weird stunts like this. Don't worry, I'll deal with it.'

Misty frowned. 'How? You think he's coming back?'

'Of course he is. You can't just walk out on your sire. If he wants to be an alpha he has to kill me. It's a rite of passage.'

'Yes,' said Misty, 'except he might think he doesn't need to because . . . Well, you haven't killed *your* alpha, have you?'

Alfie swallowed hard, squishing the desire to give Misty a warning look. 'That's different. My sire is . . .'

'I know. The Beast.'

'So he can't really be my alpha. No pack. So it's not the same.' Alfie felt himself bristle. Misty had never met the Beast, but somehow she seemed to hate him. It twisted Alfie inside to see it. Every bone in his body, every drop of his blood was branded with loyalty to his sire.

The way Alfie felt about his sire was more tender and brutal and confusing than anything he had ever known. Thrall it was called. He felt it himself when he thought about the Beast and he saw it in Leon and Misty when they looked at him.

14

Ignoring the pain in her shoulder, Iris arrived at the Institute and went to find Blake. His office door was open. She stopped in her tracks before she'd crossed an inch of fraying carpet.

Blake was perched on the edge of his desk sucking on a grubby-looking roll-up. His attention was entirely focused on Pepper and Aurelia, who were on the floor. Wrestling.

Pepper seemed to be coming off worst. Aurelia was mostly on top of her and had got her shin across Pepper's windpipe.

'The hair,' Blake shouted, waving his cigarette, 'use her hair.'

Pepper reached out and grabbed a handful of Aurelia's long blonde tresses, making her yelp.

'Uh,' said Iris, not quite sure of the right words.

Blake looked up. 'Oh, hey, Iris. Just doing a bit of training.'

Iris frowned hard. 'Training for what, exactly? Our own line of soft-core videos?'

Pepper and Aurelia had broken apart now and were both lying on the floor, looking up at Iris slightly shiftily and panting. 'Ma'am,' Aurelia said, as Iris flashed them a glance.

Blake said, 'You never know when hand-to-hand skill might come in useful. I mean look at you and that moonless lyc last night. That's what gave me this idea.'

'That's what gave you *this* idea?' Iris shook her head quickly, trying to focus. 'Look, um, whatever. Never mind that now. You three need to, uh...' *What is the phrase here. Tool up? Ship out? Go and bag me some wolves?* 'Go and bag me some wolves. Get ready.'

'What?' said Pepper. 'Now?'

'Yeah, now. Suspect lycs. Pure's already there.'

'Aren't you going to "bag" any of these wolves?' said Blake, who already looked primed for action.

Iris shook her head. 'I'll catch you up.'

Blake narrowed his eyes and looked at Iris. 'That's not like you.'

Iris gave Blake a resigned look. 'I'm supposed to be having a meeting with Cate.'

'Ah, right.' Blake knew as well as Iris that you didn't break engagements with witches. You just didn't.

'And, um,' Iris looked at Blake, she felt weird admitting this, 'that wound on my shoulder's opened up again.'

Blake reached up and trailed the backs of his fingers over Iris's shirt where it covered the gash in her shoulder. 'You should see a doctor about that, Iris.'

Then Aurelia said, 'So what's the lowdown on these lycs, ma'am? More of these moonless creatures that attacked you?'

'No, no, nothing like that. I need you to go and back Pure up. Call him. He has the address. We think these two might be Alfie's pack, but they're only suspect lycs so it needs to be strictly a grab 'em and bag 'em operation. We'll bring them in and then find the rest of the pack. No shooting them – not even tranqs., they might just be civilians.'

Pepper said, 'But if they *are* civilians, won't they sue us? Or something?'

'No, no,' said Blake. 'Cate can sort that, so long as we don't leave any worrying evidence. Like tranqs. in the blood.'

'OK, ma'am,' said Aurelia. 'We're on the case.'

The three of them trooped out. Blake turned in the doorway. 'See you later. Don't overdo it on the eye of newt.'

* * *

Pure locked his bike up on the railings and peered down into the little courtyard outside Pearl's basement flat. He couldn't see much so he pressed himself up against the wall as he crept down the steps. It was getting dark and he was glad of that. In his head he tried to recall the layout of Pearl's place. There was the kitchen as you went in, no, a little hall and the kitchen off. The bathroom was down the back, next to Flo's room. And, yeah, Pearl's bedroom was at the front. The window looked right out into the courtyard. It was the one he was passing right in front of as he crept down the steps. He hit the ground as he thought that and, at the same moment, a light in the bedroom clicked on. Pure held his breath and raised his head enough to look inside.

There was only really one moment when Pearl paused to ask herself what she thought she was doing, letting herself be alone with two men whom she hardly knew. She wondered if her idea about saying yes and being open to new things, or getting over all the crap that had happened with Martin by becoming some kind of super-slut-on-heat was really such a good idea. After all, this was her second threesome of the day. That was pushing it a little, surely? But something inside her seemed to be overriding her voice of reason. Something seemed to be telling her that resistance was useless.

Something seemed to be telling her that this was her destiny calling.

Zac was still standing in the bedroom doorway, looking as wary as she knew she ought to feel. Leon was standing very close to her by the bed.

There was something slightly odd about Leon. What with the clothes and that nasal Brummie accent, he shouldn't exude incredible, jaw-dropping sex appeal, but he did. Get those sprayed-on denims off him and maybe sort his hair out and he'd look like a film star. Those wing-mirror cheekbones. Those sultry gold-coloured eyes. And the attitude, which was probably the sexiest thing of all. Pearl glanced at his crotch, remembering the feel of his glorious cock inside her. She sucked her bottom lip.

But delicious as he was, Zac was even better. So *pretty*. Sleek dark clothes, sleek dark skin. The way he was standing right now. Catlike. A little tense, but so perfectly posed. And the accent, that easy American drawl – it gave Pearl shivers.

All three of them looked at each other. The tension in the air seemed to draw itself out. Longer and longer. And then Leon growled low in his throat and ... *snap*. In an instant, Pearl went from standing in the room listening to three sets of heavy breathing to throwing off her clothes; to watching the two beautiful guys throw off theirs; to diving onto the bed and into a warm smooth double embrace.

'So how does it work this time? You're the biggest. Do *you* get tied down?' Pearl panted, looking at Leon as Zac cradled her from behind, nipping at the back of her neck.

Leon naked was even more incredible a sight than Leon clothed. Pearl was right – he did look a hundred times better out of the denims. He had thick hard thighs and the most gorgeous weathered abdominals, half covered by a massive tangle of scar tissue. Pearl reached out and touched it, feeling like she half knew what it must be. Leon snarled at her and she pulled her hand away. He grabbed Pearl's shoulders, smashing his lips onto hers. Adrenaline spiked through her body, then washed away again as she gave in to him, letting him force his tongue possessively into her mouth. Meanwhile, Zac reached around her body and ran his fingers over her nipples, making her gasp and moan.

When Leon pulled away and looked at Pearl, his voice was low and almost vibrating. 'If you're so keen on kinky how about we tie *you* up?'

Pearl shook her head. 'Not on a first date, baby. Two guys at once is plenty kinky enough for me.'

Leon chuckled darkly, pulled her out of Zac's arms and twisted her onto his own lap. Pearl wasn't a small woman, but Leon seemed to be able to move her around like a doll. Now that she was being held by Leon and facing Zac, she got to have a good long look at Zac's naked body while Leon took over the job of biting at her neck and pinching her nipples. She reached out and ran her hands over Zac's skin. It was flawless. But then, he was so young. He must have been, what, 22, 23?

Leon pulled Pearl's head back by the hair so she was looking up at him. He was smiling a nasty animalistic smile. She held his gaze, feeling his warm chest heaving at her back. She was so turned on. She was buzzing with it. She could practically touch the pheromones coming off Leon – gingerbread and musky honey. His erect cock was grinding against the small of her back.

Leon kept up his tight grip on her hair and, with his other hand, cupped her chin and turned her head so he could kiss her. Long and slow. Melting. At the same moment, Zac leant forwards and ran his tongue over one very hard, very sensitised nipple and she moaned and twisted against both men.

When Leon finally pulled back from the kiss, he gave Pearl one last filthy look and then took hold of her by the shoulders and shoved her forwards, pushing her towards Zac, so she landed on all fours with Leon right behind her. She only had bare seconds to get used to the idea, before Leon was kneeling up behind her, sliding inside from behind. Showing her how wet she was, wetter than she would have thought possible.

She collapsed down onto her elbows, raising her arse higher in the air. She didn't seem to have any control. It was like her pussy had taken over, pushing her back against Leon. Aching for his cock to move deeper.

Leon chuckled and slapped her on the left thigh – hard enough to sting. She gasped. She thought about his rock-star hair, his rock-hard body, his attitude. She imagined the sneer on his face as he worked inside her.

He grabbed her hips, digging his fingertips into her flesh, and pushed in deeper. Then one of his big hands was between her legs, stroking her clit with rough fingertips. As soon as he touched her, it seemed to push her to the edge of her orgasm. It sparkled. 'Please.'

'You like that, baby?' he asked, his voice rougher than ever. Dirty.

'Uh,' she moaned, 'yeah.' She tried to work out how he had turned her, so quickly, into this keening, needing *thing* on the bed. She ground herself onto his cock and his thumb.

Leon chuckled and took his hand away. She squirmed back, trying to find his touch. 'Oh, yeah. You do, don't you? You dirty bitch. You like it. You're so wet, baby. You want to come, don't you?'

'Please,' she said again.

He reached out and stroked her clit again and she sighed, but his touch was only feather light this time. Not enough. Frustrating. 'No, baby, got to earn it.' He reached across her back and tangled his free hand in her hair, lifting her head up and back. The beautiful black guy was still in front of her. She had almost forgotten. Leon kept pulling at her hair, lifting her head until she was nose to nose with yet another breathtaking erection. She took her left hand off the bed to take hold of it, but the black guy brushed it away, 'No. No hands. I just want to feel your mouth, honey,' he said. *That accent.* He wasn't as demanding as the boss-man, but clearly taking his cues. He pressed the blunt tip of his cock against Pearl's lips. The rhythm of Leon pumping behind her made her rock against it. She opened her mouth and sucked.

'Good girl,' Leon said, stroking her clit very briefly again. 'Now, here's how you earn your fun, baby. Every time you make my buddy Zac moan, I make you moan. How does that sound?'

Pearl shuddered. She couldn't bear it. She needed Leon's touch on her clit. She needed it *now*. But then, Zac did moan – in response to Pearl swirling her tongue around the head of his cock – and Leon circled Pearl's clit with his thumb. Pearl felt like she was going to explode.

'Oh, yes,' said Leon, 'perfect.'

Zac tasted wonderful. That same combination of ginger-bread and newly turned earth, but, if anything, even spicier, headier, more overwhelming. Pearl gasped around the cock in her mouth, her world contracting to nothing more than her mouth, her pussy and her aching, wanting, desperate clit.

She sucked Zac hard. She worked with her tongue and her lips, taking him deep until her jaw ached. When Zac moaned Leon stroked her clit. His touch was glorious, but he never let her enjoy it for long and every time he took his hand away again she groaned, squirmed after it, often getting rewarded by another hard slap on the thigh. She was all kinds of stinging, aching, squirming, frustrated by the time Leon relented and started stroking her clit in earnest.

She was close to coming then. Suddenly. Desperate. Twisting. Trying to find the right friction. Almost there. Almost . . .

Outside, Pure couldn't stand it any longer. His skin was bristling as he crouched on the ground, peering over the window sill at Pearl being devoured by two filthy lycs. He had no doubt that that was what they were. The way they'd mauled her, dragged her around on the bed like that. One of them was even slapping her occasionally.

The dirty, kinky bastard.

He was almost ready to smash his way in alone when he heard a low whistle behind him. He turned to see Blake, Aurelia and Pepper looking over the railings at him.

'Oh thank fuck,' he said.

'What's up, Pure-boy?' hissed Blake.

'Two lycs. Human form though. W2s. And a human woman. Inside and we need to go in now.'

'We do?' said Pepper. 'Why?'

'We just do. On my mark.'

Pure heard the soft sounds of Pepper and Aurelia cocking their silver guns and fisting their silver blades. Blake might have said something, but he really wasn't listening. He flicked a glance over his shoulder, saw them ready, shouted, 'Mark', and vaulted right through the window.

15

Zac threw back his head. He was about to come. Pearl's mouth was so soft and so sweet. Through his half-closed lids he could see Leon across Pearl's cool-white back. He was close to the edge too.

At first the crashing noise confused him. He thought it might even be part of his orgasm. But then he saw the figure sailing through the window in a shower of broken glass.

More followed. *Vix*.

Zac had never seen Leon move so fast. He didn't know Leon *could* move so fast, shoving him and Pearl off the bed, shielding them both with his body.

From his position on the floor, adrenaline pumping, Zac couldn't help notice how massive and powerful Leon suddenly looked. How animal. How alpha. Naked and fierce. He could practically hear the Vix backing off.

Pearl wrapped a hand tight around Zac's and he looked at her. She nodded towards the open bedroom door. Zac was scared. He knew the room was full of Vix. He knew they'd be armed with silver guns and knives like the one that Alfie took in the eye. But, then again, maybe that was all the more reason to get out of here.

It seemed a long way to the door from where they were. Leon's terrifying display wasn't going to hold a bunch of armed soldiers for long.

What to do?

What Cate Ray – Magical Interfacing Operator – did for the Institute was very specialised. Very expensive. *Very useful*. Before the new funding they could never have afforded her. Witches did not come cheap. Which was bizarre, of course, because witches didn't actually *need* money. What with all their power and everything. They could probably just pull money out of the air. Iris had always assumed that the salary was just a point of principle.

Cate was all smooth red hair flowing down to her waist, floating ethnic skirts flowing down to her ankle. A lot of flowing. A lot of earth tones. A lot of chunky jewellery. Pure claimed Cate was gay. Iris strongly suspected this meant he'd hit on her and she'd turned him down. In which case he was lucky he wasn't croaking away in a pond right now.

Iris's briefing meetings with Cate were meant to keep her in the loop. Iris had been volunteered for the job as it was the general consensus – among Blake and Dr Tobias – that witches got on better with women. The meetings were supposed to be briefings on the week's events at the Institute, but they more frequently were just rambling conversations where Cate asked lots of questions and Iris got increasingly uncomfortable. Not least about why Cate needed a briefing anyway – didn't witches know everything already?

'So the wolf that attacked you was Alfie?'

'Um, well it's hard to say . . .' Iris's voice faded away.

Answer the question, Iris. Matthew was standing right behind Cate.

'Matthew?' Cate said and turned around. She looked right at where Matthew was standing, but then looked back at Iris with a calm expression. Iris narrowed her eyes. She knew Matthew wasn't real, that Matthew didn't really exist outside her own feelings of grief and guilt. However, she sometimes got the distinct impression that Cate could see him.

'Hmm, is Matthew distracting you?' Cate asked. 'Do you want him exorcised? Because if it's affecting your work, I could probably make a case for –'

'No.'

I knew you loved me, really.

Iris ran her tongue around the inside of her mouth. 'Anyway, don't exorcised ghosts go to hell?'

Cate made a face. 'Yeah, well, that is generally the case for ghosts. For figments of the imagination, though, I think, not so much.'

Iris nodded.

'Aren't you going to tell me he's not a figment of your imagination?' said Cate.

Iris shook her head.

'Because he's probably some kind of manifestation of your guilt over what happened.'

'I know. Makes you wonder why I can't just imagine him leaving.'

You don't want me to leave.

'Oh, I do. You shouldn't be here.'

Cate looked over, again right at where Matthew was standing, and said, 'What does he look like?'

'Like he did at twenty-one, when he died. Kind of like me if I was a boy. Small frame. Black hair that needs a cut and is sticking up on top, pale skin, long navy-blue overcoat with a ripped pocket . . .' Describing him like that to someone else, confirming that no one could see him but Iris – that no one else would ever see him again – was too much. She felt her voice catch in her throat. 'Oh, God. Oh, Matthew, I'm so sorry.'

She didn't tell Cate that this was how Matthew appeared to her now. She didn't tell Cate that for the first few years after the attack the Matthew that she saw didn't have a face, just a ripped up mess of gore; that sometimes he appeared by her bed in the middle of the night and just screamed and screamed at her until dawn. That she used to get up in the morning and have to step over his corpse to get to the bathroom.

Cate frowned. 'Iris, you clearly have some very strong feelings of guilt over Matthew's death. Why are they so strong that you are experiencing this kind of imaginary haunting? I know that bonds between twins can be strong, but how was any of it your fault?'

It's Alfie you really feel guilty about. Iris looked at Matthew, who arched his eyebrows at her and then turned and walked away, losing substance altogether before he reached the wall.

Cate followed Iris's eyes. 'He's gone?'

Iris nodded.

Cate said, 'Well, if you don't want him to come back, just don't let him. It's really that simple.' She left the tiniest beat before she said, 'Tell me about Alfie.'

Iris felt the hairs stand up on the back of her neck because the way Cate said that just then really made it seem like she must have heard what Matthew had said. Except she couldn't have. Because ... *Unless she could read minds.* Iris shook herself. 'What do you want to know?'

'What do you want to tell me?'

Iris shrugged. 'He was my boyfriend at university. It's a bit complicated because ... Well, we'd been together in our second year for a bit, but then we'd broken up. But we were getting back together. Reconciling. In the middle of that Matthew came to visit. Matt wanted to take some photos of Alfie for his portfolio. He was a photography student. During the shoot we were attacked by the Beast. Matthew died. Alfie lived.' Iris swallowed. 'But he'd been bitten.'

'Did you know about the bite?'

'Yes, but not what it meant. But after the first time he changed, well, the Beast – his sire – came to him like they do and explained it. So, we both wanted – I don't know – something. Revenge. Vengeance. Because, well, Alfie was a werewolf, Matthew was dead. I wanted to find the werewolf who'd attacked them. Kill it. This sire. I started coming up with all kinds of theories. I'd just finished my biology degree. I started researching for a thesis on werewolves. Of course, no one took me seriously, but I started working on my own anyway. There was a load of stuff in the Bodleian library on monsters. Loads of ancient texts. I was making a start on paraphysiology all by myself. I got myself a plan. Then Alfie said he couldn't help me kill the Beast.'

'What did you want him to do?'

'I'd found out about the summoning ritual. How Alfie could call the Beast by going to the place where he was bitten. It sounded perfect. Too easy. Especially as I knew how to kill werewolves by then. But Alfie refused to help. Said it was impossible for him to do it. Thrall. He couldn't betray his sire. So I told him that if he couldn't help me, I never wanted to see him again. And, like I said, I knew how to kill werewolves by then.'

16

In the end, Zac didn't have to make a choice. Pearl grabbed his hand and hauled him with her through the door. They ran through the flat. Leon shouted after them, 'Just go. Don't come back for me. Go.'

The narrow hall gave way to a big living room. Pearl pulled Zac through some French doors at the back, up some stone steps, through a gate and into a huge open space.

They ran on and tumbled through trees and under-growth. On and on until Zac felt sure no one could be following. They flopped down in the dark grass.

'Where are we, honey?' Zac panted.

'University Parks. The flats sort of back onto them,' Pearl gasped.

'Woah,' said Zac, thinking of how wonderful it must be to run and rampage through this wild space after a change. Zac had locked down every single full moon since he was bitten by Leon a year ago. 'You think we're safe from the Vix out here?' Zac's heart hurt when he said that. He couldn't bear leaving Leon behind, but Leon had told him not to go back and he couldn't disobey a direct order from his sire.

'It's dark and there were only four of them. They'll never find us. What are they? What did you call them? Vix?'

Only four, seemed like an army. 'Vix. They're werewolf hunters. They might have got them some back-up.'

'They might,' Pearl breathed, running a hand up his bare leg.

'Also, we're kind of naked.'

'You know, I had noticed that.' Pearl's hand snaked around Zac's cock and stroked it gently.

Zac knew he ought to say something about going back for Leon, but he didn't. Pearl rolled over and on top of him. She leant down and kissed him, slowly.

'Werewolf hunters. Are you and Leon werewolves, then?'

'Yeah.' Zac chased her mouth again, but she wouldn't let him kiss her.

'So are you going to change into a wolf now?'

'Oh no, nothing like that tonight. Only when it's full moon.'

'Oh.' Pearl looked up at the sky. 'OK. I suppose that isn't all that long, is it? Er, when is the next full moon?'

Zac laughed. The idea of a person not knowing when the next full moon was. But then, had he known things like that? Before? 'It's a week away.' Zac could feel the pull already.

'Oh,' said Pearl. 'A bit to wait then.' She leant down, nearly close enough to kiss. 'Actually, though, I think that what you are is so fucking hot.'

'You do? You know there's a name for people like you.' Zac rolled on top of Pearl and slid his cock inside her. She was still so wet that it felt almost frictionless. But then she tightened around him, squeezing his cock. He could tell that her orgasm was less than a breath away.

'There's a name for what?' she said. 'What do you mean?'

'There's a name for humans who get hot for lycs. It's, like, a thing. They're called sniffers.'

'Sniffers!' She sounded slightly indignant, but Pearl was so close to coming now, she could hardly get the word out.

It was late October. It was night. They were both naked. The grass was slightly damp. But Zac couldn't feel the cold. Heat was coming off him in great waves. When he came and Pearl bucked up underneath him, glowing and white in the moonlight, he really thought he did feel the earth move.

* * *

Iris was in her office, cursing as she tried to get a dressing on her right shoulder. Her make-up mirror was propped against a pile of books on her desk. It was far too small.

So, he'll be here soon.

'Who?'

Alfie.

Iris looked up at the clock. She supposed that Matthew was right. Blake and the Reds would capture Alfie's pack. *Alfie's pack!* Then he'd have to come for them. An alpha would never desert his cubs. Maybe then she could do a deal. Persuade Alfie to summon the Beast for her in return for his pack. Surely that would work. Get round thrall. Wasn't a strong wolf meant to choose his cubs over his sire? Wasn't that some kind of werewolf thing?

'Mmm-hmm,' Iris said, not looking at Matthew as she tried to fix the little sticky strips over the gash in her skin, without being able to really reach or see what she was doing.

The buzz of the entryphone made her jump. She pressed the button on the phone on her desk that connected her to the speaker outside.

'Yes?' she said.

'Iris?' said a voice that she hadn't heard for eleven years.

'Alfie!'

17

While Pepper and Blake hurried off to search for the escapees, Pure and Aurelia dragged the naked lyc that they had managed to capture up the steps at the front of the flat.

Despite having a silver gun trained on him by Aurelia and Pure's silver blade at his throat, the lyc was fighting like a motherfucker, his body jackknifing and arching as he tried to get away.

'To hell with this, we're going to have to tranq. him,' Pure yelled.

'Iris said not to. In case he's a civilian. Makes it harder for Cate to do the cover.'

'He is so not a civilian,' Pure muttered to himself, but he decided that it was best to do what Aurelia said.

They managed to get him into the back of the truck. As they forced him to the floor, the lyc yelled something Pure couldn't make out, but Aurelia shouted, 'You fucking try it.'

'What did he say?' shouted Pure, over the noise of the lyc screaming and growling.

Aurelia had let go of the lyc now, leaving Pure struggling alone. She rummaged through one of the boxes in the back of the truck. 'He said he was going to bite you,' she shouted.

'Jesus.' The shock of the threat made Pure loosen his grip on the lyc. But then, realising this gave the creature more freedom to manoeuvre himself into a biting position, he tightened it again.

Aurelia came over, armed with hardware. She was wearing tight-fitting rubber gloves and she rammed a metal head cage onto the lyc, securing his entire skull in a prison of narrowly spaced wire mesh. 'Who you going to bite now, puppy dog?' said Pure, instantly relieved to have that threat taken away.

'You're such idiots,' spat the lyc, snapping behind wire, as Aurelia buckled the neck strap of the head cage and fixed it with a padlock, 'human-form bites don't do shit.'

'Yeah, well, maybe we don't want to take any chances,' Pure said, wrestling the lyc into a pair of standard-issue rigid handcuffs.

Aurelia moved a little closer, pushing her face close to the wire mesh over the lyc's ear. 'And, you know, it's very helpful of you to make such a typical lyc threat, darling, because if you hadn't done that we really wouldn't have known for sure that you weren't a human.'

'True enough,' said Pure. 'You could have passed for an ordinary pervert if you'd been smart enough.'

The lyc narrowed his eyes at them both, just as a loud banging on the outside of the truck made them all jump. Aurelia opened the canvas at the back and Pure heard her say, 'Hello, sir,' before Pepper and Blake climbed into the truck, looking serious.

Blake eyed the bound lyc. 'You don't need the head cage,' he said. 'That one won't be infectious in human form.'

'He threatened to bite,' Pure said, wishing his voice sounded more like Blake's, less borderline hysterical.

Blake nodded. 'Fair enough then.'

'Any luck?' Aurelia asked Pepper.

Pepper looked at the naked, chained lyc with a slight wince. 'No,' she said, 'it's pitch dark out there. We'll never find them.'

'How many got away?' said Blake.

'One other suspected lyc. A black guy. One human woman,' said Pure.

'You sure the woman is human? Female lycs are rare. If there's one out there we could really do with bringing her in alive.'

'No,' said Pure, coldly. 'It was the nurse who'd given an ID on the hound Iris injured.'

'Was that the hound that got away? We really need that unstable one brought in too. He's very important to Iris.'

Before Pure could reply, the lyc in the head cage made a noise like a cross between a bark and a laugh. 'So you're looking for Alfie, are you?' he said, clearly very amused.

Blake whipped round to face the lyc so fast Pure almost shied away. 'He's part of your pack is he?'

The lyc laughed again. 'Maybe he is.' He fixed Blake with a long stare. Then he said, 'And maybe he's my sire. So if that's who you really want we can strike ourselves a deal.'

Iris felt her whole body shudder. Clinging dumbly to the phone, she looked at her face in the mirror on her desk then wished she hadn't. She opened a drawer in her desk and pulled out her silver gun.

'Iris?' said the gut-wrenchingly familiar voice on the other end of the phone again. 'Can I come in?'

'Sure,' Iris said, in a voice that sounded wrong, *just wrong*. She pressed the button that released the front door and pulled her blood-stained shirt back on.

18

Leon looked at the small wiry man who was standing too close to him in the back of the truck. He was at least ten years older than the others and smelt decidedly untrustworthy. 'You're in charge, are you?'

The man nodded.

Leon let his eyes flick around the inside of the truck. He wasn't planning on letting a few little details like the fact he was handcuffed and had a glorified salad-spinner locked around his head – or the fact he was otherwise stark-naked – faze him. Just the opposite. In fact, every time these ridiculous Vix creatures took another precaution to make sure the big bad wolf couldn't hurt them, Leon saw it as a sign that he was strong and they were weak. They were even scared of him biting them when he wasn't even in his wolf-form. *Idiots.* And they wanted Alfie. His sire. 'I need to go to the place I was bitten,' he said, smoothly. 'I can only do the summoning there.'

'Well, where's that?' said Mr Wiry. 'We're not ferrying you all over the country.'

'The gallery of the Natural History Museum,' Leon said.

'The Natural History Museum? That some kind of lyc attempt at satire?'

'It's true.' Leon grinned. *Prove me wrong, buddy.*

'You were bitten by Alfie, by a werewolf, in the Natural History Museum?'

'I was running away from it. I never thought it would follow me in there.'

Wiry wrinkled his oversized nose, then said, 'Pure, you take the wheel. We can be there in a few minutes.'

Another one of the Vix, the queer with the bald head, climbed over the back of the driver's seat and slotted himself into place. As the truck spluttered and started to rumble forwards, Leon said, 'And you'll have to take all this metal crap off of me. I can't be wearing this.'

Wiry looked suspicious again.

Leon made up some more bullshit. 'To summon my sire I need to be naked, humble before him. It's important. The relationship between cub and sire is something you couldn't ever understand. It's a sacred thing.'

Wiry frowned. 'Sacred? Don't most werewolves get killed by their cubs?'

'Yeah. Sometimes. Eventually. When the thrall breaks. Just one of the things you wouldn't understand. But I can't have this on me. Especially not metal. We don't like metal.'

'It's not silver,' said one of the other Vix in the truck. One of the women. The good-looking one.

'Doesn't matter,' said Leon. 'Well, it does. But all metal is vulgar to werewolves. He'll be able to smell it. You certainly can't have metal on your body for a summoning.' He was rather proud of how that last bit sounded. Very convincing. Even he was starting to believe it now.

Leon wasn't a clever fighter, but he knew a few dirty tricks. He knew that these four Vix would be trained and ready, expecting him to try to escape. *Wolves escape.* If a bunch of armed soldiers smashed their way in through the window of the room where Leon was having sex, he'd rather stand and face them than hide under the bed like he was doing something wrong. Leon was brave. Leon was reckless. And Leon knew his strengths.

Leon knew about the Natural History Museum, because he'd heard Alfie talk about it. One of the dreary-sounding places where he liked to hang out in his pathetic pre-werewolf life; when he had a lovely girlfriend and was training to be a doctor. Silly sod.

It had a gallery on the first floor, though. All Leon needed right now was somewhere high enough.

The museum was closed for the night. But that didn't seem to be any obstacle to Wiry, who had the door open in moments. Leon – still naked – followed the Vix up the dark stone steps and into the vast main hall. Torchlight made spooky shapes of the exhibits. The ceiling was so high it disappeared into the darkness and there was a smell of dead things so strong that it nearly bowled Leon over backwards.

'Just keep away from the dinosaur skeletons, doggie,' said Wiry at his shoulder.

Leon swallowed a snarl and led the way up more dusty stone stairs to the first-floor gallery, where glass cases housed all kinds of creepy-crawlies. Live ones this time. The sexy girl Vix squeaked a little at a case full of cockroaches and the queer guy laughed, taking her in his arms. *Silly bitch. What kind of Vix is scared of some big beetles?*

Leon moved close to the edge of the gallery, looking down into the great pit of the museum. The largest dinosaur skeletons loomed up out of the darkness. 'I need to get up on the edge,' Leon said bluntly.

'That was where you were when the wolf bit you?'

'Yeah,' said Leon and he pointed at the mass of scar tissue on his belly where Alfie had ripped his intestines away. 'I was trying to get away, but there was nowhere else to run.'

Leon climbed up on the ledge overlooking the museum, balancing himself using the stone pillars that framed the gallery. He didn't look down. He knew there were four silver guns trained on his naked back. But he knew that wouldn't matter in a moment.

His only consideration was who to take with him. He wouldn't normally consider anything so cold-blooded, but these guys were Vix. They killed werewolves.

The guy in charge was the obvious choice. Nasty-faced, wiry bastard. Best to take him, really. Him and the queer. No sense in killing the girls – they were both pretty enough.

Over his shoulder he called, 'I need two of you to link arms with me. For the ritual.' The queer and the stockier of the two girls stepped forwards. 'No. Not the girl. Needs to be a man.'

Wiry looked suspiciously at Leon. 'If you're thinking of trying to push anyone over the edge . . .'

Leon quirked a smile. 'You'll shoot me? Yeah, I figured that.'

Wiry and the queer walked slowly over and climbed up next to Leon on the ledge. They both looked suspicious. They thought Leon was planning something. They were thinking right. But if they had any clue exactly what Leon was really planning they wouldn't have climbed up on the ledge and linked arms with him. They wouldn't even have let him out of the truck.

Silver kills werewolves. Silver bullets, silver blades. Mercury too, although that was a lot harder to handle. Werewolves were pretty much impervious to most other things.

Like falling from a height.

Iris saw him before he even noticed she was there. As she walked down the stairs, he was standing in the foyer, looking at a bright-orange poster that advertised THURSDAY SPECIAL FOUR BINGO CARDS FOR THE PRICE OF THREE. They really needed to redecorate this place.

As she gazed at him, Iris's tongue twisted in her mouth. He looked amazing. Glowing. He had a dressing over one eye – final confirmation it really had been him – and his hands in his pockets. The dressing looked weirdly good on him. His jeans and pale-blue checked shirt looked faintly familiar. Either they were eleven years old or his style hadn't changed much.

Iris raised her gun, feeling a dull burn in her shoulder. She forced herself not to shake, just for long enough to be convincing.

'Hi,' she said, once she had the gun trained on him.

'Hi.' He turned. And smiled. He was beyond beautiful. And all Iris could think of as she looked at him was the way he looked when he was holding himself over her. Fucking her. His big body held over her on those beautiful hard arms. With his face flushed and a little of his dark hair wet with sweat and stuck to his face. She wanted him

so much. She'd lost her edge completely and it had been –
what? – less than thirty seconds.

Iris knew she was now holding the gun far too tight for
it to be any use. 'How did you find this place?'

'Scented you.'

'You . . . you can do that?'

'Apparently, yeah.' Alfie eyed the gun. 'You planning on
shooting me?'

'You planning on summoning the Beast for me?'

His eyes flicked down her body and up again. Very
quick. 'You know I can't do that.'

'Well, in that case I'll settle for locking you up in a cage
until you change your mind, werewolf.'

19

Iris took Alfie down to the holding area in the basement, where there were two cells and two cages. The cells were reasonable – as cells go – with bunks and small barred windows. The cages weren't so comfortably fitted. They weren't small – maybe twenty feet square – but they were completely empty of furniture and more like something for confining animals than humans.

Alfie walked in front of Iris. Once or twice he looked back over his shoulder. 'Do you want to know why I'm here?'

'No.' Iris kept the gun trained on Alfie as she walked around him and pulled open the door of the first cage – which swung soundlessly on its new hinges. She flicked the gun to indicate that he should go inside.

Alfie strolled through the door like it was the most normal thing in the world. 'So how come you aren't going to shoot me? Because you did say that if I ever came back to Oxford you'd kill me. So, counting last night, that makes twice you've failed to deliver on . . .' He tailed off, seeming to notice his surroundings for the first time. 'Oh, nice, so I don't even get a cell like a human.'

Iris shut the cage door and fixed the lock. 'Because you're not a human. Anyway, it's just a precaution.'

'A precaution against what? You think it might be dangerous to lock me in something with walls?'

'You're unstable. You flip. Change without the moon. It's safer for everyone if you're visible.'

Alfie nodded. 'Safer for *everyone*? So you have my best interests at heart?'

'Well, unless you *enjoy* turning into a wolf and killing people. You do remember last night, don't you? You know how you got a silver blade in your eye.'

'Yes,' Alfie said tightly, 'I remember. And it stinks down here, you know. It smells like blood and fear.' Alfie dropped his voice very low. 'And if you're keeping me alive for the reason I suspect then forget it. It's like I told you upstairs, I'm never going to be able to do what you want.'

Iris inhaled hard through her nose. 'Maybe we can change your mind about that.'

'Really? That sounds unpleasant, especially with the vibes I'm getting off this place. You going to "change my mind" yourself, Iris?'

Iris shook her head. 'No, I don't do that.' Her eyes flicked to his damaged eye. 'I'm more fieldwork really.'

'So that'll be what I can look forward to in the morning: some hardcore vivisection from one of your pseudo-military buddies?'

'Something like that.' What Blake did to lycs was wrong. Sick. But in this case wasn't it justified? Looking at Alfie – thinking about what Blake might do to him – was starting to make Iris weaken. She started to turn away, to close the cage door.

Alfie smiled. 'You're hurt,' he said.

'Huh?'

'I can smell it. You're bleeding. Or you've been bleeding very recently.'

'You knocked me down onto my blade. The same one I then stuck in your eye. I can't get the wound to close up properly.'

'Have you seen a doctor? You might need sutures.' Alfie paused. 'Have you got a dressing on it? I don't think it's scabbed over properly.'

'Yes, there's a dressing, but I don't think it's on right. It's a tricky place. You're right, I should get it fixed up properly. Blake can take a look when he gets back.'

'You want me to fix it?'

'No!' Iris raised her gun, stepping back.

'What's the matter? What do you think I'm going to do?'

'The sight of blood won't make you, I don't know, wolf out?' Iris asked, lowering the gun again slowly.

'Don't know, but it never has before. And anyway, what if it does? I'm in a cage and you have a gun. Aren't you a trained werewolf killer?'

Iris pursed her lips. The badly positioned dressing *was* uncomfortable. And really, what could he do to her? 'OK. I suppose you can take a look. From in there.' Iris went over to the cupboards by the door. They were mostly full of things belonging to Blake that she didn't want to think about right now. Handcuffs and chains and gags. This was so not the time to have that kind of stuff in her head.

She pulled out a first-aid kit and passed it to Alfie through the bars. He opened it and started cleaning his hands with an alcohol spray. Iris turned her back to him, unbuttoning her shirt then shucking it down her arms. She took half a step backwards so he could reach her through the bars.

'Trust me,' Alfie said with a soft chuckle in his voice, 'I'm a doctor.'

'Yeah, right. Didn't you bail out of medical school after three years?'

'Didn't you run me out of town?'

Iris felt Alfie's hands on her back. His touch, warm and kind of familiar, as he redressed the wound. She winced as he removed the sticky stitches and replaced them. He worked slowly. Dragging it out, she was certain.

Then she felt him kiss her.

And there was a long time when she didn't react. She was only in the moment where Alfie's lips were on her skin, soft and real. Blake had once told Iris she had the fastest reactions of anyone he'd ever seen, but that was before Alfie Friday had stepped back into her life and made her lose her edge.

Finally, coming back to reality, she pulled out of his hands and took a big step away from the cage, rounding on him, raising the gun, yanking her shirt back on with her free hand. 'What the hell was that?'

'What? It looked nasty. Thought I'd kiss it better.'

'Thought you'd drink my blood more like!'

Alfie looked at her like he thought she was either crazy or very, very dumb, 'I'm not a vampire, Iris.'

'I know *that*.' She was still so angry about the kiss that she was shaking. 'Oh my God. Your saliva in an open wound. You were trying to turn me.'

Alfie looked disparagingly at her again. 'I'm smooth. In my human form. It doesn't work like that.'

'Except that you're unstable. Maybe it does with you. I've heard about cub maters – lycs who try to turn women so that they can boss them around with the whole sire–cub thing.'

Alfie clapped his hand to his forehead in mock surprise. 'Oh, so you *do* understand about the sire-cub relationship, do you? Funny, because whenever we talk about me summoning the Beast for you, you act as if you really don't . . .'

'Don't change the subject. You just tried to make me into your cub.'

'Iris, I didn't. Do you *feel* like you're my cub? Do you feel like you're naturally submissive to me in any damn way at all? Because I'm pretty sure I'd notice such a cataclysmic change in our relationship, even after all these years.'

Iris stood still and looked at him for a moment. She was about to say, 'No,' when she found herself wondering. Her feelings for Alfie were so jumbled up and confusing. What did she even think? 'I'm not sure,' she said, slowly. 'Anyway it wouldn't work this quickly, would it?'

'It wouldn't work at all. That's the whole point. But, OK, I don't want you to fret about that, of all things. How about I give you a direct order? Let me see if I can pull alpha on you and see what you do.'

'I don't know . . .'

'Get on your knees and suck my dick, Iris.'

'Fuck off, Alfie, you are such a wanker.' Iris's voice was steady, hard, as she snapped back at him, but inside she was in bits. That was the last image she wanted in her head right now. She had to get out of here. Leave him. Blake could deal with him in the morning.

'Well, I think that's that settled. I did not just turn you into my cub. My cubs, when I talk to them like that, they do not tell me to fuck off.'

'Well, what a delightful picture of your home life you do paint. God, Alfie, you are so . . .' She shook herself again and turned to leave.

Alfie raised his palms, backing off. 'I'm sorry, Iris, that was stupid. A misjudgement. Let me tell you why I came here. You've got to be wondering.'

Iris turned back. 'I don't –'

'Please.'

'Alfie . . .'

'I need to talk to you. Please, I need your help.'

Iris stared at his face. The memory of his lips – soft on her back – was still confusing her. He was messing with her mind already. Alfie Friday. Heartbreaker. Coward. Traitor. The man who'd sided with the lycs and refused to help her avenge Matthew's death.

Iris dropped her gun deliberately onto the floor. It made a loud noise as it hit the stone flags and both she and Alfie flinched slightly. Her face set, she walked back to the cage until she was inches away from the bars. Too close. Danger close. 'Why should I help you, Alfie? You didn't help me when you had the chance. You're right, there's only one reason you're still alive right now. And if Blake can't make you do what I need you to do then I'm sure he will put you out of your misery, right after he's finished slicing you apart to see how you work.'

'Really? Blake will do it for me, will he? Not you though, Iris. Because you can't kill me, can you? You had your chance and you couldn't do it.'

Iris was already walking away.

20

Saturday 20 October 2007

Iris had been up all night. Twice she walked down to the basement to check he was really still there. Both times he was lying on the floor of the cage, sleeping.

About 5 a.m. she heard the truck pull up in the yard. She'd almost forgotten about the other operation of the evening.

When she got outside, Pepper was standing at the back of the truck looking shaken. She had her arm in a sling. Aurelia was climbing out of the driver's seat. No lycs. No Pure. No Blake.

'What happened?' Iris yelled, breaking into a jog as she crossed the yard. 'Where's Blake?'

'Hospital,' Pepper said bluntly, barely looking up.

'What?'

Aurelia rounded the side of the truck and looked at Iris. Her model-perfect face had a hardness to it that Iris had never seen in her before. 'We got the white one. He tricked us. Told us he would summon his sire. Blake was really into it because he said his sire was Alfie – the unstable lyc, the one who can summon the Beast – that's the one you and Blake really want, right?'

Iris nodded, not really taking any of it in.

'He took us to the Natural History Museum for some kind of ritual; Blake seemed to know about it. Then the lyc managed to jump off the gallery on the first floor taking Blake and Pure with him.'

'Fuck! Are they OK?'

'Not really. Blake's going to be all right, I think. But he hurt his arm really badly. They think they can save it but, uh, I don't know. Pure went through a glass display case. He's in intensive care.'

Iris shook her head. 'Oh God, what was he thinking? What were any of you thinking?'

'But his sire was the unstable lyc, ma'am,' said Pepper.

'Right. And that would be the same unstable lyc who is locked up in the cells right now, would it?'

Aurelia's mouth fell open. 'Oh, you are fucking kidding me, ma'am.'

Iris sent Pepper home. Both girls needed some sleep, but Pepper seemed the most likely to actually be able to close her eyes. She'd sprained her wrist nastily climbing down to get to Blake, who hadn't fallen all the way. Apparently his life was saved by a luckily placed piece of jutting masonry and his own razor reflexes. The painkillers Pepper had got from the hospital seemed to be zoning her out somewhat.

Pure hadn't been so fortunate. He'd cut himself up nastily smashing through that display case. Of course, the lyc himself was long gone by the time Aurelia got down to ground level.

Iris got Aurelia to write up a report on the incident for Dr Tobias, while she called Cate at home to let her know there'd be a mopping-up operation. Cate didn't seem to think it was a big deal. She said Blake would probably be able to spin a suitable student-prank-that-went-wrong-type story and promised to smooth the path, make sure any explanations were believed, that any discrepancies weren't noticed.

What with covering off all that, Iris might have forgotten about Alfie, locked up downstairs. Might have, but didn't. Even as she went about her solemn business, she never once stopped thinking about his cheekbones, his shoulders, his fingertips and his lips so warm on her skin.

Eventually, she was sitting at her desk, wondering if it was too late for breakfast or too early for lunch, and thinking about running out for a sandwich anyway, when Aurelia appeared.

'Ma'am.'

'I thought you'd gone home, Aurelia. It is Saturday, you know. And you need some sleep.'

'I'm just about to get going, ma'am, but I wanted to apologise. We really messed up out there.'

'Forget about it, Aurelia. It happens. We all let our emotions get in the way sometimes.'

'But you'd never have let that lyc talk Pure and Blake into standing with him at the edge of that ledge. You'd have seen what he was up to, ma'am.'

Iris picked up the mug on her desk and took a mouthful of tea. It was on the cold side, but still drinkable. She swallowed it, considering. 'Aurelia, you know, I probably shouldn't say this, it's terribly unprofessional to admit, but if that lyc had convinced me he could bring me Alfie Friday, I really don't know what he could have persuaded me to do.'

Aurelia shifted from foot to foot. 'Yeah. Except you've already got him locked up downstairs, ma'am.'

'Yeah, except for that.'

21

The cage Alfie was locked in was equipped with a bucket, but there was no food or water. He'd woken up feeling strange and light-headed.

Seeing Iris had been weird. Seeing her still so *broken*. In eleven years, he'd come to terms with what had happened so much better than she had. She needed to start letting it go. Alfie wondered if there was any way he could help her. Then again, any kind of helping her would be so much easier if he didn't have to worry about her having him tortured by the not very eagerly awaited Blake.

Across from the cages a piece of paper was taped to the wall. Scrawled on it in black marker were the words WOLVES ESCAPE. Alfie had heard that phrase before. It was kind of a werewolf slogan. A boast. Werewolves were good at escaping. If there was a possible escape route from a situation they'd find it.

Alfie had no idea why it was stuck up on the wall down here. Perhaps a reminder to whoever was playing jailer not to give any of his werewolf prisoners a crack to squeeze through. But, as he looked at it, it didn't seem that way. It felt, to Alfie, like someone had left the sign for him and whoever else might find themselves locked up down here. That the sign was an instruction: WOLVES! ESCAPE!

Alfie looked around the cage. He searched for the weak link: the bars, the lock on the door, the way Iris had looked at him every time she'd let her guard down.

Iris never did make it out for that sandwich before lunch-time. She reviewed Aurelia's report and spoke to Cate on the phone again. Cate had gone straight to the hospital. Iris thought about going there too but didn't. She did call and try to speak to Blake, but the nurses told her he was sleeping.

Eventually, she closed down her computer and went to the convenience store round the corner from the Institute and bought two cooked chickens, a four-pint container of milk and a couple of big bottles of mineral water. She tried not to think about anything too much. She just schlepped the whole lot down to the basement.

Alfie was sitting in the cage, hunched up, arms around his knees, head down. He looked up as Iris got close to the bars. He didn't look too good. Drained and weak.

He spoke before she did. His voice sounded cracked and dry. 'Iris, could I have some water, do you think? And some food?'

Iris opened the carrier bag she was holding and pushed one of the bottles of water through the bars. Alfie snatched it, ripped the top off and drank almost the whole thing in one pull.

When he finally stopped drinking, he looked at Iris; water was running down his chin and splattering on his shirt. 'Thanks,' he said, slightly breathless. 'You know about how my metabolism is, right? How a werewolf metabolism is?'

Iris nodded. To demonstrate she took the milk and the chickens out of the bag and pushed them through the bars onto the floor of the cage. Alfie tossed the empty water bottle and fell on the meat.

'Well, OK,' said Alfie, tearing at the chicken, while he spoke. It was kind of weird to watch. He really did look *animal* as he ate. 'Werewolves,' he said with his mouth full, 'need to eat. A lot. The change uses energy like you would not believe. It feels like it takes the rest of the month to make up the calorific deficiency. I guess you know that, you've brought the right things.' He set down the chicken and started on the milk. 'Also, uh, my nose is rather more sensitive than a human's.'

'Yes. I know.'

'Well, anyway, could you send someone down to empty,

er, that?' Alfie nodded his head to the blue plastic bucket in the corner of his cage.

'This isn't a hotel, Alfie. I don't have anyone here to empty your bucket right now.'

'There's no one else here?'

Iris heart sank. Telling him they were alone in the building was beyond stupid. She tried to bluff it out. 'So what? I've got you in a cage, haven't I? And as the building is empty no one knows you're here.'

Alfie sneered slightly. 'My pack knows I'm here.'

It shouldn't have been that surprising that Alfie would have a pack after eleven years as a lyc, but it still made Iris's stomach turn over to think about it. 'You were bitten by an ancient beast, a lone wolf. So if you've got a pack it must be made up of people you've infected. How many?' she said. 'How many people have you bitten and made like you?'

Alfie held her gaze, but she saw his throat move as he swallowed before he spoke. 'Two,' he said.

'As far as you know.'

'I know. That's how it works. You have to be there the first time they change. There are rules about these things. I know that you know this, Iris. You were the one who did all the reading up after Matthew. So I know that I've sired two cubs.'

'Do they have names?'

'Not that I'm telling you. They're my pack, Iris. That's more than family. I can't tell you their names.'

'I need to know, Alfie. If they're in my city I need to know.'

Alfie just shrugged.

Iris made a resigned sort of face at him. 'OK, fine. You can talk to me or we can wait for Blake. He'll have no problem getting information out of you. That's what he does. What he's good at. And he'll persuade you to summon the Beast too. Your sire. The thing that killed Matthew. Summon it so I can kill it. I know you can.'

'I can't, Iris. I can't do that. You know I can't.'

'You can summon your sire. It's part of werewolf lore.'

'Yes, but I can't betray him. There's lore and then there's ... stuff. Other stuff. Dark stuff. Iris, I know it's hard for you to understand.'

Iris started walking back towards the cage. 'So why are you even here, Alfie?

'I need the collar.'

'What? What collar?'

'The Silver Collar. It's a kind of ancient object. Legendary. I know you have one here. That's why I came. I need to control it. The moonless wolf thing. I need you to help me. My wolf and human form are breaking down. This is my last chance. The only way I can keep people safe from me.'

Iris stared at him. 'The Silver Collar. You came here for the collar?'

'You've heard of it then?'

Iris paused. 'Um, maybe. Sounds like something Blake might have.'

Alfie took a step closer to Iris behind the bars. 'Really? Please, Iris. I need it to stop me transforming without the moon.'

'Can't you just figure out what else makes you change and avoid it?'

'It's too hard. Too complex. It is mostly when I have sex, well, when I come, orgasm, but not always. About half the time now.'

Iris considered. 'Well it might depend on a number of factors: the presence of a trigger, your mood, the lunar cycle, the time of day.' Iris took another step towards the cage. She felt less angry now. Alfie's face was milder too. Talking about Alfie's problem like it was a science experiment. It reminded her of university. Of working with Alfie in the biology lab at university. Working and flirting and sneaking off to the toilets, after he'd brushed his erection against her arse and moaned softly and given her such a *look* she just couldn't concentrate on what she was doing. The way he could moan, soft in her ear. For a big man, he could express his need so gently and delicately. Although his desire – when Iris felt it focus on her – was no less powerful for that.

She shifted. She couldn't be with Alfie for more than ten minutes without thinking about sex. What was he doing to her?

Alfie said, 'I've been all around the world looking for something to control it. I found out about the collar –'

Iris's mind was elsewhere. 'Hang on, did you say sex was your main trigger? Orgasm? So does that mean you can't have sex?'

'Er, well...'

'You! *You* can't have sex. You, who slept with the entire college before we got to together. Now you can't have sex without it changing you into a wolf.'

'Well, it wasn't exactly the *entire* college. Anyway, I *can* have sex. I kind of found a way to ... Look, can we talk about the collar?'

'Can we talk about you not having sex? When did you last get to have sex? Hang on though, didn't you have sex with Pure's cousin?'

'What? With who? I can have sex. I just have to be –' he looked away from her, down at the ground and back up '– chained down.'

'Oh.' Iris gulped and hoped Alfie didn't notice. She'd already been feeling a little turned on, but when Alfie said that, said he had to be chained down for sex, she felt her pussy get hot and her nipples go stiff. She squeezed her legs together, hoping he couldn't scent her arousal. 'Oh God,' she said, her voice a little wobbly. 'But when you changed would the chains still...?'

'Spelled. Got them on my travels, along with the news about the collar, which was what we were talking about.'

'OK. Right. Do you always have to be chained down to have sex? I mean didn't you used to like to be the one who...?'

'Yes. OK, fine, if we must have this conversation then, yes, if I'm planning to orgasm and someone else is in the room, then, yes, I have to be chained down. Subject closed. Listen, the collar. Is it here or not?'

'Yes, it's upstairs,' Iris said weakly. 'In Blake's lab.'

'Great. Let's go get it.'

Iris looked at him. 'If you think I'm letting you out of there . . .'

'Listen, um, just a minute. I've got something for you.' Alfie was rooting in the pocket of his jeans. He pulled out a slim black leather wallet and from it a little black velvet bag. He held the bag out to Iris through the bars of the cage.

Iris stared at it. 'Uh?'

'Take it.'

Iris cocked her head, but a moment later she did reach out and take the bag.

'Look inside,' said Alfie.

'All right, all right.' Iris opened the tiny bag. Something glinted. She pulled out a familiar-looking ring. 'Your grand-mother's ring,' she said.

'It's your ring. I gave it to you when I –'

'Yes I know you did. But I gave it back.'

'Threw it back, technically.'

'Well, yes. I think in those circumstances ownership usually reverts to the –'

'Yeah. I know. I get that, but . . .' Alfie shrugged and in that moment looked so ridiculously coy and boyish Iris had to blink the image away. 'Well, what use is it to me? It's silver.'

'But you used to wear it before. It was your ring.'

'I can't wear it now. I started stinging in the hospital after . . . That's why I took it off.'

Iris looked at him open mouthed. 'Oh my God. That's why you proposed to me in the hospital? Because your ring was hurting your finger! I thought it was all about how you'd seen your own mortality, realised how close you came to nearly losing me when you'd only just got me back and, and, and all that other stuff you said.'

'It was. All that was true. Still is. Take the ring, Iris. I want you to have it. Call it a fair exchange. For the collar. Let me out of here and take me to the collar, Iris.'

Iris stared at him. Held his gaze for a long time. Then she put the ring back into the velvet bag and slipped it into her pocket.

Iris wanted to let Alfie out of the cage more than anything. She wanted a part of his deranged experiments with collars and chains and moonlight. She wanted him. She wanted to find that collar, fix it around his neck and then see if he wanted to test it out by fucking her over her desk. Her hand was already on the door of the cage. It was like a kind of madness. Like a spell he had cast over her. 'Hang on.' She stopped. 'I can't just let you walk around. What if you get, uh, excited and change?'

'It doesn't work quite like that. It's not instantaneous. Have you got any sedatives? Or tranquillisers?'

'Even so, it would be suicidal to . . .'

'Well, why don't you get your gun?'

Iris shook her head, feeling like she might be coming to her senses. 'Still too dangerous. You could get out into the street.' But then she thought of Alfie chained to his bed – actually she hadn't really shifted that image since he'd mentioned it – and she looked over at Blake's cabinet. 'Hang on though . . .'

Iris walked over to the cabinet and opened the door. In amongst all the paraphernalia glinted a pair of handcuffs. Knowing full well she was in the throes of a seriously deranged idea, Iris said, 'Put your hands behind your back and stand right up against the bars so I can fix these on you.'

'But they're not spelled are they? They won't change if I change.'

'No, they won't change. So I reckon they'll probably break both of your arms if you flip while these are fixed on. That'd probably give me a fighting chance against your wolf form.'

Alfie didn't say anything. He just did as Iris requested, moving close to the bars then turning around with his arms braced behind his back. Iris tried not to touch his skin as she locked the cuffs into place, because the way he felt – so warm and so smooth and so familiar – was making her heart beat too hard.

His shirtsleeves were pushed up just a little, midway up his big perfectly shaped forearms, and the way the cuffs held his arms rigid and slightly tense made the muscles flex and tauten. Once he was locked into the cuffs and he turned around inside the cage, Iris saw that the way his arms were pulled behind him also made his chest expand and his posture change.

Trying not to look at him too much, not too think, Iris let Alfie out of the cage.

Behind her on the stairs Alfie said, 'It would work I'm sure, I've thought it through and I can't see how it wouldn't. I'd take it off for full moon, but it could control me between times. Then I could still lock down for the moon like normal and that way I would be safe. Completely controlled.'

'And you could have sex without being chained up,' Iris said.

'You sound a bit disappointed about that.'

Iris stopped walking and turned around. They were still in the stairwell, climbing up to Blake's second-floor office and lab. Iris was on the step above Alfie, so they were eye to eye. She looked right at him, beautiful posture and all. 'Believe me, Alfie, if I wanted to chain you up and have sex with you I could have done it by now.'

'Really?' Alfie said. 'So this is a pretty ethical, professional organisation you're working for is it?'

Iris turned away and carried on up the stairs.

22

In Blake's office, Iris watched as Alfie looked around. 'So this Blake seems like an interesting guy: bibliophile, scientist, werewolf torturer. So where's the collar?'

Iris nodded to the door in the far corner. 'In the lab.'

Alfie crossed the room. When he reached the door he twisted sideways, trying to get his cuffed hands into position to turn the door handle.

Iris watched him for a second, slightly incredulous, then walked over. 'God, Alfie, you could just ask me to open the door for you.'

As Iris opened the door she couldn't help notice how close they were to each other again. She stopped, caught his eyes on her, felt the warmth of his body, even the beat of his heart.

Alfie walked in first. 'Well, isn't this fancy ... Oh.'

Iris struggled for a moment to see past his big body. 'What? What? Oh.'

A perfectly plain silver collar was right in the middle of the island workbench in the centre of the lab. Blake hadn't even put it away. Iris ran her tongue over her bottom lip. 'Is it silver? Real silver, I mean. It looks like silver.'

Alfie swallowed, visibly. 'Easy way to find out. Put it on my skin.'

Iris fetched it and walked back to where Alfie was standing just inside the open door. She hesitated for a moment, wondering which part of his body to use. Everywhere suddenly seemed too intimate. If it was silver, it might mark him and even scar. She didn't want to do that to his face. His hands were still cuffed behind him. In the end she flipped open a couple of his shirt buttons, revealing a small V of chest. She pressed the silver collar to the latte-coloured skin just below his collarbone, noticing too late that she was biting her lip.

A split second after the collar touched his skin, Alfie yelled and jumped back, stumbling into the glossy white wall behind him. 'OK,' he panted, 'that's silver.' His chest was heaving, his shirt was half open and there was mark like a burn or a brand striping across his collarbone. After long moment of eye contact with Iris, Alfie said, 'You look a little flushed. Did that turn you on?'

'Maybe,' Iris said. 'That's not relevant. But how you can wear a collar made of something that damages you like that.' Iris pointed at the angry mark on Alfie's chest. 'Well, that really is something we need to figure out.'

Alfie shook his head. 'No, it isn't. Just put it on me.'

'But...'

'Makes no difference what it does. It's my last chance. It's kill or cure. Go on.' He raised his chin slightly like an invitation. Iris swallowed and stepped over, opened the collar up on its hinge and snapped it around Alfie's neck. Alfie recoiled, jerked his head around, then stilled. 'Actually...'

'What?'

'It's actually OK.'

'It is?'

Alfie shrugged. 'Yeah, it kind of tingles a bit. Maybe it's spelled or something because it really doesn't hurt nearly as much as it should.'

'Well, I guess now we need to find out if it works. Blake probably keeps some adrenaline around. If anything flips you that will. We should do it in the cage though, for safety.'

Iris pulled open a drawer. Blake's lab was completely disorganised, as far as Iris could tell, but it seemed to make sense to Blake. However, she got the right drawer. Full of syringes. She grabbed one and an ampoule of adrenaline.

As Iris turned around, Alfie said, 'You don't need that, Iris.'

'I don't need what?'

'You don't need to use adrenaline to see if I flip. I told you what my main trigger is. Why don't you kiss me, Iris?'

Iris swallowed. 'You know damn well why, Alfie.'

'Remind me.'

Iris took a step forwards. She had already been very close to him to put the collar on, now she was right in his personal space. 'It killed Matthew, Alfie.'

Alfie blinked. 'Yes, I know and I can see how you're getting over that by joining a werewolf-killing organisation and sleeping with a werewolf torturer. Because he is fucking you, isn't he? He fucked you last night, right after I nearly bit your head off.'

Iris started, moved back a little. 'What? How do you...? Oh, God, you didn't smell that on me, did you?'

Alfie grinned. 'Nope. Just guessed. So he's your boyfriend is he, this torturer? That must make for an interesting sex life.'

'No more interesting than yours.'

Alfie dropped his voice very low. 'You ever pretend that he's me? You ever think about that? You ever remember how it was with us?'

Iris swallowed hard, shaking her head.

'I thought about you last night. After the change I get so horny. Depleted. I went upstairs, used the chains to make sure I was secure and all I could think about was how much I wished you were there with me while I was touching myself. Kissing me while I was chained down.'

'If you're trying to seduce me, Alfie, it isn't going to work.'

'Really, well, I'm sorry about that.'

'Well, I'm not.'

'No, Iris, I mean it, I'm really truly sorry about this.' As he spoke, Alfie sprang towards her, bringing his hands out from behind his back.

He fell on Iris, knocking her into the island workbench. Iris's injured shoulder was alive with fresh sparky pain as the whole thing clattered over behind her. Alfie was still on top of her.

She was cursing inside. Her reflexes should have been sharper than that. But she'd thought he was handcuffed. *How long had he had those cuffs off?*

'Sorry,' Alfie said again as he started rummaging amongst the equipment and utensils spilt over the bright-white floor, keeping one big hand on her chest, holding her down.

Iris struggled and Alfie turned to look at her, all the charm gone. He was feral, scary. 'Where's the key, Iris?' he said, his voice soft but threatening.

'What key?'

'The key to the collar. In case I need to remove it.'

'I don't know. There wasn't a key. Uh –' Alfie slid his hand up to Iris's neck.

'Alfie, please.' Iris stopped talking as he started to increase the pressure. She stared right into his gold-coloured eyes. It was like the park all over again. The way those eyes had looked at her. She kept staring back at him and eventually he loosened his grip. 'Maybe Blake knows,' she half-coughed. 'Let's go to my office. I can call him at the hospital.'

'Huh. We'll see. Excuse me a moment.' With his free hand he worked his way into the front pocket of Iris's jeans. His fingers fumbled around. His other hand was still on her neck. Purple clouds edged into her vision. Iris started to see stars. A moment later, he pulled his hand free and reached over to try the other pocket.

'Aha!' he said, pulling his hand out and brandishing a tiny silver key in Iris's face. 'Well, it was nice to see you again, Iris. Not really what I would have wanted for our reunion, but never mind.' He pocketed the key and moved his face closer to hers. With one hand still on her throat, he reached up and stroked a lock of hair away from her face, soft and loving. 'You really think that boyfriend of yours could've tortured me as you have?'

His face was so close now it was going out of focus. Still dazed, Iris closed her eyes.

And Alfie kissed her.

His lips were hot and familiar, slightly urgent. His mouth opened up wider and he tasted like the sating of a craving she hadn't previously been aware of. He shifted his body so he was covering her. Big, long, borne on his heavy arms. 'Iris,' he said. He said it right into her open mouth and his voice was thick with desire. God, it was all so familiar. It felt like a dream. But then his mouth was suddenly harder, firmer on hers. Greedy. He'd got a hand in her hair, holding her head so he could force his tongue deeper into her mouth. She couldn't help herself. She took it. She wanted it. She wanted Alfie more than she could believe. These weren't the sweet youthful kisses they had shared eleven years ago. This was different. Spiked by pain and loss and longing. Viscous and bruising, Alfie was biting her bottom lip, forcing her mouth to open wider. She could feel his chest through her shirt. He was so hard, hot and smooth. Iris was light-headed with it.

'Alfie,' she said, shaking her head as she pulled her mouth away, 'no, this is –'

'I know,' Alfie said. He pushed out his tongue and licked her bottom lip. 'But it isn't like that, Iris. We are testing the collar, remember. I have to fuck someone to find out if it works and who better than a trained werewolf killer?'

Iris felt herself startle, all senses on alert. 'You can change. You could change if we do this. You're not cuffed any more. Alfie, I'm not armed.'

'You weren't armed before,' Alfie said, sitting back, straddling Iris's body and starting to undo her buttons.

'No, wait, wait,' Iris said, batting his fingers away. She scrambled out from under him, got shakily to her feet, and pulled open the drawer she had been looking in before. Next to the ampoules of adrenaline and other chemicals were Blake's tranquilliser darts. It looked like more than a hundred, different strengths, ready to be loaded into Institute rifles. Iris grabbed a substantial-looking one and turned. 'OK?' she said, holding it up. Alfie nodded. 'I'll just leave it within reach,' she said, setting it down as she willingly returned to her spot underneath Alfie Friday.

Iris looked up at him. His nipples were hard under the cotton of his shirt. His erection was firm against her belly. He always had been – and still was – the most beautiful man she had ever seen. This was so dangerous, and that had nothing to do with the paranormal. As Alfie got her shirt open and then started undoing his own, Iris reached out and took hold of the fly of Alfie's jeans.

Alfie stripped for her, so casual about his nudity – a classic werewolf trait borne of circumstance. He wore nothing but the collar, sparkling bright against his skin in the winter sunlight coming through the greasy windows of Blake's lab. His big body coiled shell small as he fitted himself into the gap between Iris's widespread legs. He paused a moment before his head disappeared from view, 'Now,' he said, in a voice that was barely even a whisper, 'let me see if I can remember how you like it.'

Alfie's tongue twisted against her. Long strokes. Slow. Teasing and familiar. Nostalgic patterns that said everything. Alfie's tongue against her, around her, inside her. Not words. Something darker and scarier than language. Something no one could have said to her and made her listen. *It's still him.* Werewolf, traitor, coward, heartbreaker: Alfie Friday is still the one. The only one. It felt as though his tongue was twisting tighter and tighter around her heart.

Iris sighed, reached down, wound her fingers in Alfie's hair and heard him moan into her. His tongue slid twice over her clit. The sparky sensation was almost-but-not-quite too much. She twisted, cried out, looked away. And Alfie was off her, up, out, inside, over her, overwhelming. He fucked her and he knew. He'd brought her so close with his tongue.

So fast, all so fast. Alfie had always been strong, had always fucked hard. Not like Blake – who did fuck hard, but deliberately hard – Alfie fucked hard as if there was no other way he could do it. The floor was shiny smooth; Iris was being driven backwards. She had to put her hand up to stop her head banging against the toppled island workbench. She'd completely lost track of where she'd carefully put that tranq. dart.

Alfie was coming. His face twisted and so familiar. He was holding his big body on one strong arm, his other hand holding the collar at his throat. Iris felt her own orgasm too, rushing over her. Alfie was a werewolf. Not changing. Still him. But she could see the wolf too. She closed her eyes. The wolf was still with her as she came.

And before she was over the last ripples of pleasure she heard a voice saying, 'I'm so sorry, Iris,' felt something like a sharp scratch on her arm and realised she was losing consciousness as she listened to the sound of breaking glass.

23

Back home at last, Alfie found the house quiet. Still no Leon or Zac. He felt strange, slightly hollow and empty inside. He found Misty in the kitchen. She was looking out of the window into the damp, unloved back garden. The radio was playing gently. Something classical.

'Hi,' he said.

Misty turned, clearly startled. 'Alfie?' Her face seemed to morph through every emotion: relief, anger, love, relief again. 'God, Alfie, babe, where have you been? I thought you'd ... I thought you'd gone too. I thought everyone had gone.'

'I haven't gone anywhere,' said Alfie, sitting down at his spot at the head of the kitchen table. There was a pot of tea sitting in the middle of it. Alfie started examining the cups in front of him, looking for the cleanest one.

'Oh, Alfie.' Misty was still frozen by the window, looking at him as if he might be a dream. Then, like something had snapped into place, she ran. Ran across the room and flung her arms around his big shoulders, kissing his face again and again. Her kisses felt nice. Familiar. She let go of him and took a step back. 'I don't know what I'd ever do if ...'

Her voice trailed away as Alfie moved, taking a cup and leaning forwards to pour his tea, and something flashed, a glint of light reflected across Misty's face. Her expression changed. 'What's that?' Misty reached for the collar.

Alfie let go of the teapot and it dropped an inch, landing on the table top with a clunk and a slight splattering of tea. He clapped his hand over the collar and pulled back, gritting his teeth against the sting in his palm where he was touching the metal. 'Don't touch it. It's silver. Real silver, I mean.'

'What?' Misty gaped at him. 'Does it hurt? I never thought it would actually be made of ...'

'No. Nor did I.' Alfie reached for the teapot again and this time succeeded in pouring some tea. There was a long pause and then Misty said, 'How's your eye?'

'It's getting better.'

'It looks terrible. The dressing's coming off again. Let me get some more gauze.'

Alfie took another sip of his tea while Misty took some packets out of drawers and bustled over to the table.

Iris had woken up on the floor of Blake's lab and found a tiny strip of clear plastic on the floor where Alfie had been standing before he hit her.

She wrote a note for the discreet cleaning firm that Dr Tobias employed, asking them to take some extra time cleaning up Blake's lab and the basement cells. She called an equally discreet firm of glaziers and asked them to come out urgently and board up the window Alfie had jumped through.

After that she'd stayed at work as long as she could before she went home. It'd got late. She felt strange. Empty and deflated.

Iris was more of a person for keepsakes than she would ever admit to. She had three shoeboxes full of her past lives on top of the wardrobe. When she got home she went and found the university one. The lid fell off as she pulled it down and out spilt a thousand memories.

The photo she wanted was right there. Right on the top like a lucky charm. Alfie, aged 21, taken that very night. His last night on earth as a human.

Great idea. Dig that out. That'll cheer you up.

Iris didn't need to look around to see that Matthew was standing behind her.

The photograph was one of the shots that had been developed from Matthew's camera when they'd found it.

It was of Alfie, shirtless in the moonlight. It was the only one Iris had kept. The rest had been spooky, predatory and overtly sexual. This was more of a candid shot. Alfie caught off-guard and laughing at something with his teeth showing.

God, but Alfie was beautiful. Back then he was bursting with a kind of golden glowing youth. His kisses had been rich with it. Charisma and promise. Virile and slightly twisted. He'd had a scheme once about fucking at as many Oxford landmarks as possible. He'd bent her over Magdalene Bridge once very late at night. Fucked her, while she looked down at the silent Thames and writhed against his big thick fingers. Bright young things. Another time, he'd made her come in a tight dark corner of the Pitt Rivers museum, jamming his knuckles in her mouth.

The picture made Iris's eyes start to prickle for all kinds of reasons. Behind Alfie, high in the sky, was a fat white moon. It was weird seeing human Alfie standing in front of a full moon. Not right. Like it must be some kind of trick photograph. It made Iris shiver with the wrongness of it.

Now his body was different and the same. Half his left shoulder was missing. He had scars everywhere. She'd noticed masses of them on his hands. He locked down, didn't he? The wolf tried to escape.

WOLVES ESCAPE.

24

Monday 22 October 2007

First thing on Monday morning, Iris sat opposite Dr Tobias in his spartan office. Just a desk and two hard chairs. He didn't even have a computer. Iris had no idea what he did when he was in here. Not that he was in here much.

Dr Tobias could have been anywhere between 45 and 75. Iris had never seen him in the field – he had already retired from wet works when Iris had joined the Institute – but he had trained Iris for months in his expansive basement, back in the days before they had their own building. From the way he handled weapons, the way he spoke about lycs, the way he held his jaw when he fired a silver gun, Iris just knew he'd made more kills than she ever would.

But there was no hint of his hardened side today. Even while he was giving Iris a dressing down, he was light of voice and gentle of tone. 'So, on Friday night a lyc found his way here. You just happened to be in the building and you locked him in the basement overnight, but he escaped on Saturday morning.' Dr Tobias did that steepling thing with his fingers and Iris found she was shifting her weight from foot to foot. Awkward and embarrassed.

'Yes. I'm sorry.'

'What I don't understand is how he got away. To tell you the truth, Iris, I'm not even sure we should be keeping live lycs at all. But if we are to keep them, I expect you to at least keep them locked up, not give them a guided tour.'

'We were getting the Silver Collar.'

'Ah, yes, the Silver Collar. The extremely rare artefact

that he stole. Somehow. Even though you had him handcuffed.'

'He must have picked the lock, Dr Tobias, I...'

'Yes.' Dr Tobias picked up a piece of paper from his in-tray. 'I read your report. He picked the lock with –' Dr Tobias paused for a moment as if unable to comprehend what Iris had written '– the plastic strip from the lid of a bottle of mineral water?'

'You know the piece you rip away to get the bottle open? I found it on the floor afterwards.'

'Yes, I do see. "Wolves escape" – you've heard that saying, I'm sure. So, anyway, he then overpowered you, tranqued you and exited by jumping through the window.'

Iris nodded. 'Yes.' She swallowed hard.

Dr Tobias shrugged. 'Alfred Friday, rare and unstable; so important to Blake – you know what a completist he is – and important to you because of your obsession with the Beast, which we do all understand and, frankly, it might be what makes you so very good at your job.' Iris tried to say something, but Dr Tobias held up a finger and stopped her. 'But he really isn't so important to the Institute. Firstly, if his thrall for his sire is really so strong as all that, he likely would have let Blake torture him to death before he betrayed his maker. Secondly, this Institute is about keeping people safe from lycs. Friday is a very diligent wolf. He locks down. He takes care. The flipping was an issue but even that was pretty well controlled. He abstained from anything that might cause him to change form, and now he has the collar, well...'

'You don't want me to try to bring him back in?'

'I think there's little point. It seems clear from your report that he came here to steal the collar. Now he has it, I doubt he'll stay around. I'm a little concerned how he found us, though. The last thing we want is lycs able to walk in here whenever they please. Does Cate need to rework the cloaking spell?'

Iris shrugged. 'He said he found *me*.'

'I see.' Dr Tobias raised his eyebrows, but his mild

expression didn't change. 'Blake's doing well. Making a strong recovery as I'm sure we all expected he would. He ought to take some leave but I'm sure none of us will be surprised to see him back in the office in a few days. Although his arm is rather badly damaged. We might have to face the prospect of his not being able to do fieldwork for some time. How is your injury?'

'Healing fine.'

'Good, because it looks likely you'll be two men down next sweep. William – Pure – well, there were some bad moments there with his condition. I had to ask Cate to take some steps.'

Iris shivered at Dr Tobias's expression. 'What steps?' she asked cautiously, hoping he didn't mean what she thought he meant.

'We can't afford to lose a trained Red right now, Iris.'

'You fixed him with witchcraft? But we never ... Our policy is that...' Iris stopped talking and looked down, fidgeting with her shirt cuff.

'I know,' said Dr Tobias. 'It was my decision to break that policy.'

Under her breath Iris said, 'You didn't break it for Jude.' Dr Tobias either didn't hear or didn't react. Iris wasn't sure what else to say. She had a niggling sort of feeling that what had happened to Pure was her fault. That she had made the bad calls early on that had led to him plunging off the gallery with the lyc. But she didn't know how to express any of that. 'Is that all, sir?'

'For now.'

25

Friday 26 October 2007

The collar was working just as he'd hoped it would. Alfie had gone almost a whole week without flipping. That was practically a record. So they were all set. It was full moon that night. Misty would do her transformation for Omega and then they would go back to London.

Just him and Misty. Because the one blot – and it was quite a big blot – on Alfie's perfect horizon was that Zac and Leon had never returned.

Misty was resolute when he told her. She was changing the dressing on his eye and tutting about the way it still wasn't healed. 'It'll be like old times. Just you and me. The original twosome.'

'Maybe we should wait a little longer.' Alfie felt something like a twinge in his heart. He sighed, staring down at the grain of the table.

'They're not coming, Alfie. Leon and Zac have known where to find us all this time.'

Alfie let his top teeth slide over his bottom lip. 'But how will they find us if we leave? If they want to find us, I mean.'

'Well, Leon can summon you if he wants to.'

'Yeah, but Zac can't. I don't like to think of Zac all alone, he's only been a wolf for a year. He can't even summon Leon unless he goes back to Texas.'

Misty walked around the table and leant against the edge right next to Alfie's chair. She looked down at him. 'Zac isn't your responsibility, babe. He's Leon's. He's probably with Leon right now.'

Alfie nodded, but there was a lump forming in the back of his throat.

When Blake returned to work Iris couldn't believe how tired he looked. His arm was strapped up in a technical-looking sling. His slim face was pinched and drawn. His eyes were like shadows in his skull. He'd never had a lyc get the better of him before.

Iris had visited him in hospital once. It had made her feel emotionally weird. Seeing Blake sitting up in his hospital bed had given her a flashback of seeing Alfie in the same position, bare-chested and bandaged, screwing up his forehead to tell a slightly besotted WPC that the thing that had attacked him and Matthew had 'maybe been a bear'.

She hadn't told Blake, until now, about Alfie's capture and escape or about the Silver Collar being stolen.

But now he was back he'd have to know, so she'd gone up to his office with some tea and got him up to speed on everything that had happened. He seemed surprisingly unfazed by the loss of his collar.

'Aren't you pissed off?'

Blake shrugged. Iris had brought him the photo Matthew had taken and he was running his thumb over Alfie's gloss-finished face. 'Not greatly. That was the plan, after all, wasn't it? Good to make it a proper field test. Plus, it'll kill the stupid lyc bastard.' He ground the pad of his thumb right into Alfie's smile.

Iris felt her whole body flood with emotion. She twisted inside as she tried to respond without it showing. 'What?'

'It'll kill him. It'll stop his changes outside the moon fine, but once moonlight hits him – two magics that strong working in conflict will rip him apart.'

'Oh.'

'I mean, his whole plan would work fine if he combined it with lock down. Locked down for the moon and used the collar the rest of the time. I did a few calculations and

I'm almost certain that would work. But he'd have to take the collar off every full moon.'

Iris suddenly brightened. 'But that's what he said. He knew he couldn't wear the collar all the time. He said he'd take it off for full moons.'

'Oh yeah? And how's he going to get it off?'

Iris remembered Alfie looming over her, his fingers invasive and intoxicating, working around her pockets, seducing her. 'He took a key,' Iris said softly.

'Did he now? The clever boy. But that wasn't the key to the collar, was it?'

In the cellar of the house, Alfie got ready to lock himself in. The cellar was pretty solid, but he had his cage too as a double layer of protection

He had a combination padlock for the cage door and two small bolts on the inside that were too fine for his paws to manipulate. But he still felt twitchy looking at it. WOLVES ESCAPE: he'd proved that at the Institute. They only need the tiniest crack to slip through.

He went upstairs and fetched the muzzle from his bedside cabinet and put it ready beside the cage. He checked the time, hours yet, but he should probably try the collar. Take it off and put it back on again. After all, once he was safe in the cellar . . .

He took the key he had taken from Iris from its spot – it was safely stowed inside a matchbox balanced on the light switch. He ran his fingers gingerly around the stinging metal of the collar looking for a keyhole.

There wasn't one.

He ran his fingers over the metal again, wincing as the silver started to make his fingertips smart. Definitely no place to put a key. In fact, now he let himself really explore the thing around his neck, ignoring the sting, he couldn't even find the join where it closed, or the hinge where it opened. Iris had definitely held it open. But now it felt like a completely smooth circle of metal encasing his neck: no end, no beginning.

He looked at the key. He remembered pulling it out of Iris's pocket. He knew then, as he stared at it, that the key Iris had in her pocket at that moment wouldn't have been the key to the collar. It would have been the key to the handcuffs she had put on him.

Alfie unbolted the cellar door and ran up the stairs. Misty was standing at the open front door, dressed in a long black PVC raincoat. 'Oh, Alfie, babe. I'm glad you're still on the loose,' she said. 'Could you give me a hand with the cage?'

Alfie nodded. He picked up the cage sitting in the hall and stepped out into the rain. His shirt was open a couple of buttons and, as he slid the cage onto the back seat, he noticed the taxi driver was looking at the collar. He couldn't resist playing up to what he knew the guy was thinking.

As Misty came down the steps he said, 'Have you got someone to help you with the cage at the other end, Mistress?'

Misty gave him a slight frown. 'Ye-es?'

Trying not to smirk, Alfie dropped to his knees on the wet pavement and kissed the toes of Misty's high-heeled boots. 'Would you like me to lick the dungeon floor clean while you're gone, Mistress?'

'Oh, stop it, babe,' Misty said, pulling her foot away and laughing.

'Can I pleasure myself with a dildo after I've locked myself in the cage tonight, Mistress?'

'Alfie! Not fucking funny.'

'I'll take that as a "no" then, Mistress.' Fixing his face into a more serious expression Alfie caught her laughing eyes. 'Misty,' he whispered, 'I can't get the collar off. I'm going to have to go back to the Vix HQ.'

'Babe, you can't.'

'I don't have any choice. I know if I don't get this off in time it'll be bad.'

Misty's face was set. Hard. 'You can't.'

'I have to. I can lock down there if I need to. In fact, I probably won't have any choice.'

'They'll never let you out again.'

'I can get out of there. Always. Don't worry.' Alfie got up, winked at the taxi driver and opened the car door for Misty. She climbed in, looking bewildered.

He stood out in the rain until the taxi was out of sight, then he looked at the sky, made some mental calculations and set off at a run.

'Anyway –' Blake grinned at Iris '– I've found something else for you to do. Keep your mind off Butch, here. You know how some websites are monitored for, I don't know, nefarious activities?'

Iris frowned, caught out by his change of tack. 'What, by the police?'

'Police, MI5, GCHQ, whoever. Well, while I was in hospital I got to wondering if lycs or any kind of paranormals use the internet.'

'You what? Look, if you've found some kid's homepage where they claim to be a werewolf you can investigate yourself, broken arms or no broken arms. If you think I'm hunting down every web-based nutter who –'

'No, Iris, it's a bit more than that. When Cate came to visit me, I got her to magically hack me into the databases of websites that are being monitored by the authorities. Then cross-referenced that against mentions of werewolves and Oxford and, well, I think I found something.'

'OK. What?'

Blake started fiddling with his computer with his left hand. Iris leant over his desk to see. 'OK, look, there's this encrypted site, but the encryption isn't hard to break once you figure out it's in Sumerian.'

'Sumerian?' Iris's forehead crinkled as she looked up at him, leaning over her. She could feel his breath on her neck. 'Doesn't than mean vamps or witches, though? Lycs don't use ancient languages.'

'Yeah, I reckon there might be some vamp involvement. In fact, I think this is a cross-species set-up. It's basically a way for paranormals to make money. This is a website where, uh, "interested" humans – you know, sniffers and bloodfuckers – can pay to do all kinds of paranormal-related weird stuff: have a vampire drink their blood, sleep with a succubus, hunt ghosts, watch a werewolf transform.'

'Holy shit. And you say the authorities are aware of this.'

'Well, the site's on some kind of watch list. That's how I found it. I expect whoever's got their eye on it thinks it isn't real. And maybe it isn't, but there's this ...'

Blake clicked a link and a virtual poster filled the screen. Iris read aloud, '"Omega Entertainments. Exclusive new event, first time in Oxford. Rare female lycanthrope transforms into a wolf before your eyes. Full safety guaranteed."' Iris looked at the date. 'That's tonight.' She tipped her head back to look at Blake again and raised her eyebrows. 'Full moon.'

'Worth checking out, don't you think?'

'I can't, Blake.'

'Why not?'

'You know why. Because I have to find Alfie. I have to find him before moon-rise.'

'And how are you going to do that?' Blake asked. 'Wander the streets calling for him. "Here, Fido!" Does he answer to that?'

'Blake.'

'He's probably left town. He came here for the collar. Why would he even stick around? Oxford is full of people who want to kill him.' Blake paused. 'Like you.'

Iris ignored this. 'I have to try.'

'You have to get me a WXX. I can't do it on my own, Iris, my arm is busted. I busted it trying to bring your damn guy in. You owe me, Iris, and I need you to take this.'

'Blake, are you pulling rank on me?' Iris narrowed her eyes. Whether Blake was *technically* Iris's superior had always been an unresolved issue and one of many points of tension between them. Blake was older and had been doing the job longer. But Iris, well, Iris was better.

Blake swallowed. 'No, baby, course not. Just, face it, he's already dead. He should be dead by now anyway. Eleven years a lyc, body breaking down. You have to let it go. Let him go. You always used to tell me you already had. Now, how about you and me nip over to this address? You can tranq. the WXX. Come back here. Stick her in the basement, pick up the girls and we'll go and shoot some monsters. Destroy your demons. Just the way you like it, baby.' Blake reached out and touched Iris's neck, at the back, just under her ponytail. Blake wasn't really good-looking – his face was all sharp angles. He didn't have an amazing body – just more angles. He was short. But there really was something about him. Physically, he couldn't have been more different from Alfie and, yet, there was something about both of them that was so similar.

Iris leant back into Blake's touch on her neck; it was giving her gooseflesh on her arms. She looked up at him. He was making so much sense. *Let him go.* 'I guess.'

Blake took his hand away, back in business. 'You know, it's shocking what certain interested men will pay to watch a WXX transform. They're so much rarer that WXYs. We won't even take silver. Just the tranqs. Hey, when we've got her maybe we could even set up some shows ourselves, make a bit of money off her.'

'Yuk.' Iris screwed up her face. 'That is so wrong.'

'But you'll come?' Blake gave a small tight smile.

'OK, I guess.' As Iris heard herself say this, she felt weird and disjointed, like she was coming apart from her body. Like she shouldn't really be saying that she was going to go out with Blake and investigate some weird-ass paranormal cabaret act and leave Alfie to die as soon as the moon rose.

She almost didn't notice when Dr Tobias gave a delicate cough from the doorway. 'Good afternoon, Iris, Blake.'

'Hey, doc,' said Blake, 'you off?'

'Yes. Very soon. However, I just wanted to let you know that our Mr Pure White has made an excellent recovery and has been discharged. He isn't ready to return to work yet, but he did want to pop in tonight and say hello before you go on your sweep. He sounded very keen to touch base.'

Iris swallowed. 'Pearl,' she whispered to Blake, 'it'll be about Pearl. No one's heard from her since...' A little louder she said, 'That might be a bit difficult, sir. We're going to leave early for the sweep tonight. A lead on a WXX.'

'Well, Blake will still be here, won't he? Surely you're not going out in your state,' said Dr Tobias, eyeing Blake's injured arm.

Iris looked at Blake. 'I can take Pepper and Aurelia instead.'

Blake looked a little put out, but said, 'Yeah. It's fine. I'll talk to him.'

Misty got set up in Omega's big basement room. It turned out that she didn't need her own cage. Omega had provided a spectacularly huge one set on a raised dais.

Omega wasn't a werewolf herself. She wasn't even a paranormal. She was more of a broker. Someone who sorted things between the human and the paranormal world. She had been on at Misty for years to do these transformation shows. There was always a big demand for werewolf kink in Oxford. Omega had offered to fly Misty in by helicopter before now. Misty had never dreamt of saying yes until Alfie had found a really good reason for them all to come here.

Four years ago when Alfie had told Misty he was a werewolf, naturally, she hadn't believed him.

He'd shown her his grandmother's ring. He pressed it against the skin inside his wrist. He held it there until there were blisters – which only took a few seconds – and Misty had said, 'Yeah, well, that's just an allergy.'

But he so clearly wanted her to believe. He said he hadn't told anyone in such a long time. They were sleeping together by then. Casually, but joyfully – experimentally – feeling superior because of their mature understanding of no-strings fun, of emotionless sex.

Except for Misty it had never been emotionless. Not from the first day they'd met.

Less than a month later, Alfie had taken Misty to a lock-up garage he rented in Ealing. It was full moon. Inside he had given her a gun, which she had shrieked at and dropped before he gave her a serious look, then shut himself inside a sturdy cage and told her to watch.

That night, Misty felt like she had had to change everything she believed about how the universe worked.

So, a couple of months later, when Misty had been blindfolded and tied to Alfie's bed and Alfie had screamed as he came and pulled out of her, perhaps she should have recognised the sounds he was making.

'Alfie?'

No response.

'Babe?'

Alfie's hands were on the rope around her wrists, ripping it away. As soon as she could, Misty tore off the blindfold. 'Babe?'

Alfie lifted his head. At first he seemed to be looking out the window. His face looked strange, blistered and swollen. Misty followed Alfie's gaze to the night sky and the moon. The crescent moon.

Misty turned back to Alfie. His body was wet with sweat, heaving. 'It isn't full moon,' Misty said.

Alfie looked at her. When he spoke, his voice wasn't a voice at all. Not human. But the sounds he made were words.

Two words.

'Get. Out.'

26

As far as Blake was concerned he wasn't too injured to have gone and sat in the van while Iris scooped him a WXX. Who knew what he'd be missing stuck in the office?

Bloody Pure. And, just as Blake thought that, Pure himself, like a sulk made flesh, suddenly stuck his head round the door. 'Hey, Blake. Are you the only one here?'

'Pure. Yeah. Dr Tobias said you were coming. The others have left for the sweep already.'

'Right, actually I'm kind of glad it's you.'

As he strode into the room, Pure looked remarkably fit, considering how badly he'd been hurt. He'd lost some weight and a little of his lean muscle. There was a single livid scar that divided his face in two. But even that looked cool on his otherwise dreamboaty face. Considering how badly Blake's arm was mangled, he couldn't help thinking it was unfair. Pure, who had fallen all the way to the ground and right through a glass case containing a stuffed dodo, looked like he'd practically shrugged the whole thing off.

Blake knew that was because Pure had got the witchcraft. God knows how much that had cost. While Blake had got nothing but the NHS's finest. But he knew Dr Tobias was almost certainly secretly pleased about what had happened to Blake's arm. Tobias had been trying to get Blake to take a desk job since Jude had died.

Bloody Pure. Fully fixed by the witch and still so young and so incredibly good-looking. And with it all only compounded by the way he moved with a gawky unsure grace which seemed to imply he didn't know how devastating (and lucky) he was.

He remembered Iris commenting on it not long after

they had recruited him, asking Blake if he thought Pure was gay or straight. Even now, looking right at him, a mind as shrewd as Blake's couldn't begin to fathom where Pure's sexual priorities might lie. And now, swirling with resentment and boredom, Blake wondered if there might not be a really easy way to find out.

Pure slid onto a chair in front of Blake's desk. 'Blake, it's full moon tonight. I'm really worried about Pearl. What if one of those lycs bit her? She'll be transforming tonight.'

'Well...' Blake began to do a steepling of the fingers move he'd learnt from Dr Tobias, and then stopped because his right arm was still in a sling. 'We now know that for almost all lycs in W2 form a bite is harmless. So we can be pretty sure that –'

'But there's that one that changes at other times isn't there? He's on the loose too.'

'Yes, but he was collared by Iris before he escaped so we can be pretty sure –'

'Collared?'

'Yes, you don't need to worry about that, but we made him safe. So there really is no need to worry. We'll find Pearl soon enough. Meanwhile, why don't we have a nice cup of coffee and I'll show you some literature on lycs that you might enjoy?'

Blake stood up and went over to the little kettle he kept in the corner of his office. He flicked it on to boil, manipulating cups and coffee one-handed. 'Now,' he said turning back to Pure who had stood up and moved a couple of steps over towards him, 'did you know that there are about twenty male lycs to every female?'

Pure shook his head. 'No.'

'Well, it's true. Although very little is known about lyc social structures this has led to some very interesting speculation. Have you considered, for example, that a lyc pack could easily be entirely male, as females are not needed for reproduction of the species?'

Pure was frowning at Blake. 'Er, I'm sorry, I...'

'A lot of packs are wholly or for the main part made up of male lycs, WXYs they tend to get called now. Of course, they do lure human women into their lairs for carnal reasons, much like what happened to your cousin. But there has been some speculation that lycs, that WXYs, enjoy each other.'

Pure shook his head. 'You mean the male lycs have sex with each other? Well excuse me if I don't fall over in shock. Did you think I thought there were no gay lycs? Like gay guys never got bit or something?'

'Well, quite. In fact, I have some books here, some illustrated books . . .'

Blake turned to his shelves and – using the intricate cataloguing system he kept in his brain – placed his good hand on the spine of the exact book he was after without even looking. 'I think you'd like this one.' He shoved the heavy volume at Pure, who took it, stepping back.

'Wow,' said Pure, flipping the pages and giving a little gulp, 'this is pretty hardcore.'

Blake leant forwards, tapping a fingernail against a drawing of what could only really be described as a were-wolf orgy. Muscular men, some half transformed into wolves, writhed with other creatures, fully transformed. Cocks and jaws and teeth and claws. It was shocking and grotesque. Blake had always found the picture freakishly arousing. 'This part here is, I think, particularly interesting. A rite between sire and cub, passing knowledge, power, down to the newer lyc.'

'Y-yes. Interesting.'

Blake moved closer; close enough to trail a finger on Pure's shoulder. 'Lycs aren't just dumb animals, I guess.'

'I guess.'

That was all the encouragement Blake needed, he leant over and, in a sudden darting movement, pressed his lips to Pure's. They felt cool for a moment, but rapidly getting hotter, needier, more eager. Pure let out a sigh that was all desire and sank into the kiss, giving more, faster than

Blake would have ever imagined. Pure was far taller than Blake, but somehow he still seemed to be the submissive partner, letting Blake drive into his mouth.

The image from the book was still in Blake's head as Pure fell to his knees on the hard unforgiving institutional carpet. Blake's lips were still tingling slightly from the kiss. He actually wanted to put the brakes on a little, kneel down himself and insist on more kissing first, but Pure already had other things in mind. He was fumbling with Blake's fly, liberating an already hard dick.

'Want to suck your cock, sire,' Pure said.

Blake was taken aback. He wasn't sure that he wanted full-on lyc role play. But suddenly, now that it was on offer, it felt very right. 'I know. You need to take it,' he muttered as Pure started to lick his dick. 'Take it all. You need to learn from your sire.'

'Teach me.' Pure's eyes were huge. Blake kept telling himself that this was a nonsense, that lycs don't do this. But somehow he could see why the lie was so compelling. 'Force it down my throat, sire. Show me the ways of the wolf.'

With his good hand, Blake pressed his fingers on Pure's bare scalp. Pure's mouth fell open and closed softly around Blake's dick. Blake moaned, leaning back against the bookshelves. 'That's right, my boy,' he muttered, somehow, strangely, he couldn't quite bring himself to say 'cub', 'take it, take it all for your sire.'

27

Alfie had spent a good half an hour casing the Institute from the outside. The fire escape seemed a good bet. It went past the window of Blake's lab, the one he had jumped through on the way out last time. The window was still boarded up awaiting repair. He was all set for some breaking and entering. There was a while until moon-rise, but he was banking on most of the Vix being busy preparing for the night's action.

The fire escape was almost too easy to climb. The boards on the window gave in to his crowbar. Clearly no one was expecting him to return. He dropped through the window into the lab without a sound.

It was dark in the lab, but just as he remembered it. He moved silently, starting with the cupboards mounted above the long workbench that hugged the wall. Chemistry equipment, bottles of various liquids and powders, chains, weighing scales, incongruous books. *Books*. The collar had no keyhole, no fastening of any kind. So how to open it? Paperwork might be the most useful thing right now. The next room was Blake's office. The room full of books.

He slid himself up against the wall next to the door and eased it open a crack, holding his breath. What he saw in the office was surprising and, for one or two moments, confusing.

Two men. One kneeling in front of the other. Both muttering strange things about 'sires' and 'the ways of the wolf', but Alfie knew right away that these men were not lycans and at first his brain wouldn't seem to process what he knew this must be. Two men – two werewolf hunters – role-playing as lycans for kicks. Or at least, some weird idea that lycan sires get their cubs to suck their dicks to pass on knowledge.

Yeah, actually, we tend to just tell them stuff.

But, as he watched, the weirdest unsanctioned image flashed into Alfie's mind. He thought of Leon. His own dick stiffened in his jeans as he thought of Leon on his knees; that surly mouth opening for him. Those snarling lips taking Alfie's dick just because Alfie was the sire and the alpha and Leon knew his place.

Alfie got very aroused very quickly, watching and imagining. It was the moon too, of course. The moon, so close. Calling to his blood. He leant back against the wall, opened his fly, fisted his cock. Aching. Thrusting into his own touch. He jerked himself off quickly, his mission forgotten. He came hard, fast, his whole body jackknifing. His head hit the wall behind him, hard.

When he opened his eyes the older of the two men, the one who had been standing – the one with his arm in a sling – was right in front of him. He was holding a knife to Alfie's throat. The point pricking just under the metal of the collar.

'Don't worry, Alfie, it's a solid silver blade.' The man grinned nastily, like he'd done something clever.

'Blake, right?' Alfie said, smiling right back. 'You torture werewolves and fuck Iris. I feel like I know you already. What you were doing in there just now was kind of interesting. "The ways of the wolf"? So tell me, does Iris know about your little role-play games?'

It was only a chink, but it was enough. Blake's face clouded with confusion for a fraction of a second. Enough for Alfie's elbow to slam into Blake's forearm, sending the knife flying. Alfie shoved Blake back and to the ground, using his injured arm against him. Then he turned, making mental calculations about the distance to the broken window.

'Don't move!' Alfie froze. That was a different voice. Someone behind him in the open doorway. Someone who sounded like he was going to be able to back that state-ment up with something lethal. 'Turn around very slowly.'

Alfie turned, raising his hands. An extremely pretty bald guy with a scar down his face was aiming a gun at him from the doorway. Alfie's eyes flicked to Blake, who was smiling again. 'I know,' Alfie said, 'silver bullets. I do know that you're werewolf hunters. I do get that.'

'Not really hunters, more *researchers*,' said Blake smoothly, sitting up. 'And it looks like you've just become our latest subject.'

Alfie looked from one man to the other and back again. 'You want to be careful with that.' He nodded at the gun. 'It might upset me. You know who I am, don't you? This close to moon-rise anything could flip me.'

'Not so,' said Blake. 'You're collared. Safe. Practically neutered.'

'You sure? I mean, how much testing have you really done? You've never got your hands on an unstable wolf before. What do you reckon, Blake? You reckon your collar will hold me?'

The pretty guy with the gun went pale.

Blake smiled a nasty smile. 'I'm willing to take that risk. And Pure here is trained to deal with your kind – in either form. Besides, werewolf, when the moon rises and the light hits you with that thing locked around your neck, your body will almost certainly rip apart with the two conflicting magics working at once. So, I think if I just wait an hour or so, you won't be quite so perky.'

As Blake relaxed into a tiny moment of smug self-satisfaction, Alfie threw himself at Pure. Pure was looking at Blake and didn't react in time. Alfie's sudden weight and momentum sent Pure flying backwards through the doorway into Blake's main office. Alfie ended up on the floor holding the gun. He yanked Pure into his lap, shoved the gun against his temple and coiled his free arm around his throat.

'OK. So, how about you tell me how to get this collar

off.' He pushed the barrel of the gun harder against Pure's temple.

Blake laughed. 'You won't like it.' Alfie narrowed his eyes. Blake was still laughing as he spoke. 'It can only be removed by the person who put it on. And I don't think Iris has any plans to do that this evening.'

'Iris. Fine.'

Alfie sniffed at the air. He could scent Iris anywhere in this city.

28

The house where the werewolf transformation show was taking place was large, set back from the road and facing a park. A park which just happened to provide perfect cover for spying.

Iris, Pepper and Aurelia found a spot hidden by some large trees and some larger shadows. Pepper and Aurelia seemed in high spirits, laughing about the idea of seedy little men jerking off as they watched a female werewolf transform.

'I mean,' said Aurelia in her cut-glass voice of privilege, 'how hot can it possibly be, darling?'

Pepper laughed. She wasn't usually one for mirth on the job, but clearly this subject was just too funny.

'Sniffers,' said Iris.

'Sniffers?' said Aurelia.

'That's what lycs call them. People who get off on it. The idea of, you know...'

Pepper said, 'The idea of what?'

'Of lycs,' said Iris.

'Heh,' said Aurelia, 'they likes the lycs.'

They watched in silence as another four or five ordinary-looking men crept up to the house. Each one paused, looked furtively around, dug in their pockets for sheets of paper, checked and double-checked before ringing the doorbell.

'Yeah,' Aurelia said at one point, while watching a grey suited man looking up at the impressive house and frowning, 'I was surprised something so freaky was happening in a place like this too.'

'Ma'am,' said Pepper, 'what exactly are we going to do? I mean, I've watched nine men go in there and that's without anyone who was already inside. Plus the WXX. There are only three of us.'

'I've been thinking about that, too. I think we should call the police.'

'The police,' Aurelia sounded highly surprised. 'I thought we didn't involve the authorities, worked outside the law, remained – what was it – deniable.'

'Well, we do, but I still think we could call the police, as concerned neighbours, and get them to go in first.'

'But what about the WXX?' said Pepper.

'Well, we know it'll be in a cage to protect the punters. Maybe if we followed up, posed as, I don't know, police vets, we could just tranq. her and take her away.'

'Police vets?' Aurelia said.

'Yeah. Why not? I'll call Cate, get her to cover us for it.'

Iris couldn't get a signal on her phone from their current position, so she ducked further into the park.

She called Cate first, telling her what she needed and giving her the GPS co-ordinates from her coms. Then, after a short pause for the spell to whirl through the ether, she called the police and reported some very odd goings-on in the house on the edge of the park. They were only too happy to help and promised a swift and appropriate response.

Iris was about to head back to Pepper and Aurelia to watch the fun, and feeling pretty pleased with her plan, when she was suddenly overwhelmed by the twin sensations of hot flesh pressing against her back and cold metal pressing against her temple.

'Hi,' said Alfie who had just emerged from – where exactly?

Iris swallowed. 'Hi. That gun feels familiar. Blake's?'

'You recognise it? Does he press it to your temple often, then?'

'Not as often as he'd probably like to. Blake's gun? Silver bullets, then?'

'Still kill humans though, right?'

'As far as I know . . .' And then, like a sudden rush, Iris

remembered how much she needed to see Alfie. 'Oh God, though, I need to tell you –'

Alfie jabbed her with the gun. 'Shut up, Iris. Can we just assume that as I'm the one with the gun you're going to be the one doing what I say –'

'No, Alfie wait –'

'I said "shut up". We don't have much time.'

'Alfie, seriously, you need to take the collar off,' Iris said, and at exactly the same time Alfie said, 'Blake says I need you to take the collar off me.'

'What? Me? Why me? I can't ... I don't know anything about the collar.' Still less with the ever-threatening gun pressing, although, in truth, Iris was noticing the gun far less than Alfie's warm muscular chest pressed against her back or his big arm, tight around her waist.

'Iris –' he pressed his face into the angle of her neck and shoulder, licking the sensitive skin there.

'What? What are you doing?' Iris's voice cracked as she let her head fall back. Alfie buried his head tighter into her flesh and nipped at her skin. Then she was twirling around in his arms, he was pushing her back against a tree. He was kissing her again.

'We have to be quick,' he said, almost as part of the kiss. 'You can't take the collar off me until afterwards and you have to take it off before ...'

'The moon'll kill you,' Iris said, talking into his hair as he moved down her body, his teeth and lips and tongue everywhere.

'Yes,' said Alfie. 'So quick.' He wrenched her trousers down, lifted her, used the tree for extra support and practically seemed to set her down on his cock.

Iris jerked. Too much, too soon. 'Alfie!'

But Alfie's hands were there on her clit. Those fingers again. Those fingers that had made her come so many times. He was supporting her with the tree, with the angle of his body. Her feet were off the floor. He brought up the hand that wasn't jammed down between their bodies and touched her face. Then he pushed two of his big fingers into her mouth. Filling her there too. In. Out. Stopping her cries as her orgasm began to rush fast towards her. He held her there. Found her tipping point, her edge and held her on it, stilling his cock inside her, his thumb on her clit, his two big fingers fucking her mouth. Iris shuddered, waiting for her moment.

Ever since Alfie had left town Iris had fantasised about this – fucking Alfie and racing the moon's rise to orgasm. In her fantasies she had been cheating her own death in the jaws of the wolf. In this real-life version of her fantasy the stakes were different. But no less high.

And he made her wait, playing chicken with the moon, not more than ten seconds, but each one felt like a lifetime, before he let his thumb slip over her clit one more time and thrust into her cunt and her mouth. Iris threw her head back and came, consumed by his body.

When she opened her eyes, Alfie grinned at her, his face tight in the dark. 'We really must stop meeting like this,' he said.

Iris twisted in his arms and reached down to the pocket of her trousers which were halfway down her thighs.

Her fingers closed around the two tranquilliser darts she had stowed there.

'You need to take the collar off now, Iris, don't wait. The quicker you do it the further away from civilisation I can get before I change.'

With the fingers of her left hand still curled around the darts in her pocket, Iris reached out with her right and ran a finger along the edge of the metal at Alfie's throat. 'Does it hurt you?'

'No. It kind of tingles, but, I don't know, it's hard to forget that it's there.'

She held his gaze a moment more. Then said, 'I guess it's my turn to be sorry, Alfie.' Her left hand was a blur coming out of her pocket as she stabbed one of the darts through his blue shirtsleeve into his upper arm.

He looked at her open-mouthed. Words started to shape

on his lips, but he was unconscious before he hit the ground. Out cold, lying on his back in the dirt.

Iris had fallen with him, she was lying on the ground in a bundle of her clothes. She touched the collar. There was an almost inaudible *snick* and it came away in her hands. She stowed it in her pack. Underneath the collar, Alfie's skin was red – sore and blistered. Iris swallowed and gently touched the place where he was wounded.

When she took the collar off him, it was like she didn't need to think about what she was doing. Her will just seemed to happen. That same dream state compelled her now too, as she looked at him. Alfie, asleep. So real. So familiar. She lowered her head, placed her lips on his and kissed him. He didn't move – didn't wake like Sleeping Beauty – but his lips were very slightly parted and she slipped the tip of her tongue a tiny way into his mouth. Her pussy went thump. She couldn't believe how much she still wanted him.

She was losing herself. Forgetting her mission, her job, the time . . .

29

In the basement of Omega's place Misty was feeling pretty pleased with herself. She could tell, when she peeked around the red velvet curtain, that the room was filling up nicely. Misty was getting a – very large – flat fee for doing this show, so it made no difference how full the room was, but it was still nice to feel appreciated.

'Misty.' Omega startled her. It was strange that Omega had managed to sneak up behind her without her noticing – Omega was not the kind of women who was built for stealth. She was Big, Busty, Blonde, Brassy. All those capital Bs. 'Misty, will you get in the cage? The moon's nearly up. The moonlight'll be in here in a moment. If you change before we get the curtain open they'll be in trouble.'

Misty was thinking, If I change before you get me in the cage they'll be more than in trouble. But she didn't say that, there wasn't time. She shucked off her robe and climbed into the big cage.

Oh, for a cage like this at home. She could stand and stretch out in this beauty. So damn civilised. Even Leon couldn't complain about locking down in something like this. They should get a place in the country. Settle down somewhere with room for a big cage like this. Just her and Alfie. Part of her really liked that idea. A tiny part of her brain started to whisper to her that the collar was working. That maybe it would make things all right between them again.

She struck a pose, legs splayed, hands behind her head like a Saxon salute, then turned her left leg so that the scars on her inner thighs were clearly visible. The curtains were opening.

She barely had time to register the sea of faces, the awe

and arousal in their expressions, before the moonlight hit her and she stretched into it, arching, lengthening, reaching for something inside herself. As the door to the basement burst open and the room filled with cops, Misty was beyond caring about anything but the light.

Iris felt the moonlight start to leak through the canopy of trees above them. It curled around branches and licked through every tiny gap. She squeezed her eyes closed, but beneath her lips she felt Alfie change.

She pulled away from him, shocked, repulsed and confused. She rubbed her lips with the back of her hand to take away the impression of fur and fangs. Beneath her the enormous wolf made a low sound. A growly purr. Iris yelped in surprise and sprang back. She pulled the second tranquilliser dart from her pocket and stabbed it into the hound's front leg. It stilled again. Sleeping, looking like nothing more than an oversized dog.

Iris shook herself. She had some rope in her pack and she used it to tie the animal's paws together – the way Blake always did with his hound captures. Alfie's clothes were lying on the ground next to him. Iris stuffed them into her pack too. As she did so she felt something hard in the pocket of his jeans. Blake's gun.

30

As Iris walked back to the road, she wondered why she hadn't noticed any sirens. The road was full of cop cars.

Pepper and Aurelia melted out of the park and were suddenly flanking her on both sides.

'Where have you been?' Aurelia asked softly.

'Nowhere, just got distracted. Briefly.'

Aurelia looked at Iris a little oddly, but didn't ask anything else.

'Are we covered, ma'am?' said Pepper. 'Did you speak to Cate?'

'Yep,' Iris said as they got near the first police car. 'What do you reckon we are then? Still going to go with police vets?'

Aurelia snorted. 'Yeah, tonight on BBC1, Police Vets!'

'Animal handlers?' said Pepper.

'Yeah,' Iris said. 'I like that. It's practically true.'

The first cop that tried to stop them got Iris's biggest beamiest smile and the words, 'Hi, we're the animal handlers.'

'Oh, thank God,' said the cop, not hiding his relief. 'It's downstairs. Nasty-looking creature.'

Iris led Pepper and Aurelia into the house and they found their way to the basement by following the trail of bewildered-looking men. Some were quiet and guilty-looking, others were protesting: 'What *is* this!'; 'I've done nothing wrong!'; 'What, so it's illegal to watch a dog in a cage now is it?'

'Actually, ma'am,' Aurelia hissed, her head close to Iris's, 'they have a point. What are they supposed to have done?'

Pepper was the first into the big basement room,

already snapping, 'Animal handler,' as Aurelia and Iris followed behind. The room was long, easily running the full stretch of the big house. Chairs were lined up facing a raised stage, on which was a large cage almost the size of the ones in the Institute's basement and inside that a sleek black hound. Smallish. A WXX.

'Oh, good,' said the middle-aged paunchy cop who was standing by the cage. 'Glad you're here. She's going crazy, poor thing. Not quite figured out how to get this cage open yet, but . . .' He was fiddling with the door.

For a moment Iris didn't get it. The hound in the cage was snapping and snarling – a dangerous dog and then some – yet the cop was cooing, 'Poor love, you don't like it in there, do you?'

It was Pepper who shouted, 'No! Don't!'

But the cage door was already swinging open. From the expression on the cop's face he didn't expect it to unlock so suddenly. He also didn't expect the hound to lunge out and send him hurtling backwards. He landed on the floor below the stage, toppling several chairs as he fell. The hound was on his chest, its fangs a whisper from his neck.

Iris heard Pepper and Aurelia start to take aim next to her. They had tranqs. She didn't. Her tranqs. were gone. But she did have . . .

She knew how much Blake wanted a live WXX, but she also knew she was a better shot that either of the girls.

'I got it,' Iris shouted, lunging forwards and pulling Blake's gun out of her pocket.

The wolf was on the floor before she had even finished the sentence.

Pepper rushed across and covered the wolf's body with a PVC raincoat that had been hanging in the wings. She got the face covered before any of the cops noticed the woman it was rapidly becoming.

Pure had gone home. Blake had put him in a taxi. He looked even greyer and more shaken up than when he had been talking about Pearl. Poor bastard.

It wasn't long after that that Blake heard the truck come chugging into the yard. Slight concerns about Pure were shoved out of his mind as he felt himself suddenly thrill to the idea of a WXX of his very own.

He raced down the stairs, through the auditorium and out into the yard. Iris stopped him before he climbed into the back of the truck.

'Hang on, Blake.'

'Where is she? Did you get her?'

'No we . . .' Iris stopped and inhaled. 'There was a situation. I had to take her out.'

Blake felt himself sag. 'But Iris, the tranqs.'

'Yeah. I had to use my tranqs on someone else. You might be able to work out who if you think about it. It must have been you who told him where to find me.'

'You tranqued Alfie and you killed the WXX! How did you even kill – oh.' Blake felt a lump forming in his throat as he looked at Iris. 'My gun. Alfie had one of my guns.'

Iris nodded her head.

'Where's the body?'

'The WXX? We got rid of it, sir,' said Aurelia who was walking round from the front of the truck with Pepper.

'No reason to keep it,' said Iris.

Blake was shaking his head. 'I could have done an autopsy.'

Iris took a step forwards so she was very close to him. 'Or sold it. What does a WXX body go for these days?'

'Fuck off, Iris,' Blake said back, his voice low but not as low as hers had been. 'Like you're the image of professionalism. For example . . .' Blake pushed past Iris and climbed into the back of the truck. Inside, unconscious and roped, was a huge hound. Nearly as big as the Beast. 'So this is the other side of our friend Alfie, is it?'

Iris climbed up on the footplate. 'Yep. That's him.'

'So, you want me to kill him for you?' Blake had already picked up the gun – his own gun – that was lying on the floor of the truck. He placed it up against the huge hound's chest.

'No!'

'Why not? What are we keeping him alive for?'

'Aren't you the one that thinks we *should* keep them alive, for information?'

'Aren't you the one that thinks that we shouldn't?'

Iris bit her lip. 'Alfie's different,' she said.

'Yeah?'

'I need him. To kill the Beast.'

'Oh, God, Iris, will you just drop that damn excuse and tell the truth?' Blake said, throwing down the gun. He jumped to the ground, pushed past Iris and started to walk back across the car park. 'He's never going to do it,' he shouted. 'His sire is an Ancient Beast. The thrall is too strong. And you know it.' Blake stopped and turned. Iris was still standing just in front of the truck staring at him. 'You're a total hypocrite, Iris. At least admit the real reason you can't kill him.'

'You don't know anything about it, Blake.'

Aurelia and Pepper were both just standing watching – clearly loving every moment.

'Fine,' Blake shouted, 'fine.'

Iris turned away and went to get a gurney with Pepper and Aurelia for Alfie. She didn't even care. *Bitch*.

Blake stood and watched for a while. When Pepper and Aurelia came back he walked back over to the truck. He looked at Iris. 'You're driving,' he said.

'You're coming?'

'Yeah, let's go out and kill some motherfucking monsters.'

31

Pepper felt kind of embarrassed about the scene she had just witnessed between Iris and Blake. What was the deal with those two? She was glad when Iris told her to sit up front with her. She was nervous enough about her first full-moon sweep without the sight of her bosses trying to kill each other.

It wasn't until their third stop out in the countryside beyond Old Marston that they saw some hounds. Scrappy mongrels in the trees. Just like the fake ones from the training session.

Iris, Pepper and Aurelia prowled forwards with their guns tight in their hands.

'Hang on,' said Blake, in a low voice that was so insistent it wasn't really discreet. 'I thought we agreed to tranq. them.'

'No, Blake.' Iris wasn't really whispering either. 'We didn't. We didn't even bring tranqs.'

'I did,' said Blake. 'Please, Iris. What if they lead us to a whole pack?'

'Blake, I just said they are not pack animals. They are clearly strays; look at the state of them. Either their sire rejected them or their pack kicked them out. They won't know anything.'

'You can't be sure. What if they do? What if they're something to do with Alfie? Part of his pack? They'd be a good bargaining chip with him if they were.'

'I thought you said he'd never . . .' Pepper watched as Blake and Iris just stared at each other for a moment. Then Iris said, 'No, Blake. Let the girls take them. Aurelia, Pepper, let's see what you can do.'

But as Aurelia and Pepper started to move on the

hounds, Blake was with them. Ignoring Iris's shouts. Pepper tried not to look nervous.

The whole thing was a blur as she and Aurelia moved on their quarry. Aurelia got hers with the first shot, just before they started to bolt. Blake was next, firing with his left hand, but still bringing his hound down with ease. Pepper swallowed. The black hound, the last one was running away. She gave chase. By the time she had hit her target she had a long way to walk back to where the others were.

Aurelia met her halfway. 'Did you get it?'

'Yeah. In the end.'

'Where's the body?'

'Back there. Sorry, was I meant to bring it?'

'Don't worry, I'll deal,' said Aurelia, sprinting off into the dark.

Pepper headed back to the van, past Blake, who was carrying the brown hound over one shoulder. He grinned at her.

Iris was already standing by the van. Pepper was expecting a reaction from Iris, but she didn't say anything. Blake got into the back of the van and just stabbed the hound with a second tranquilliser dart before starting to rope it up. Pepper got in after him.

As soon as Aurelia returned, the truck rumbled off.

Pepper said, 'What did you do to the bodies of the hounds we shot, Aurelia? Do they always turn back into humans like that WXX?'

'These didn't,' said Aurelia. 'Some do, some don't. I don't know why ...' She glanced at Blake who was still coiling rope around his hound's front paws.

'Uh, strength of the one form over the other? The way the lyc would rather be seen? No one knows.' He shrugged.

Pepper watched the muscles in his arm where he'd rolled up the sleeve of his red shirt. He wasn't a big man, but his frame was taut, hard with understated muscle. He had one arm in a sling but the way he'd carried that hound – he hadn't even broken a sweat. And the way he was tying it up one-handed was making Pepper think some very unprofessional things about him indeed. He was a capable man. Probably capable of anything.

Pepper turned her attention back to Aurelia. 'So, what did you do with the body?'

'Oh, we have this powder. I'm not sure how it works. Cate takes care of it. Purple stuff. Purple and turquoise. Real pixie dust. We sprinkle it over the body and, pouf!'

'Pouf?'

'Gone.'

'Gone where?' said Pepper.

'Away,' Blake grunted, finally tying off the last ends of his ropes and sitting back. 'God, you kids don't know you're born now we can afford the marvellous Cate Ray and all her glorious magical assistance. Before we had a witch on staff we used to work the magic ourselves – and we were all pretty bad at it, even Dr Tobias. Iris, in particular was horrendous at magic.'

'Only because it doesn't make any logical sense,' Iris shouted from the driver's seat. Pepper hadn't realised she could hear them.

'Heh,' said Blake, getting off the floor of the truck and sitting down next to Pepper, 'logical sense. Yeah, 'cause, in our business logic is so very key. Anyway, before, we used to use these amulets the doc bought from some contact of his. They were kind of like, I don't know, clip-on things. They made sure the hound wouldn't turn back into a human. So you had to get it clipped on quick in case it was one of the ones that flip back instantly. Then, you had to bury it.'

Pepper shuddered. 'Bury it? Wasn't that weird?'

'It was certainly time-consuming,' said Blake. 'There were only three of us. If we killed a hound we had to leave someone behind to bury it. Can't go freaking out the public by leaving hound bodies all over the place.'

'Do you ever . . .' Pepper stopped herself, stumbling over a tricky question. 'Do you ever think about the fact that they're people. That the hounds you kill are really people?'

Blake sort of smirked and looked over at the back of Iris's head expectantly.

'They're not people,' Iris shouted. 'They know what they are and if they're letting their wolf form run loose like this on full-moon night then they're not people, they're monsters. They could make themselves safe. They don't. And it's not like they have families and friends to miss them like we do. Once they get bitten lycs reject their families, everyone they cared about before, to be loyal to their sire and their pack. To other monsters. They are unbelievably dangerous. If the creatures we encountered out in the field cared at all about keeping people safe they'd be one of the fifty per cent who kill themselves within the first year. Yeah, it's awful for them, but once they're bitten it's over. A lyc doesn't live for more than a few years after it's bitten anyway. The bite's always fatal – just in some cases it's a very slow death.' Iris stopped talking. She hadn't turned around, but Pepper felt like she knew the impassioned, slightly flushed look that Iris would have on her face just from her tone of voice.

The last stop of the night was a multi-storey car park. Not a usual stop, but Iris saw it and, in her words, it set off her wolf-dar.

The multi-storey was, despite the fact it was brightly lit and full of signs of humanity, the spookiest place they'd swept yet. On Iris's instruction, Blake and Aurelia took the lift and started at the top, while Iris and Pepper headed up from the bottom.

'Check in on the coms at least every two minutes,' Iris had said to Blake's back as he disappeared through the door to the stairwell.

It happened when they got to the third floor – entirely deserted apart from one turquoise SUV. As they walked slowly across the concrete, the thing – Pepper couldn't bring herself to think of this one as a 'hound' – leapt out from behind the lone vehicle and made straight for them.

It was easily twice the size of the creatures they'd seen

earlier. Huge, hairy and like something from a nightmare. Pepper recognised it instantly. The dirty-grey and chocolate-brown pelt. The size. The copper-coloured eyes. This was the Beast. Iris had devoted three entire lectures to this creature. Its history. Its savagery. The fact that when it was in its wolf form it was impervious to silver bullets.

The creature landed on the concrete in front of them, snarling and vicious, its huge claws boring holes in the concrete. Iris pushed Pepper behind her, forcing her into the gap between Iris's back and the wall.

The creature snarled at Iris.

'Here you are, Beast. I knew I'd see you tonight,' Iris said in a slow threatening voice.

Pepper didn't understand it. Iris had told her quite clearly that there was no point trying to talk to, or otherwise reason with, lycs in wolf form. They had no rational comprehension. And yet, when she looked over Iris's shoulder, the creature did seem to be listening to her.

The creature snarled again and Iris said, 'I'm not going to let you have her. I know you never attack me. And there's no one else here.'

Silence then. Pepper watched the wolf as it looked at Iris almost sulkily. Tension seemed to crackle in the air.

Tension that was instantly diffused when – across the other side of the car park – the door to the stairwell banged open. Aurelia and Blake, on their way down. The two of them froze in the doorway, staring at the creature.

'No! Blake, Aurelia,' Iris shouted, 'Beast.'

Aurelia slammed the door shut again but the creature was already hurtling across the strip-lit concrete towards them. Iris followed, then Pepper.

Iris started to shoot. Pepper could see the bullets were hitting their target, but they didn't seem to faze the creature at all. They just bounced off. Despite the fact she had heard Iris describe this in lectures, she didn't believe it until she saw it – the hot metal pellets rattling off onto the ground. Iris was still shooting as she disappeared through the doorway where the wolf had followed Blake and Aurelia.

When Pepper got through the door after them she could see Blake was holding the creature off with gun fire from somewhere down the stairs and Aurelia was doing the same from above. Again she could see that silver bullets and tranq. darts were hitting the creature over and over and just bouncing off. But the hail of fire did seem to at least be enough to hold it back from making an attack.

With Aurelia from above, Blake from below, Iris and now Pepper coming towards it, the creature was pinned. Backing away from them into the dead end in front of the lifts. Pepper saw Iris pull out her silver dagger.

'Hold,' Iris shouted and the gun fire stopped. Iris looked at the creature again. 'OK, so we know bullets aren't your poison. But how about something more old school, like a silver blade. Will that go through your damn fur coat? Something's got to kill you.'

As Iris lunged, there was a soft *ding* and the doors of the lift behind the creature slid open. It sprang backwards out of Iris's path, leaving her sprawled on the floor. Pepper held her breath. Iris was scrambling to her feet, looking as if she was going to leap into the lift too, but at the same moment Blake came thundering up the stairs, screaming, 'Don't be so fucking stupid, Iris!' and threw himself at her, shoving her clear of the lift as its doors slid closed again.

In the silent stairwell the four of them looked at each other in bewilderment. 'Did the Beast just . . . ? Did it just take the lift?' asked Pepper, unable to believe what had happened.

'Seriously,' said Aurelia, flipping some blonde hair out of her face, 'now I've seen everything.'

Blake was on top of Iris on the floor. 'Fuck's sake, Blake,' Iris muttered. 'I had him. I reckon the knife might have done it.'

'It would have killed you,' said Blake.

Iris shook her head. 'It never attacks me.'

'Yeah. It never used to attack Jude either, until the two of you had it cornered. It would have killed you if you'd gone after it into that lift.'

Iris sighed and shook her head. She was staring at the closed lift doors where the Beast had disappeared. Blake, still on top of her, ducked his head down and tried to kiss her, muttering something about his reward for saving her life. Iris pushed him off her, and Pepper turned jealously away.

Back at the Institute, Iris watched Blake trying to get his trussed-up lyc onto the gurney with one working arm.

'You can't take that down to the basement,' she said. 'I've got Alfie down there.'

'Basement's mine,' Blake said gruffly, hoisting the hound onto his shoulder and then onto the gurney. 'Anyway, it'll be good for Fido to watch me take this one apart. Let him know what's in store for him.

'Blake, no, I don't want you to . . .'

'You don't want me to persuade Alfie to summon the Beast for you? Well, in that case, Iris, I have to ask you once again why you are keeping that creature alive.'

Iris scrambled for a response. 'I thought you wanted him. For experimentation.'

Blake dropped her gaze. 'Fine.'

Iris looked at the unconscious hound on Blake's gurney. She couldn't bear it. She knew it was a packless creature. It wouldn't have anything to tell Blake about the huge werewolf packs he was desperate to find. She pulled her gun and, before Blake even realised what she was doing, she shot it in the head.

32

Saturday 27 October 2007

Iris had watched Blake go. Storm right out of the yard, leaving her to deal with the lyc's body. He had told her to tell Dr Tobias that he was taking some leave.

After powdering the lyc, she'd gone down to the basement to find Alfie human and sleeping. Naked. She fixed the Silver Collar back around his neck and stuck a new piece of gauze over his eye.

Then she – finally – reached out and put one hand on his smooth, perfectly shaped bicep. Her mouth went dry and her pussy got wet. Her fatigues were covered in grass and mud and dirt from the floor of the car park. Her hair was matted with sweat. But with Alfie lying naked in front of her, she had never felt so sexy. She reached out with her other hand and touched his hard cock.

Once, Alfie had masturbated for her. Stood up next to the bed and touched himself. Made a slow-handed show of it while she lay there watching. He'd stopped and started to Iris's instructions, biting his lip when she made him pause too long, until she couldn't resist stroking herself too.

Iris let her hand work Alfie's cock up and down a little. Just a light touch. Not enough to rouse him or arouse him. Just so she could feel him. Real.

She took her other hand from his arm and slipped it into her underwear, just for a second, teasing herself a little and then thinking better of it. Then she bent down and – compelled by the strangest feeling – slipped her shiny finger between Alfie's slightly parted lips.

Alfie stirred slightly. Iris pulled her finger away, turned and left him in the cage.

Pepper and Aurelia were lounging across the sofas in the staffroom. Aurelia was bored and she could tell by Pepper's face that she was too. It was never easy to relax after sweeps.

'How about the hound Iris had trussed up in the park, eh?' Aurelia said.

'Yeah,' said Pepper as she rolled off her grubby white socks. 'Where did she get him from?'

Aurelia shrugged. 'Big chap, and, woah, was he heavy. And Blake said it was *him*?'

'Him, who?'

'You know. *Him*. Alfie. Iris's big werewolf passion.'

'What?'

'God, Pepper, like the whole reason Pure and Blake nearly died. Because Blake let that lyc try to summon his sire. And that sire is Alfie. And Iris has a filthy-dirty-and-wrong thing for him. Pure told me all about it. You know how it is, thin line between love and hate. All that. She's spent so much time hating lycs that she's fallen for one.'

'Ooh. So this Alfie,' said Pepper, then she paused. 'Right, so who is Alfie, exactly?'

'Oh, well, story is that he was, like, Iris's boyfriend or something. He got bitten and infected and that's why she's working for the Institute. Because a lyc broke her heart.'

'Aww.' Pepper was playing with her bare toes, but not in a way that grossed Aurelia out. Pepper had neat little feet. Sweet and peachy coloured. 'But that's weird. I mean if she loved him what would it matter? I mean he'd only be a hound once a month.'

'Yeah, and we all have our monthly issues, darling,' Aurelia snorted half to herself.

'But, really, if she *loved* him. I mean, it's not like it would have been his fault. Like, he would have gone out and got himself bitten on purpose.'

'I don't know,' said Aurelia, 'but according to Pure some

heavy stuff went down and that's why Iris is so, uh, so *intense*, now.'

'Intense? Well I guess that's one way of putting it. So what do you reckon she's trying to do, working for the Institute? Kill him or cure him?'

Aurelia shrugged, and then she said, 'Well, surely she could have killed him last night. She had that gun.'

'Right,' said Pepper. 'Oh, but hang on, though. Isn't Iris with Blake? The way they talk to each other I always thought...'

'Oh, well, kind of. That is such a car crash. They were married when Pure and I started. Hadn't been married very long and they were separated not long after that. I don't think they've got properly divorced though. And, of course, darling, they're still doing it. They think no one knows but it is so obvious.'

Pepper laughed. 'Maybe that's why Blake was so pissed off that Iris had her old boyfriend tied up in the back of the truck.'

'Yeah.' Aurelia laughed. 'Who wouldn't be?'

The staffroom was on the third and topmost floor of the Institute, right at the top of the twisty maze of rooms and offices. It had no windows apart from a skylight in the roof. Aurelia followed Pepper's eyes as they drifted up to the square of sky. It was purple, growing paler mauve as they watched. Pepper said, 'I wonder what he looks like?'

Aurelia ran her bottom teeth over her top lip. She knew what Pepper was thinking about. 'Alfie? Well, he was actually pretty hot as a wolf.'

33

'This job has the best perks,' Aurelia breathed, staring through the bars of the cage at Alfie asleep on the floor. 'He's magnificent.'

'He's better looking than Pure.'

'He's even better looking than that black guy – the one who got away last week – and he was seriously fit.'

'Do you think all lycs are, uh . . . ?' Pepper started to trip over her words. Aurelia glanced over. She noticed Pepper was blushing.

'What?' Aurelia said. 'This hot? Don't know, darling, but those two guys we saw doing Pure's cousin were pretty yummy and that Japanese girl from last night, she was cute too.'

'Him, though . . . Fuck.' Pepper shook her head as if she couldn't believe what she was seeing.

'I know.'

Alfie was wondering whether to open his eyes. He was so tired – drained – but the floor was very hard and it was difficult to sleep listening to all the chatter. Not that it wasn't nice chatter to listen to, pretty good for his ego. An ego that was a little bruised now he realised that that bitch Iris had tranqued him and brought him back here. Again. *Just how many times am I going to have to escape from this place?*

Those voices. Women's voices. Young women. That kind of company would be nice about now. Show Iris just how much he didn't care about her and her inability to refrain from locking him up in this bloody cage. *Iris.* Why could he scent her so strongly right now?

He felt far worse than he normally did after the change.

Must be the tranqs. Iris had given him. Worse than sedatives. Much worse. His mouth was dry. His eyes were gritty. His head was fluffy inside. Contrasting with his outside which felt decidedly unfluffy. He could do with one of Misty's coffee enemas right now. Except she never did really give him a coffee enema did she? Just threatened it that one time when he wouldn't get out of bed and Leon was really pissing her off.

Cubs! And weren't those girls Iris's cubs, if you looked at it with a wolf head on?

That decided it. He dredged some energy from somewhere and snapped his eyes open, rather satisfied by the way the two girls jumped back from the bars. 'Morning, ladies.'

They *were* pretty. One in a more obvious long hair, long legs way. The other was stockier, short mousey hair. In fact, he'd almost put her down as a dyke if it wasn't for the way she was staring right at his cock.

'Hello, darling,' said the prettier blonde one. 'Are you Alfie?'

'Yeah,' said Alfie, sitting up and twisting around to set his big bare feet on the floor in front of him. He gave Blondie a long loaded look. 'You want to come a little closer and tell me what big *teeth* I have?' He felt something like a tingle of power, even as he reminded himself that he didn't believe in Lure. He looked at Blondie and smiled.

She smiled back. Alfie caught the scent of her in the air, as she moved a little way towards the bars. He stood up, his erection pressing hard against his belly. He walked over. So close he could almost touch her, could almost kiss her, could almost fuck her right through the bars. For all the use that would be.

But her friend caught her by the shoulder. 'Aurelia,' she hissed, 'isn't Alfie the lyc that attacked Iris out at the parks?' And she jerked her head in the direction of the WOLVES ESCAPE notice taped to the wall.

Aurelia turned. 'Yeah.'

But the other girl's eyes were wide, scared. 'Aurelia, that

means he's the lyc who changes. Who can change when it isn't full moon.'

Aurelia jumped back from the bars. 'Fuck. Right.' Her eyes met Alfie's. Livid.

Alfie shook his head, trying to get his thoughts in order. The stocky girl was right. What was he thinking? 'Yeah,' he muttered, 'fuck, yeah, sorry. You better not come in.'

'You were trying to get us killed,' Aurelia said.

'No, I ... Hang on though.' Alfie hands moved to his neck, felt the collar there and snapped away again as the silver stung his fingertips. 'Oh. It's OK. I've got the collar on. Iris must've –'

'What collar? What are you talking about, werewolf?' Aurelia snapped.

The other girl touched her shoulder again. 'Hey, don't be like that with him. He's just woken up after his change. Some of them don't even know who they are when that happens. And he was tranqued. Although, hey, that actually gives me an idea.'

With an excited smile, the stocky girl turned and dashed off up the stairs. Aurelia looked at Alfie through the bars. After a few moments she said, 'That true? Did you just forget how dangerous you are?'

Alfie shrugged. Did he? Now it seemed weird to imagine that he could ever forget that.

When the stocky girl came back and Alfie saw what she was carrying, he jumped away from her, backing up until he was pressed against the far wall. 'Oh, no. Look, I'm sorry. I didn't mean to.'

Stocky Girl shook her head. 'What's wrong? It's just to be on the safe side.' She was clutching a tranquilliser dart in one hand and a rifle in the other.

'Not that again. God, I still feel like I've been stuffed and mounted from last night.'

Aurelia smirked.

'Go on,' said Stocky Girl. 'Aurelia can go inside and I can mark you.' She fitted the dart into the chamber of the rifle she was holding in her other hand and hoisted it onto her shoulder. She squinted into the sights. 'If nothing happens I won't have to use it.'

Alfie looked at Aurelia. Her mouth quirked into the prettiest smile. He remembered that other idea he had. The one about sticking it to Iris for making him find out how disorientating that stuff was in the first place. He smiled back at the girl. 'All right,' he said, 'and then if that goes OK, maybe we can swap around.'

'What?' said Aurelia, her hand already on the first bolt of the cage door. 'Me and Pepper screw while you hold the gun?'

As she crossed the cage and put one manicured hand on Alfie's chest, he caught Pepper's eye and said, 'Well, maybe that'd be good too.'

Pepper looked a little sour, but he was already turning his attention to the long blonde wet dream standing in front of him. Not Alfie's regular type. In fact, Pepper fitted his small brunette template more closely, but she was certainly nothing to complain about and he still felt like he had a cloud of Iris's scent around his head. Iris's arousal. He was practically delirious with it.

Trying not to think about that too much, he grabbed Aurelia and wrenched her shirt open in one move, crushing her to him. Aurelia moaned. Alfie shook himself – a professionally trained werewolf hunter, overcome with lust, taking risks like this. It was crazy. He opened his eyes and looked into hers. They hunt all night, he thought, just like us, maybe it leaves them a little pent-up to.

It was artless, that first fuck, vulgar and quick and raw. He kissed and stripped Aurelia, then pushed her down to the floor. He fucked her on her hands and knees, while she held onto the bars of the cage for support. She looked beautiful. Her hair all over her smooth flawless back. And even as he came inside her, rolled her over and licked the taste of himself from her until she came too, he thought only of Iris. The scent of her all pervasive, like it would never fade away.

Naked, still hard, Alfie got up and walked over to

Pepper; she was still on the other side of the bars. He put his arm through and grabbed hold of her, pulled her close enough that he could kiss her against the metal and let her taste the cocktail in his mouth. All the time she had been watching he hadn't been able to tell which of them she was looking at. And even now, as her tongue came out and she crushed herself to the bars of the cage to lick and kiss his face, he couldn't tell who she was trying to get more of.

So it might have been the taste of Aurelia – rather than the Lure he didn't believe in – that got Pepper into the cage, still grasping a tranq. dart she had removed from the gun.

'Plenty more for you, baby,' he whispered as he pushed her up against the wall and kissed her. His erection was already hard against her hip. It was always like this after the change. It never ended.

He held her against the wall so she could look over his shoulder and see Aurelia lying naked and sated on the floor of the cage. He kissed and nipped the hollow of her neck – it hardly took anything to make her come.

34

Later, when Alfie, Pepper and Aurelia were all lying on the floor of the cage, panting and glowing, Alfie put his plan into action.

He rolled over and snatched the tranquilliser dart Pepper was still holding in her hand. At one point, she'd scratched the tip of it against his bare hip, while she sucked his cock and Aurelia had watched them with lusty eyes. He'd licked his come off Pepper's face and he'd kissed her afterwards. *Oh, God, the kissing. Kissing, never enough kissing.*

Pepper started when he grabbed the dart, but he was too fast and sank it into her leg. She looked at him with her eyes stretched wide. So betrayed it made Alfie wince. But he didn't have time to think about what he was doing. He was on his feet and pulling Aurelia to hers, twisting an arm up behind her back.

'Where is she?' he barked, shoving Aurelia hard up against the wall, grazing her beautiful face on the exposed stone. Alfie yanked Aurelia's wrist hard and made her yell and squirm in his sex-sticky arms.

'Where's who, you idiotic brute?' Underneath her defiance she sounded scared.

'I heard you saying you saw a female werewolf last night. A WXX, you said. A Japanese girl. Did you bring her in?'

'No. We didn't bring her in. Now let me go, you filthy animal.'

'You better not be lying.'

'Or what, you'll kill me twice over, werewolf?'

Alfie pressed his lips up to her ear. 'I'm not going to kill you. And I am not an animal.'

'Well, nice job not acting like one, dog breath,' Aurelia spat. At the same time, she braced herself against the wall and threw herself backwards, catching Alfie off guard and making him stagger back across the cage. She spun around, launching herself at Alfie to tackle him, but he dived away in time and she landed on the floor. Alfie took his chance to put the door of the cage between her and him.

As he was drawing the bolts shut, Aurelia sat up and narrowed her eyes at him. 'I can have a whole bunch of Reds down here in a second –' she began.

'Yeah,' Alfie interrupted her, 'except . . .' He was already bending down, grabbing Pepper's tranquilliser gun, still loaded with the second dart. Aurelia opened her mouth, probably meaning to scream, but too late.

Alfie found his clothes in a messy pile on top of the cabinet by the stairs. He pulled on his jeans. He couldn't be bothered with the rest. He never felt the cold.

The other cage was empty. He checked the two cells too. No sign of Misty. So now his only problem was the fact that Iris had locked him back into the collar. And after the way things had worked out last night, he knew that wouldn't do at all.

Showered and changed, Iris had been up in the staffroom looking for Aurelia and Pepper. When she hadn't found them she wondered if they had decided to go off home without telling her. Didn't seem like them. And they were scheduled to have their usual sweep debrief at eleven thirty.

As she stepped over the threshold of her office she was pulled off her feet and into a threatening embrace that was really getting all too familiar.

'Oh no, who let you out?'

Alfie's right arm snaked around her neck; his big sinewy muscles were tight against her windpipe.

'Let's just say girls will be girls.'

Iris shoved her right hand back and grabbed Alfie's balls

through the crotch of his jeans and twisted. *Hard*. He yelled and his grip around her neck slackened just enough for her to duck under it. Iris whirled around. Alfie was doubled over a bit, enough for her to kick up and aim for his chin. But he recovered too fast. He grabbed Iris's leg and yanked her off balance. Then she was on the floor on her back and he was on top of her pinning her wrists in one big hand.

Oh damn. That did not go well.

Iris looked up at him. He was shirtless. Hot and smooth and glowing and pinning her down. 'What do you want, Alfie?'

'An apology'd be nice.'

'An apology?'

'Yeah. Something like, "Alfie, I'm sorry I tranqued you and locked you up in my evil Institute again."'

'It's not an evil Institute.'

'Is if you're a werewolf.'

Iris didn't say anything. Alfie's face was very close to hers. It was making it hard to concentrate.

'Well?' he said.

'I'm not apologising to you, Alfie. I did what I thought was best.'

'I stopped by Blake's lab on the way here.' Alfie squirmed around on top of her and rooted in his pocket with the hand that wasn't pinning her wrists. He pulled out a familiar-looking pair of handcuffs. The rigid ones Iris had put on him last time he was here. 'Look what I found,' he said, holding them up so they caught the light. 'Do you think we should keep them? Put them in our memory box?'

While he was holding the cuffs, he wasn't using that arm to support his not inconsiderable weight. He had suddenly got a whole lot heavier. 'Alfie,' Iris gasped, 'you trying to crush me?'

Alfie laughed, but he let go of Iris's wrists and sat back, straddling her body. Iris pulled herself up on her elbows.

'Look what else I found in your boyfriend's lab,' Alfie

said. 'It really is quite a treasure trove.' He pulled a gun out of his pocket. 'Just how many guns does your boyfriend have?'

Iris didn't answer that question because, as she opened her mouth, Alfie stuck the gun barrel right in it. She tried to pull her head away, to spit the gun out, but Alfie dropped the handcuffs and used his free hand to hold her head still by the hair.

'Take the collar off me, Iris,' he said. His voice was in that dark place again.

Iris shook her head as far as she could.

'Iris, you have to take it off me. There's some trick to it. If you take it off, I'll put it back on myself. I swear.'

The gun tasted smoky and dirty. She could bring herself to imagine where it might have been – one of Blake's guns. She was pretty sure Alfie wouldn't shoot her. Then again, she was also pretty sure that he was telling the truth about putting the collar straight back on. *Wasn't the collar all his idea?*

Iris reached up and the collar fell away in her hands, revealing the red band of soreness around his neck.

'Thank you.' Alfie pulled the gun out of Iris's mouth.

'Pervert,' Iris muttered.

'Uh-huh,' Alfie murmured, pulling the gun away and leaning down to kiss her. Iris opened her mouth, let him in. His tongue darted between her lips, but only for a second, then he pulled away. 'And talking of perversion,' said Alfie, as he picked up the handcuffs, 'how about you go and handcuff yourself to that chair over there?'

Iris sucked her bottom lip, searching out the last of the taste of him. He tasted of sex. Not his usual enigmatic muskiness – just pure sex. She shook herself. Losing her edge again. 'How about I . . . ? No! What if you flip? I won't even be able to run away.'

'Yes,' Alfie said darkly. 'What if I do flip? No collar on now. Really it would be best if you didn't annoy me, Iris. I'm not feeling all that stable as it is. Plus, I have this.' Alfie pulled something else out of the pocket of his jeans and held it up so she could see it. It was a syringe, a hypodermic needle full of clear liquid.

Iris felt her stomach turn over. 'What's that?' Her voice was shaking. This was way scarier than the gun.

Alfie smiled. 'It's not for you, Iris. It's adrenaline from Blake's lab. Do you fancy some experimentation into my condition? Laboratory conditions?'

Iris squirmed underneath Alfie's thighs, but she was going nowhere. 'What would you do to me if you changed?' she said, wondering if she sounded even the slightest bit calm. 'Kill me or make me like you?'

Alfie shrugged. 'That's the really fun part. You never know in advance quite how it's going to go. So, I suggest you give some real consideration to doing whatever I tell you. Now, take these handcuffs, trot over to that chair, strap yourself to it and I'll think about not injecting myself with this nasty stuff, what do you say?'

'I think, I say . . .' But Iris's planned defiance died in her mouth as Alfie pushed the point of the needle harder into his bare chest until the skin started to indent around it. 'I think, I say, OK then. Good idea.'

'I knew you'd see sense,' Alfie said, climbing off her.

Iris did as she was told, sitting down then locking her wrists into the hard cold embrace of the handcuffs behind the chair.

'Well,' Alfie said, putting the hypo down on top of a filing cabinet. 'Now, maybe we can behave like adults.'

Iris rolled her eyes at him. 'What are you talking about? You have your collar. I'm not going to be coming after you. We're done.' Except for the fact that they hadn't yet run into each other without having sex. And Iris was now handcuffed to a chair. Her pussy thumped.

'Almost, just one last thing,' said Alfie. He picked up the collar delicately, from where Iris had left it on the floor, holding it gingerly by the edges and wincing. Just touching it was painful. Iris could see him gritting his teeth as he placed it round his neck. He pushed the two halves together, but they didn't slot home like they did when Iris had done it. The things just sprang apart. Like the two halves didn't fit.

'Dammit,' Alfie muttered. 'How does it work?'

'I don't know.'

He walked over to her and bent down so she could see the back of his neck.

When his face was practically in her lap, a realisation hit her. She was turned on. She was wet. This close, there was no way he wouldn't be able to tell. Lyc senses and all. Iris swallowed. 'Can you look?' Alfie said. 'If you can see how I need to do it.' The butt ends of the collar halves looked perfectly smooth. Nothing to join the pieces together. *Is that what they looked like before?* Iris couldn't remember.

'I don't know,' she said again. 'I don't know how I did it before. Should I try to call Blake? He might know. It's not really my . . .'

'Yeah. Not your area.' Alfie turned his head and held Iris's gaze. 'Except, it is and you know it is.'

'What?'

'This thing is spelled so only you can work it, isn't it?'

'Um, well, if it is then it's the first I've heard about it.'

Alfie straightened up and leant against Iris's desk. He looked down at her. 'What do you think I should do to you, Iris?'

Iris swallowed. 'What?' She looked at Alfie's crotch, which was very close to her face. He was hard. He could smell her and he was hard. *Oh God, but without the collar, if he* . . . Iris twisted at the cuffs again, wondering how Alfie worked that trick with the lock pick. 'Alfie? Are you going to change on me?'

'Not if you tell me how to put this on,' he said. He moved suddenly to straddle the chair, his big thighs pressing against hers as he lowered himself until he was practically sitting on her lap.

'Alfie, I can't. I don't know how. I really don't . . .'

But Iris never finished, because Alfie leant forward and covered her mouth with his hand. 'OK, forget the collar.

Maybe we should talk about something else: Brazil, for example.' He sounded just a little breathless. Iris squirmed. She looked up at his smooth bare chest. His nipples were hard too. 'I've been meaning to tell you about what happened in Brazil, haven't I? When sex started making me change into an enormous homicidal wolf, guess what I had to do?' Alfie took his hand away from Iris's mouth.

Iris took a deep breath. 'Stop having sex. We've talked about it.'

'Which was tough.'

'It would be for you.'

Alfie ignored this. 'So I went to Brazil because there was this she-wolf pack there and I had heard that their alpha had ways of controlling shape-shifters. And did she ever, not in the way I thought, but she found a way to control me.'

'Alfie, I don't really want . . .'

Alfie's face was so close to hers. She squirmed when he said, 'It's not up to you, though, Iris. *I* want you to know. When Hera had me chained up so she'd be safe if I flipped, she used to make me go the longest time she could without reaching orgasm. Because that would be when I'd change and it would be all over for her. Sometimes she could keep me on the edge for hours, days. She taught me everything I know about prolonging things. What could I do? I hadn't been able to mate for so long. I was on my knees. She liked that. Taunted me about it. She loved how dependent I was on her. She used to make me beg her for it. Filthy werewolf. Filthy unstable werewolf. Beg me. Beg to be allowed to come.' Alfie ran his fingertip over Iris's lips. 'Every. Single. Time.'

Iris swallowed.

'That's right. See. You used to like to see me come, didn't you? I knew you'd like this story. She liked to hurt me too, you know. Scratching. Biting. She had this belt with a solid silver buckle. You know what silver does to me, right?'

Iris nodded, looking at the gauze taped over his eye. Her mouth was so damn dry.

'The marks she left on me some days ... That's how I know I can heal wounds made of silver.'

Alfie's hips were moving a little as he spoke. Slightly, but Iris could tell. But hers were too. There was only the tiniest bit of dead air between her denim-covered crotch and his. 'Alfie ...'

'She'd fuck me too.' Alfie was getting very breathless. This was so damn dangerous. 'She had this silver-coated dildo. When she fucked me with that thing – it hurt and healed me in a way I can't even describe. I was incoherent on it.' And Alfie reached down and touched himself between the legs, slow and sensuous. Even through his jeans, Iris could picture his erect cock precisely. She squirmed in the chair. Too, too dangerous.

'Alfie this is –'

Then Alfie kissed her. And everything changed.

Iris melted under his mouth, squirming and wriggling in the cuffs. She pulled her mouth free. 'Let me out of the cuffs; I need to touch you.'

'No, I don't trust you, Iris,' Alfie whispered. His mouth was back on hers then. He had a hand up under her T-shirt. He fumbled underneath it for a moment then breathed, 'Fuck it,' and started to rip it away; shredding it as easily as if it were made of tissue paper. Then he slipped his hands down into her bra and pinched both her nipples at once, very hard.

Iris yelped. For a moment the pain was everything. Intense. Too much. But then he gave her back his mouth, sweet and hard – melting and nostalgic and delicious – and the pain twisted into pleasure.

'Shame, though,' Iris gasped as she moved her mouth free. 'If I had my hands free I could see if you still have that hair thing.'

'What hair thing?' Alfie asked as he kissed his way down her throat.

'That thing about having your hair pulled.'

'I don't know what you're talking about,' Alfie said. Iris could feel his smile against her skin. He squirmed and rolled in her lap. He kissed and licked her mouth, bit her ears, ran his stubbled jaw over her chin and neck. Slowly, slowly she started to turn inside out.

His hard cock seemed bigger, jutting, rubbing against her clit as he ground into her. She could have kissed him like this forever. She rubbed herself on his cock and wondered if this alone would be enough to make her come.

Ew!

Iris's eyes flew open as her heart sank. She was screaming at her subconscious. But it didn't work. He was here. Matthew was here. He was standing by the end of the desk, just a few feet a way.

Iris pulled her mouth free. 'Alfie,' she whispered.

Alfie lifted his head. 'Shush,' he said. 'Hey, talking of "things" do you still have that same place on your jaw where...' He licked his way across her cheek and bit lightly on the spot on her jawline that made every hair on her body stand on end. Alfie chuckled and grazed his teeth along the spot, over and over. She melted into complete incoherence. She couldn't help it.

OK. OK. Fine. I can deal with it. You're doing it with the man who got me killed. Who wouldn't help you avenge my death. The man who ... Matthew was practically jumping up and down on the spot. *You're doing it with a werewolf!*

'Matthew,' Iris whispered. 'Uh, I thought you knew.'

Alfie lifted his head. He looked at Iris and then followed her gaze and stared at Matthew. 'Leave her alone, Matthew.'

Iris didn't know if she was more shocked that Alfie was talking to her hallucination or that her hallucination did what he said. Matthew looked sadly at Alfie, then turned and walked away.

'How did you ...?'

'Oh.' Alfie nodded. 'Right, yeah, well, I can explain it to you in more detail another time, but I was bitten by the Beast before Matthew was, so, in the grand hierarchy of werewolves I outrank him, even though he's dead, which means that I –'

'No, no, no. What I meant was: how could you see my hallucination?'

'Hallucination?'

'Yes. Matthew – he's a figment of my imagination.'

'Not a ghost?'

'I don't believe in ghosts.'

'You don't believe in ... Iris you kill werewolves for a living, you hang out with a witch, and yet you don't believe in ghosts.' He shook his head. 'How about maintaining internal consistency sometime?'

'What? Matthew is real?'

Alfie laughed. 'Oh, Iris, I'm just messing with you. Of course he isn't real. Matthew is very, very dead. The hideously mauled corpse? The identification from dental records? Details like that stick in the mind.'

'But you just looked at him.'

'I looked where you were looking.'

'You knew it was Matthew.'

'*You* said his name.'

'He did what you told him.'

'Well then, what does that say about you? Look, Iris, much as I love metaphysics and you are very, very, *particularly* sexy when you are conflicted –' he stopped and kissed her nose '– But I'm not a porn star and I really can't keep it up all morning for you while we chat about Matthew. Weren't we in the middle of something?'

Alfie smiled and got onto his knees in front of her chair. 'Fairer if I take care of you first, otherwise ...' He grinned at Iris and, when she seemed to look a little flushed in response, he ran his finger along the seam of her jeans. Right between her legs.

Iris moaned and Alfie said, 'God, you, the smell of you. It's been following me all day. In fact, it's been following me for eleven years. Sometimes Iris,' he said unfastening her jeans and pulling them down as she shifted her weight, 'I feel like I've been trying to fuck you out of my system ever since we split up, but everything I do, every other woman I go with, every time I come I only think of you.'

He pulled her underwear away and slipped his tongue inside her.

Iris felt like she'd been on the edge of an orgasm ever since he first pinned her down on the floor. His tongue twisted around her clit and she slid forwards in the chair after more. Alfie laughed and put one big hand on her belly to hold her in place. Iris pulled uselessly at the cuffs behind her back.

Alfie was laughing. His breath arrhythmic and delicious on her hot wet cunt. 'Please,' she said, and she was laughing a little too, although she didn't know why. But this was Alfie. Alfie was back. It would all be OK. He'd never loved anyone but her. They could work it out. How could they not? When he could make her feel like this.

His tongue again. Long and flat top to bottom. Then in, around, his teeth near her clit. A lick. Two of his big fingers coming up. Fast. In and out. Then more. More inside her. Stretching her tight and sensitive. Must be three fingers now, bigger and thicker than most men's cocks. Iris's head went back and he thrust harder. His mouth covered her clit and sucked as his fingers fucked and drove her into an orgasm so long and strong that she almost lost consciousness.

35

Alfie held Iris's chair as she bucked and came in his mouth. When she finally opened her eyes, he smiled up at her from the floor at her feet and said, 'So just before I let you out of those cuffs and we sort out the collar so I can fuck you until you have another one of those, are there any more women in the building I'm going to have to make come before I leave?'

'Alfie, for God's sake,'

'Oh, come on. It was just your two pretty little puppy-hunters. I had to go through them to get to you, Iris. I just wanted to get to you.' His voice cracked with desire. 'That reminds me,' he said, stopping what he was doing for a moment to look up at her, 'they said Misty showed you a clean pair of heels. Four-inch ones, I expect.'

Iris still looked slightly floaty. 'Huh? They told you what?'

'Last night. You encountered Misty.'

'Who's Misty?'

Alfie stopped. 'Oh, damn. That was one of the names I was trying to not tell you last time I was here.' He smiled and shook his head. 'She's one of my cubs.' Alfie smiled again. His cock was already so hard from the scent of Iris's arousal, which was seeping into everything around him. He was getting high on it. Dizzy. 'I guess it doesn't matter now, we were planning to get out of town soon anyway. I know a coven where they'll probably be able to de-spell the collar for me.' Alfie looked at Iris and was just thinking about saying something rash. Something stupid about her coming with them, when he noticed that she looked a little bit pale. 'Iris?'

Iris spoke fast and Alfie began to realise something was

very, very wrong from the first syllable. 'Alfie, your cub. Misty. She's a small black wolf, right? And a Japanese girl. Pepper and Aurelia said they'd seen her last night?'

'Yeah. They said she's got away.'

'And last night she was doing some kind of show where –'

'Yeah, I know, seedy as hell, but the money is unbelievable and we need it so ... I know, I'm like her pimp, except really she pimps herself...'

'Alfie!' Alfie stopped talking. 'She didn't get away.'

'What? Is she here?'

'There was an accident.' Iris's throat moved as she swallowed. 'It was me. I had Blake's gun. I took it from you.'

Alfie stood up and took a couple of steps away from Iris, as if he was trying to escape from something awful. Something that he knew was coming even if he didn't quite know what it was. 'What? Where is she?'

'She was attacking, Alfie. She got out of the cage. She was, you know, doing this show. I had to. There were innocent people in the room, one exit, no way for the hound to get out except by going through us all. I had to.'

Alfie could see by the look on Iris's face that she was terrified. That she thought he was going to hit her, hurt her. Maybe he was. Somewhere a tiny part of his brain that wasn't in shock noted how brave she must be, to tell him this, when she was tied up and at his mercy. Brave, but stupid. Actually, make that just plain stupid.

Alfie was viciously angry, but he wasn't quite changing. He was close but not quite there. Suddenly he realised how much he *wanted* to flip, right now. To lose his rationality and not have to be responsible for anything he might do. But anger wasn't his only trigger.

Not thinking, not looking at Iris, he stormed over to the filing cabinet and grabbed at the syringe of adrenaline, but he fumbled it, too hasty, too angry. It rolled away and smashed on the floor. 'Fine,' he shouted, 'fine. There are other triggers. Better triggers.'

Orgasm. He started to undo the top button of his jeans. 'Alfie, what are you . . . ?' Iris was staring at him, like she couldn't believe what was happening. He was shaking, jumping from foot to foot. His hands itched. He fumbled with the zip, staring back at Iris. Iris looked right back at him. Looked him right in the eye. Alfie was shaking his head in confusion. Was he really about to try to do what he appeared to be about to try to do? Was he actually going to make himself come so he'd flip and kill Iris?

Iris started to struggle, fighting the cuffs so hard that the whole chair tipped over and she fell back. Alfie let go of his jeans – he'd barely even got the top button undone – and rushed over. Iris screamed when she saw him looming over her.

'Get the fuck away from her, werewolf.'

Alfie spun around. Blake. Blake was pointing a gun at him.

Iris's office had one window. High and small but he could make it with a run-up.

Iris looked up at Blake standing over her tipped-up chair. Her head hurt. Alfie was gone. She'd heard the window breaking.

Behind Blake, Iris could see the ceiling. Dirty foam tiles. 'I thought you'd gone,' she said, softly.

'Yeah, I had,' Blake said as he crouched down next to her over-turned chair. 'But I had to come back. And, OK, I came back to apologise for some stuff too. I *was* thinking that it was none of my business if you wanted to keep Fido alive. And I was going to say that to you, but, actually, well, it looks like I was right after all.'

'Yeah,' said Iris weakly, 'I guess you were.'

Blake started to take off his white coat. 'What exactly were you doing though? You're not very dressed, Iris. Did I interrupt some kind of sniffer thing? Was he changing for you, because, really, he ought to be the one secured if you're going to –'

'No! God, no. It wasn't like that,' Iris said as Blake sort

of wrapped his coat around her body to cover her. His touch light. Professional. 'Um, the WXX was part of Alfie's pack. One of his cubs. He found out and, well, he wasn't exactly pleased.'

'Seriously? He found out you killed his cub and you've just lived to tell the tale? Jesus.' Blake's hand grazed Iris's left breast, just above the nipple. Iris gasped. Despite everything else, she was still turned on – hot and wet and buzzing with it.

Blake looked at Iris and bit his bottom lip. 'That wasn't for me, was it?'

'No.'

Gently, Blake managed to pull Iris's bra cups back over her breasts and finished covering her up as she lay on the floor. 'So did he handcuff you to the chair before or after you told him you killed his cub?' He said it lightly, but sounding puzzled.

'Actually,' said Iris, 'I handcuffed myself to the chair.'

'Right. You sure you aren't a sniffer? Do you know where the keys to these cuffs are?'

'No. Actually, I don't think they're here.'

'I'll get a hacksaw from the basement.' Blake said that as if getting his estranged wife out of a pair of handcuffs with a hacksaw was part of his normal day-to-day business.

'OK. Blake, just kiss me first.' Iris didn't know if she wanted Blake to kiss her because of Alfie or in spite of him. But he did and it was very, very sweet. As his tongue melted against hers, she started to think that she and Blake might have some kind of future after all. Blake could chase her monsters away.

'Well,' said a cool voice from the door, 'maybe I shouldn't ask.'

Blake leapt to his feet looking uncharacteristically flustered. 'Dr Tobias. We've had an escape.'

'Another one? I don't know why we don't just install a revolving door.' Dr Tobias sighed, running a hand through his sparse grey hair. 'Iris, if you do encounter Alfred again

I think it might be best if you shot him. I know he's interesting, to both of you, but I think the trouble he's caused us . . .'

'He took the collar again,' Iris said. She was still on the floor.

'Did you put it on him?' asked Blake.

'He knows that would trap him. He took it with him. He said he'll try and get the spell removed.'

Dr Tobias and Blake both laughed. 'Spell,' Blake scoffed. 'It's not spelled.'

'Then why am I the only person who can work it?'

'Because, that's how the collar works,' said Dr Tobias. 'You are the person the werewolf trusts most in all the world.'

Blake bent over Iris. His face filled her world. 'Or, in other words,' he said, 'depending on which translation you read, Alfie is still in love with you.'

'Oh.'

Iris was still trying to process that information when she realised that she could hear Pepper and Aurelia shouting for help from the basement. Iris didn't know it was possible to hear sounds from the basement up here. But Aurelia had quite a pair of lungs.

36

Once, when he lived alone and changed alone and the moon had made sense, Alfie had a little list that he had compiled mostly for his own amusement.

Things werewolves can't do:

1. Hold down a proper job
2. Eat tofu
3. Wear silver jewellery
4. Fall in love
5. Be fallen in love with

The first three were mild inconveniences. Alfie had learnt to live without his grandmother's silver and diamond eternity ring which he had worn on the little finger of his right hand for nearly a year. From her death to the night he woke up in hospital to find it was stinging his finger.

The last two items on the list were trickier. And far more melodramatic. Werewolves kill the things they love. Sooner or later. No matter how good and careful they are. Cages rust, locks pop, time gets forgotten on nights when moon-rise is early. If you lived and loved with a werewolf, it was borrowed time.

Which was why Misty had been so perfect. Alfie had been sure that Misty wouldn't be falling in love with him any time soon, because Misty was always in love with someone else.

It had worked like this. Misty would pop round on her nights off, sleep with Alfie and, in return, Alfie would listen to Misty talk endlessly about whichever man she was madly crushing on that week.

That particular night it had been this guy who she had

only spoken to once, in the bar she sometimes went to after work. Misty had the weirdest taste in men.

'Leon's really hot,' she had said. 'Blond. Lots of hair. I love lots of hair.' Misty was still talking about this guy when they got into the bedroom. 'I know you'll think he's arrogant, babe. You always think the guys I like are arrogant. And, actually, you're pretty arrogant yourself, but this time, yeah, OK, he is quite arrogant. But I like that. He's confident. Maybe just a bit too confident. You're confident too. Too confident. If you two met ... Woah. Scary, babe, scary.' Misty laughed and turned. She was standing in front of Alfie's bed. He took a step closer and kissed her. It stopped her talking, but that wasn't the only reason why he did it.

Misty was small and Alfie was big. Misty was five foot one and built like a bird. Whereas Alfie was built like someone had read the plans wrong and inadvertently scaled everything up. Alfie noticed the differential most when they kissed.

Misty went soft as Alfie got hard. Still kissing her, he pushed her back onto the bed. He had been expecting her and was wearing just his jeans, nothing underneath. He shed them without breaking the kiss, shucking them down his legs. Once he was naked he got to work on getting Misty into the same state.

He was cursing under his breath in less than a moment. 'Misty, baby, you knew you were coming here, you knew what we'd be doing. Did you have to wear something so tricky?'

'I thought you said you liked it?'

'I do, but ...' Alfie's voice trailed off as he wrestled with her fastenings some more. Misty was wearing a tight black dress. Modest and revealing at once. It buttoned right up the back from ankle to neck with tiny black buttons. It covered everything but her feet, hands and head. But it was so tight and clingy it might as well have covered nothing. Eventually Alfie got enough buttons undone to pull the thing away. Like Alfie, Misty had decided against underwear today.

He sighed as he felt the way her golden-toned skin melted with warmth as he pressed her body against his. Misty's mouth tasted like marshmallows. He rooted in the drawer of his bedside cabinet and found some rope. He twined it around the bedhead and secured Misty's wrists without even breaking the kiss. As soon as she was secure he felt himself get harder.

He slipped a blindfold over her eyes and then ran his tongue down her body, over her salt-and-sweet breasts, nipping at them until she tipped her head back and moaned. Alfie pressed his face into her crotch. The sensations overwhelmed him.

Of course, he had tied Misty up and gone down on her many, many times before – wolves like to use their tongues – but this time it felt a little different. Her sweet musky scent was headier somehow, as if his sense of smell was a little more acute than usual. That should have been the first warning sign – but he never noticed.

Enjoying the extra intensity, Alfie ran his tongue lightly over Misty's clit, lapping at her, until she was rolling from side to side on the bed, her legs wrapped tightly around his head.

He waited until she was right on the edge before standing up, taking a second to roll on a condom, and then pushing into her. There was no friction for a couple of moments. Alfie felt like he was floating. Then Misty started to come around his cock. The spasms rippling through her and into him.

For one second he thought the sudden intense feeling that rocketed through him was the start of an orgasm.

He was right and wrong.

Iris, now sawn free of her restraints, followed Blake back up into his office.

'You really are going, though?' she said, as he threw

equal quantities of books and weapons into a leather holdall with his working arm.

'Yeah,' he said, 'but only for a few weeks. I'll be back by next full moon.'

'But what about everything that's happening here?'

'Nothing's happening here, Iris.'

'What if Alfie comes back to kill me?'

Blake shrugged, but it seemed to be more a shrug that meant 'You know he won't' than a shrug that said, 'I don't care.'

'Well, where are you going?'

'I'm going to get my bloody arm fixed, Iris. I can't go on like this. I need it fixed. So I need a witch.'

'Can't Dr Tobias get Cate to fix it.'

'He could,' said Blake, 'but he won't. He wants me like this. He wants an excuse to keep me behind a desk. He'll be livid if he finds out I was out last night. Besides, witches and me have something of an understanding. Don't wait up, Iris.'

37

Alfie arrived home with his fingers blistering from holding the collar. He tried to remember why he'd left his shirt behind in the basement. At least if he'd had that he could have used the fabric to protect his hands.

There were two people sitting at his kitchen table. Two people that made him feel every single emotion at once. Zac and Pearl.

'Zac,' Alfie said.

Zac looked at him warily. He seemed anxious. 'Alfie,' he said softly. Next to him Pearl drew her body close half hiding behind him. Alfie spotted the gesture at once. He could smell it on her too. *She's his ... Woah. Zac's got himself a cub.*

'Where have you been?' Alfie asked.

'Looking for Leon. We were attacked by the Vix. They took him.'

'Vix didn't have him when I was there. Why are you here, did you come back to lock down?'

'Not just that. For Leon. I need my passport.'

'Your passport? You're going to go and summon him?'

'What else can I do? I need him. So I've got to go back to where I was bit.'

Alfie looked at Pearl. 'You sired her,' he said.

'Yeah.'

'How come you sired her if you locked down?'

'It's complicated, Alfie. It's between us.' Zac held Alfie's gaze. It was different between Zac and Alfie. Sometimes it wasn't so obvious because Zac was so young and hadn't been a wolf very long, but, although Zac respected Alfie as his alpha, Alfie wasn't his sire. What Zac had done was between him and Pearl. And maybe Leon.

After Leon had bitten Zac, Alfie had taken him quietly to one side, pinned him up against the wall by the throat and gut-punched him. Right in his bite scar.

'You and Misty'll come to Texas too, right?' Zac was saying. 'And Pearly of course. She's part of the pack now.'

Alfie swallowed. In that moment when he'd come through the door and seen Zac and Pearl he'd almost forgotten. When Zac said her name, it hit him all over again. He walked over to the table and sat down heavily in his chair. There was nothing to drink. No tea. *Because she's not here.* Not here making endless cups of tea. Alfie looked at Zac across the kitchen table and said, 'I've got something I need to tell you.'

When he explained about Misty, Zac got up from the table, screeching his chair back, quick and jerky. He walked over to the window and stared out at the scrubby garden.

Alfie could tell from the way his shoulders were moving that he was starting to cry – and he didn't want Pearl to see. Alfie got up from the table, holding up his hand, signalling Pearl to stay where she was, and walked over to Zac. The moment Zac felt Alfie at his back he turned and crumpled into the offered embrace.

Alfie didn't cry. He was the alpha. But holding back his tears made his throat ache.

Pearl said, 'Can I do anything?'

Alfie looked at her. 'I don't suppose you could put the kettle on?'

'So is that what female werewolves do, make the tea?' She probably didn't mean it how it sounded, didn't know how directly it seemed like a reference to Misty, but Alfie snarled at her.

Zac pulled out of Alfie's arms. 'I'll do it.'

Pearl said, 'No, it's OK. That was a stupid thing to say, I'm sorry.'

But Zac was already crossing the room, sniffing back the last of tears. Alfie watched the two of them start to make tea together. His new pack. Just like old times. Except he was different now. And suddenly he could feel that difference rising up through his body. He realised all in a rush how very unstable he was. How he was lucky to have even made it home. Grief felt like a cannonball in his stomach, growing bigger and bigger until it was ready to burst right out of him. Rip its way out. He took a couple of steps across the room and grabbed hold of the edge of the kitchen table. 'Zac,' he said, 'I . . .'

Pearl turned. 'Are you OK?'

But Zac knew. In split-second moves he'd flipped open a drawer and pulled out a hypo of sedative. 'You need this, man?'

Alfie nodded. He could feel it coming. Zac was racing across the room with the syringe. Alfie felt the very edge of the change before the needle was in his arm and it all went dark.

Back at home that night, Iris took a shower.

She had weird red marks on her wrists from the cuffs. She'd also got an absolute beauty of a bruise coming up on the side of her face where she'd hit the floor. Being injured wasn't that big a deal to Iris. She had that kind of job. She got hurt at work. The stab wound in her shoulder still wasn't completely healed.

Ever since she'd got home, he hadn't left her alone. Not Matthew, who was remarkably absent, but Alfie. Iris couldn't stop thinking about his weight on her lap. His hands in her hair. His lips on hers.

She remembered Blake telling her that Alfie was in love with her. Even if he had been, he certainly wasn't now. Not now she'd killed Misty. His first cub. There wasn't really any way back from that was there?

Iris towelled off, taking extra care around her injuries. She wondered if Alfie had left town yet. She was already certain she wouldn't ever see him again. She needed to stop thinking about him.

She'd brought the ring home. The one Alfie had given her in the basement. She'd put it on a leather thong and tied it around her neck. She fiddled with as she walked through her flat to the bedroom.

She had Alfie's shirt too. It had been left in the basement, but he hadn't taken it.

She put it on and climbed into bed. All the time still telling herself that she had to stop thinking about him, that she would never see him again, that anytime she got close to Alfie it never ended well.

All the time surrounded by the heady scent of his warm skin.

38

Friday 23 November 2007

It was getting colder. The air smelt like winter. Like Christmas. Nearly a month after Alfie had leapt out of her office window and out of her life, Iris – all her injuries now fully healed – pulled her bike up the steps in front of the Institute and right there, in the foyer, stood Pure.

Iris dropped her bike onto the carpet.

Pure turned and looked slightly oddly at her. His face was drawn and hard. He'd grown a very slight shadowy crop of dark hair on his previously bald head and the pinkish scar that ran down his face bisected his mouth giving him a permanent sneer.

'Um, hey,' said Iris, 'are you back?'

'I want to talk to you,' Pure said. His voice sounded *damaged*. As cold as the air outside. Fixed by witchcraft. He should have died.

'Oh. OK.'

Pure's hard expression flickered for a moment. Then he said, 'I want to ask you something.'

'Right.' Iris folded her arms. She was pretty sure this was going to be an uncomfortable conversation. She really wished Blake was here. Blake would do this better.

'Um, I was wondering why you weren't trying to find Pearl any more?'

'What? I am trying to find her.'

'No, you're not. What have you done?'

'Well, I haven't done anything as such. Not lately. But resources . . . Uh, and she was a lead on a lyc that Dr Tobias said wasn't really a priority. The trail went cold at her flat and we've had nothing else to go on. It's been a long time now. If I knew any way that we could trace her I would. I'm sorry.'

'I'm sorry too, ma'am.' Pure pulled himself up. He was considerably taller than Iris. 'I'm sorry I listened to you. I was right. We should have gone and got her out of there. Out of that pub, before, when I wanted to.' He met Iris's eye. 'Because we never managed to bring in either of those lycs she was with and if we'd just got her out of there then at least she'd be OK.'

In the end Zac and Pearl had locked Alfie in the cellar. His body just wouldn't stabilise. The grief did weird things. He was a wolf a lot of the time. Lucid moments were rare, but when he was aware of what was happening he was scared. He thought his body might have completely lost it. He'd heard stories of lycs who ended up permanently changed into wolves. He'd always thought they were legends.

However, as the days wore on, as one week slipped into another the changes got less frequent. Alfie started to become more human.

He'd spent the last week entirely himself – rational, mourning, pining, thinking about how things could have been different. He relived those last moments with Misty, kissing her feet on the wet pavement.

Zac and Pearl had taken good care of him, bringing him food. The constant changing meant Alfie had never known hunger like it. He felt as if he was being eaten from the inside out. He had had no doubt that if he had been free he would have been deadly, but instead he had torn at the walls of the cellar and slaked his hunger with raw steaks slid under the door on sheets of newspaper when he was a wolf, and then with cooked steaks slid under the door on a plate now he was more human. Zac had said at one point that Omega had come good with the rest of Misty's money. Pearl had said that all the butchers' shops within walking distance now knew her by sight and were giving her special deals.

Alfie got quite used to subterranean confinement. It felt appropriate. His eye was almost healed finally. The vision not quite as pure and sharp, but near enough. He wasn't up to much in terms of guiding and leading his pack – what was left of it – but that didn't seem to matter. From the sounds he heard a lot of the time, it was pretty plain to him that Zac and Pearl filled that alpha-wolf void in their lives by having frequent and athletic sex.

He clung to the plan. The one they had been talking about in the kitchen before he lost it. That they would leave Oxford, go to Texas and Zac would summon Leon. It helped to have a plan. They needed to put the pack back together.

He had the collar in the basement with him. He examined it – as far as he could without losing the use of his fingers. But nothing seemed to make the two halves lock together into a circle. Clearly the thing was spelled.

Which meant it wasn't quite over for him and Oxford yet.

After guilt-tripping Iris, Pure took Pepper and went over to the John Radcliffe Hospital and asked around after Pearl. No one seemed to know anything, even though, thanks to Cate's magic, they clearly would have loved to have helped if they could.

Pure started to wonder if he had been too hard on Iris Maybe she was doing all she could to find Pearl. Maybe there *was* nowhere left to look. After all, the police hadn't found anything either. His Auntie Saff had reported Pearl as a missing person – for all the good that had done.

Dejected, close to giving up, he started looking for Pepper, and he found her talking to a tall Asian girl – another nurse – who was very familiar.

As he approached she broke into a huge smile and said, in a loping cockney accent, 'Oh my God. Pure White, look at you, with your new manly scar, you gorgeous fucking bastard.'

She pulled him into a crushing embrace, and he caught Pepper's amused grin. He gasped, 'Hey, Flo. Long time?'

Flo released him and Pepper said, 'This is Pearl's flatmate, but I guess you know that, right?'

'Yeah,' said Pure, shimmying a little to get all his internal organs back where they should be.

'She might have something for us,' Pepper said, grinning.

'Really?' Pure cocked his head on one side, puzzled. 'But hasn't Iris been in touch with you? Iris Instasi-Fox?' Because, surely, if Iris were doing anything to find Pearl at all she'd be keeping in touch with her flatmate.

Flo made a non-committal face. 'Not really. Well, she did call once. But no, no one has come back to me for a while now.'

'And you have something else? Something about Pearl?' Pure asked.

'Yeah, I think so. Well, it's a bit of a weird story. I was at this party, talking to this bloke. At first I thought he was chatting me up, but it soon turned out he really just wanted to tell me about this beautiful girl he was crushing on. This guy worked in a butcher's shop on Cowley Road and he said there was this crazy-beautiful girl coming into his shop everyday to buy pounds and pounds of steak. I wasn't really interested and he kept on insisting that she really was so absolutely amazing looking and blah, blah, blah. So, eventually he gets his phone out and shows me a picture he's taken of her. Covertly, natch. And guess who it was?'

Pure, who had been predicting the end of this story as soon as Flo had said that the guy was a butcher, said, 'Pearl.'

Flo nodded. 'Right. And one day he followed her. Saw where she was taking all the steaks. This house off St Clement's. It's weird though. I mean, she can't still be around, in Oxford, can she? Else why wouldn't she have let us know she's OK?'

Pure knew what he wanted to say. That he was sure

that she had been bitten. That when someone became a werewolf their pack replaced their friends and family. How old allegiances died. But instead he said, 'Give me the address.'

39

The only coven Alfie knew well was the Clement's and Castle, who met in the botanical gardens at four o'clock most Fridays.

His first problem was finding them. They'd have a cloaking spell up. All he could do was wander up and down the orderly flower beds, trying to look paranormal, trying to look like someone who was looking for some witches.

But nothing. He hadn't spoken to anyone from the C. and C. for five years. Maybe they didn't even meet here any more. He sat down on a bench in front of an ornamental fish pond and sighed.

After no more than a moment or two, a woman in full business dress, including seamed stockings and disproportionately high heels, sat down next to him and crossed her legs. 'Hi,' she said, with a small nod.

Alfie nodded back at her. He wasn't in the mood for talking.

The woman said, 'Look, can I ask you something? I warn you, it's awfully crass.'

Alfie turned and looked at her. Under her office-bitch uniform she had a sweet heart-shaped face framed by wavy brown hair. He nodded again.

'Fancy a fuck?' said the woman.

'What?'

'Fancy a fuck with a bored business woman who's run away from her dull conference, but has just seen the hottest stud in the whole of Oxford and just had to ask?'

'Uh, what? Stud?'

'Well, OK, I was improvising. But "stud" does kind of

suit you. Look, I don't usually do this. But, oh, it was so worth a shot. What do you say, gorgeous?'

'I say, sorry, but I can't.' Alfie shifted on the bench. 'I have, uh, some problems.'

'Oh,' said the woman. Then she gave him a very meaningful stare. 'I understand. The goddess's little joke, eh? Take a glorious package like you and then cut corners where it really counts. There are pills you can take now, you know.'

'I'm not impotent. I'm a werewolf. If I have sex with you I'll turn into a wolf and rip your head off.'

'Oh. Right,' said the woman looking completely unfazed. 'So you're here to see the C. and C. about that are you?'

Alfie frowned at her. 'You know about the C. and C.? I thought you were in town for a conference.'

'Oh, yeah,' said the woman, lightly, 'that. That was a lie, actually. But, I'm right, aren't I? You're looking for the C. and C. And you can't find them, can you?'

'No. Who *are* you?'

The woman laughed, 'I'm a witch, dumbbell.'

'Then why did you tell me all that stuff about a conference?'

The witch rolled her eyes. 'Because I was trying to get you into bed.'

'You were trying to ... But, you're a witch; couldn't you just cast a spell over me, or something?'

The witch gave Alfie a pitying look. 'Well, of course I *could*, but really, you wouldn't believe how fast *that* gets old.' She paused and caught Alfie's sceptical expression. 'Look, sorry about the lying. I have kind of a compulsion. It wasn't a lie about wanting to fuck you though.' She turned slightly and held out a pale hand. 'Lilith.'

Alfie took her hand and shook it. 'Lilith? Good name for a ...'

'For a witch, yeah, I know. It's my real name. Weird, isn't it? I mean, pretty much everyone else in the coven has a normal name. We've got a Tracey, a Sarah, a Cate – and then there's me, a Lilith.' She laughed. 'So you want to try to speak to them. They're not very male friendly you know.'

'Really? I thought they were a pretty liberal coven.'

'Nah. They did used to be. But there's been a change of management. You can bring men to meetings, but they have to be humbled.'

'Humbled?'

'Yep. That's naked, basically. Well, you know, head bowed, eyes cast down, but really, it's the naked part everyone notices.'

'Oh, well, really, naked is no problem.'

'Right, right. Werewolf. Even so, though, I know those girls and the minute you walk into their midst naked, looking like you do, well, they'll eat you alive.'

Alfie smiled. He was smiling more genuinely than he had for a weeks. 'And you say that like it's a bad thing.'

In her office, Iris raked her hair away from her face and noticed that her fingers were stiff with tension. 'Pure,' she said, trying to sound soothing, 'I'm sorry, but I don't see what I'm meant to have done. I did speak to Flo, but I can't contact everyone connected to Pearl every day in case something new has come up. We don't have the resources. You've seen how we operate.'

'Flo has met someone who's seen Pearl and you didn't know. You should have been on that. What have you even been doing since your boyfriend last absconded?'

A low voice from the doorway said, 'Pure, that's enough.' Blake was leaning against the frame. He glanced at Iris and gave her a broad, slightly scary grin. Iris's heart leapt. He was back. She was suddenly shocked to discover how much she'd missed him.

'But, sir,' Pure said, turning to Blake, 'we need to help Pearl.'

Blake walked into the room flexing his fingers. All his fingers. His arm looked fully healed. 'Your cousin was seen with some suspect lycs –'

'Suspect!' Pure interrupted. 'You saw what that one did! He jumped off the fucking . . .'

'That doesn't make him a lyc,' said Blake. So cool it was making Iris feel uncomfortable. 'Pearl has disappeared. We're all very sorry about that, but the reason we were interested in her was because of the unstable lyc and the fact that she might know where he is based. Something I'd still like to know as that lyc has a very valuable piece of my property.'

'He's probably left town by now,' Iris said, to nobody in particular.

'But Flo knows someone who saw Pearl going into a house.'

Blake lifted his chin and eyeballed Pure. 'A house, where?'

'Off St Clement's. Student area – all rental accommodation. I went and checked it out with Pepper. It looked deserted. I think we should raid it.'

Iris was about to say that she didn't agree, that they shouldn't bother, that it would be a waste of time, when Blake said, 'Yes, so do I.'

They were out loading up the truck when Iris said, 'I thought you wouldn't make it.'

Blake looked a little confused. 'What? No, I was fine. Witches just wanted a small favour. Take out some vampires that were bugging them. Easy-peasy. Look.' Blake pulled a crucifix out of the pocket of his lab coat and waved it around. 'You want this? Not a lot of use to me. Give it to your mother or something?'

Iris gave him a look. 'Make it back before full moon, I meant. I thought you might not make it back before full moon.'

'Oh.' Blake paused for a moment. 'Hey, though, look at this.' He took a step away from the back of the truck and dropped to the ground. He had done five push-ups before Iris quite realised what he was demonstrating.

'We can rebuild him,' Blake cried.

Iris started laughing as he kept doing frantic push-ups. One-handed now, taking his full weight on his previously damaged arm. His white coat flapped around in the breeze.

It was good to have him back.

40

Since Zac had bitten her, Pearl had felt a lot of things. Mixed things. Strange and changed. Her old self had fallen away. Things she used to care about seemed petty and silly. Childish things. Now everything made so much more sense. She knew who she was. That Zac was her sire. That Alfie was her apha. She also wanted to eat and have sex. A lot. A lot more than before.

She rolled over in bed and pressed her naked body against Zac's. The amount of heat coming off him was just delicious. Her hand snaked down and circled his cock. He groaned, 'No, no, sweetcakes. I'm spent. Being a werewolf don't give you any extra powers in that direction at all. Well, except that day after that change, but this ain't it, baby.'

Pearl closed her hand around his cock. 'You know, you'd think it would.'

'Well, if that's what you were hoping for I'm afraid . . .' Zac didn't finish his sentence. He often didn't finish his sentences. Not when Pearl had her hand on his cock, anyway.

'Well then, tell me a story.'

'Anything for you, honey. What sort of story?'

'Tell me about what happened in Texas.'

What happened in Texas? Pearl knew Zac had lived there for the first twenty years of his life and yet she felt sure he would know what she meant. In the tiny amount of light in the bedroom Pearl saw Zac smile. 'OK. What happened in Texas.

'Well, when I left high school my family didn't have a lot of money. I was smart enough for college, but not smart enough for a scholarship, so that was kind of the end of my education. I needed to get a job and my mom knew this old lady who ran this weird bookstore. It was kind of gross, that store. All dust and the funky smell of damp paper. But Mom got me a job working there and the first thing I did was get her catalogue onto a damn database. The old lady's mind was fading – she used to manage all her stock from memory – so when I showed her she could use a computer to fill the hole where her brain used to be, she thought I was some kind of a god. After that she pretty much turned over the day-to-day running of the store to me. She spent most of her time off acquiring new stock. Which was why I was on my own the day they turned up.'

'The pack?'

'Yeah. Well, Misty and Alfie. Course, I didn't know their names then. In came this tiny Japanese girl dressed, well, kind of like a Catholic schoolgirl actually – short skirt, tie, knee-highs. And this big guy was with her. I was a bit cold with him because, looking at the way his girl was dressed, I kind of took him for a bit of a pervert. Of course, it wasn't like that with them. No one, not no one, told Misty how to dress. Heh, the thought of Alfie pulling alpha on her over that.' Zac laughed, but it was a weirdly sad laugh.

Pearl wondered whether getting Zac to tell this story might not have been such a good idea. 'So they weren't a couple then?'

'Misty and Alfie. Nope. That all stopped after he bit her cause she was too freaked out. Sad, really. Misty was with Leon for a while, I think, but that was quite a car wreck the way she tells it. Leon always used to say that it was Alfie that couldn't deal with it. I don't know. Also, I know Alfie thinks it's not right to get it on with your own cub.'

'Isn't it?'

Zac grinned. 'It don't cause me any problems.' He leant down and licked Pearl's stomach but she giggled and pushed him off.

'So it's OK?'

'Well, I do know that Alfie's not always right about

everything. Like he says you can't choose who your cubs are, but we managed OK. Leon is always saying that if he met a hot girl he'd bite her and make her his cub so she had to do everything he said.' Zac shrugged. 'Then again, if Alfie had had a choice he would never have bitten Misty, would he? Or Leon. And I don't think Leon would have chosen me as his cub.'

Pearl watched Zac's face for a moment. As he looked down, she reached out and touched his chin. 'Hey,' she said, 'we will find him. Leon. Alfie said as soon as he gets back from the coven.'

'Yeah, I know.' Zac still sounded sad.

Pearl nodded. 'Tell the rest of the story,' she whispered.

'Alfie was looking around the shelves, Misty was going through the database with me asking for various titles on werewolves, none of which we had. Then the door went and this guy in denims with long blond hair walked in. I didn't really pay much attention to him. He went straight over to Alfie. Then there was some scuffling and snarling and I looked round and Leon'd got Alfie up against one of the bookcases with a knife to his throat. Leon was saying something about killing him.

'I ran over then, but they totally ignored me. Leon had the knife pressed right into Alfie's neck. There was a little blood there. I said I was going to call the cops. They still just ignored me. Alfie was telling this guy that he didn't have the guts and Leon was just snarling really and Misty was screaming at both of them. I had the phone in my hand when Alfie said something like, "Do it then, cub. If you're ready for it, fucking do it." And then Leon just dropped the knife on the floor. Alfie took him by the neck then. Pushed him against the opposite bookcase, went in real close and licked the side of Leon's face. He said, "Anytime you want me, pup. I'm waiting for you." Leon just wrenched himself free and ran out of the store. A moment later, Misty and Alfie started muttering something about it being full moon and Leon not coming back to the hotel to lock down. Next thing they're fighting about Alfie going after Leon, Misty was saying he shouldn't. Then Alfie was gone and Misty was crying and I ended up making her some tea, of course – 'cause British, so, tea.' Zac paused. He had been running a hand up and down Pearl's leg. 'Sorry, is this weirding you out? Bit weird to be talking 'bout Misty like this.'

Pearl smiled. 'No, no, it's good. Well, maybe not good, but it's interesting.'

'Right, well, somehow Misty stayed too long and, oh, by this time I'd figured out that they were werewolves. I kind of knew about that stuff 'cause of working where I worked. So I offered to lock Misty in the storeroom for full moon. Not a great option but not too bad. So I ended up having to stay all night because of that and then about midnight, maybe a bit later, this huge wolf – Leon – smashed into the store. Really smashed right through the door, splintered it. It saw me and just attacked me. I'd have been dead right then, except Alfie's wolf came right after Leon and they were suddenly both fighting each other. But by then Leon had already bitten me so that was kind of that.'

'Woah,' said Pearl. 'So you knew straight away.'

'Yeah, I guess I did. I ran away from the store while the wolves were fighting, naturally. Got myself patched up. But in the morning when I came back all three of them were there waiting for me. My pack.'

'And they brought you back here?'

'Well, we went all over, but eventually, yeah. Here.' Zac looked at Pearl. 'Here,' he repeated.

Pearl was stroking Zac's cock again. She'd been doing it for a while. She chuckled as Zac arched into her hand, getting harder. 'You know,' she said, as she began to move faster, 'perhaps we should go downstairs. Those people who knocked on the door might come back.'

'Oh, forget them,' Zac gasped, bucking and writhing under her hands.

Pearl shifted position to straddle Zac's twitching body. She lowered her head until her lips were a whisper from his erection. 'You think?'

'Yeah. Anyway, we shouldn't answer the door without Alfie here. Could be anyone. Could be Vix.'

'What?' Pearl said just before she took his cock into her mouth.

'Oh, nothing.'

41

Alfie followed Lilith down the scrunching gravel path. When they got inside the cover of the trees, Alfie casually took off his shoes, shirt, jeans and underwear. He folded them all up in a neat little bundle and tucked it under some tree roots.

Lilith was staring at him. 'You ever thought of modelling?'

Alfie squinted at her for a second, then bent to pick up the little canvas bag that contained the collar. 'Not after what happened last time.'

Lilith eyed Alfie's behind. 'Shame. You should consider it. We don't really do anything at the C. and C., but some covens do a nice line in merchandise. Calendars, stuff like that. I can see you as werewolf hunk o' the month. I think Mr April.' Her tongue flicked over her lips. 'You'd look good wet.'

Alfie shook his head.

'Wuss. And do you need to be carrying that scrappy bag? It does ruin the whole kind of man-slut image I wanted for you.'

'I need the bag. Also, not a man.'

Lilith moved closer and slipped an arm through the crook of his elbow, 'Sure.'

She took one step forwards – pulling him with her – and everything shifted.

It was like they'd stepped through an invisible curtain. The whole scene before them changed. About twenty women were now sitting around amongst the trees. Some were in street clothes, most were in Witch-Lite – a mass of floaty fabric – and one was dressed like she was about to go trick or treating, pointy hat and all.

It seemed warmer through the cloaking, even though they were under the canopy of trees the light was richer, more honeyed. Sunlight dappled the mossy ground. It was witch world – just slightly better than where the rest of us live.

'OK,' Alfie whispered to Lilith, 'so who's in charge around here?'

'Oh, right,' said Lilith. 'That'd be me.'

Alfie stared at her. 'What? You're the new management? It's you that insists that all men be naked?'

Lilith turned and placed a manicured fingernail on Alfie's bare chest. 'Yeah, although, actually, "insist" might not be the right word. I haven't ever enforced that particular rule before. I actually brought it in just after I saw you, really. But, you know, I think I should keep it. Only for certain men, though.' She stopped and smirked. 'For "studs". Otherwise, you can imagine the horror a lot of the time. Ew.' Lilith grinned broadly. 'Now, see that, over there –' she pointed to a tree stump which was carved roughly into the shape of a seat '– well, that's my ... hmm, I want to say "throne". Would that sound bad? "My throne"?'

'Well, you are the ... What are you?'

'High Witch. Actually I'm the High Witch of more than seventeen covens. And yes, you're right. I *am* the High Witch and that *is* my throne.' She paused and fixed Alfie with a look as if the two of them were conspiring together. 'You know it would be absolutely the perfect thing if you could follow me and kneel at the foot of my throne, until I give you permission to address us. How would that be?'

'I get the feeling I don't have a lot of choice about it.'

Lilith shrugged. 'Sure, if that works for you.'

Alfie raised his eyebrows slightly – but only when he thought Lilith wouldn't notice – and followed her through the witches, who parted elegantly to let her pass. Most of them bowed or curtseyed and greeted her with, 'Lilith', or 'Your Highness', or 'Your Ladyship'. One voice called, 'I see you've brought dessert, ma'am.' Another, 'Yeah. Ninety-nine per cent fat free, too.' Alfie was quite relieved to be busy keeping his head down and his eyes averted as he took his prescribed place at Lilith's feet.

The meeting got going and the talk seemed to oscillate between the mind-bending (stuff that sounded like it might be obscure hardcore science, but Alfie couldn't fathom a word) and the mind-bendingly trivial (cats, chocolate, who's turn was it to store the large cauldron).

Eventually Lilith said, 'And now, we have a special guest star here to appeal to our benevolent sides.' She gave Alfie a little kick and hissed, 'Werewolf, you're on.'

Alfie got to his feet. At least forty witch eyes stared at him in a way that made him seriously wonder if he was going to get out of this meeting alive.

He tried to clear his throat and then one of the witches shouted, 'Are you going to say anything or are you purely decorative?'

Alfie coughed. 'Um, I'm a werewolf,' he said, his voice sounding less steady than usual. 'I was bitten eleven years ago by one of the Ancient Beasts, right here in Oxford.'

A witch with long red hair said to her neighbour, 'God, not him. I hate that Beast creature. I get enough of him at the office. Ew.'

Alfie tried to keep talking over the chatter. 'Um, yes. My lycanthropy has become unstable recently and –'

'What are your triggers, Butch?' shouted the witch dressed in the long black dress and black pointy hat.

Another witch said more quietly, 'It'll be sex, just look at him. Bound to be sex.'

'It's, uh, high emotion,' said Alfie, 'and sex. Um, usually orgasm.' This was met with what could only be described as cackling. 'I've spent the last four years trying to find a way of controlling these other changes and I have had some success with a silver collar.' The witches murmured. It seemed clear to Alfie that they knew what a silver collar was. He took it out of the bag anyway and held it up, his fingers smarting where he touched it. 'But the one I have I got from Vix and it's spelled so that only a member of Vix can use it. I just need the spell removed so I can control my body.'

Lilith took the collar. 'Strange,' she said. 'You talk as if this is one of many collars. It isn't. This is *The* Silver Collar. As for it being spelled,' she continued, 'I don't think it is. No one has added any magic to this. I don't think that would even be possible. But it does have certain safe-guards built in. The werewolf can't manipulate it itself.'

Another witch, the one with long red hair, said, 'It's a precaution so the wolf inside the man can't gain control somehow and remove it. It's made so only the person the wolf most trusts can use it.'

Lilith nodded. 'Ah, yes, Cate, I forgot you were our werewolf specialist. And I think she's right. The magic that is troubling you is part of the collar itself. Can't really be removed without destroying it. Although it is interesting that the person you trust most in the world is one of the Vix. They're the ones who kill werewolves, aren't they?'

Alfie nodded.

Lilith looked sort of sad, distant. 'Poor, poor boy. Can't have sex unless he's tied down and muzzled to protect his partner. Can't even play with his magnificent cock unless he secures himself.' Lilith looked right at Alfie's groin as she said that, then reached out and lifted his chin with her hand. 'Maybe we could at least do something for you. Something that would please us as much as it does you. You see, I can hold your form myself perfectly well while we enjoy you.' She smiled a long slow smile and all around Alfie, the witches got to their feet.

In split moments, the witch's hands were all over him, pushing him back onto his knees, anchoring him to the ground, pulling his knees apart, stroking his inner thighs. Mouths crushed onto his, kissing and nipping. Floaty fabric caressed his skin and drifted over his eyes. Fingernails grazed his nipples. When a tongue slid over the bite scar on his shoulder, he closed his eye so tightly he saw stars. More hands tangled in his hair and pulled his head back hard, forcing him to look up. Lilith was standing over him.

'Thank you so much for this,' she said. Alfie gasped as he felt two different tongues swirling over his balls. 'We do get so *bored* of all the lesbian orgies. Sometimes one just wants … Well, would it be awfully vulgar to say "cock"?'

Lilith snapped her fingers and the witches pulled away, leaving Alfie kneeling on the ground, tingling and thrusting into nothing. He was teased and aroused to the perfect point of need. He could barely think about anything but his swollen kiss-bruised mouth, his erect nipples and his hard, desperate cock. Lilith stepped closer and straddled his lap, sliding herself onto him, her tailored skirt gliding up to her waist.

She kissed him. *Kissing*. She tasted like everything Alfie had ever desired: chocolate, steak, Iris, death. 'Poor boy,' Lilith whispered. 'Poor sad boy, perhaps there is more I can do for you.'

'Perhaps?' Alfie gasped.

Lilith nodded. 'Something to fix you.'

'Fix me.'

Lilith put her hands on Alfie's face. He felt her tighten around his cock until he thought he was about to come. 'Well,' she said, 'anything is possible. It depends what you really want.'

'What I really want?'

Lilith kept moving on his lap. 'Yes. Do you want her? Or do you want to forget about her?'

'Iris?'

'Yes. You said you'd been trying to fuck her out of your system. Want to try and do that properly? There's twenty-seven of us.'

'Twenty-seven! I, I can't,' said Alfie. 'It's only after changing that I can –'

Lilith put one long manicured finger to Alfie's lips. 'We're witches, werewolf, witches. You don't have to worry about anything like that.'

She moved against him once more and again and faster. Still with her hand covering his mouth, she moved on his cock until he came.

When Alfie's breathing slowed he looked over and saw that the witches were lined up, the queue of them snaking back into the trees. He swallowed and moaned. He was still hard. A short blonde was at the front of the queue, she came casually over and lifted her skirt. She straddled him and shoved her tongue quickly and roughly into his mouth.

Alfie looked over her shoulder at the others. So they were all going to fuck him? All going to make him come? And that was going to make him forget Iris? Did he even want that.

There seemed to be a lot of them, he thought, as the blonde kissed him to panting arousal. Twenty-seven, Lilith had said. Did that include her? So he had 26 left, including this one who was working his magically hard cock inside herself. Twenty-six – like the letters of the alphabet. So she's A – all he needed to do was get to Z without going insane.

The blonde made him come quickly. She was very tight and hot and wet. She kissed a lot. Kissing.

Another fuck and C and D both sucked his dick. One after the other. He was still getting hard but the fourth time he came, into a white-haired witch's mouth, it felt like fire being ripped out of him. That was the first time he screamed.

But they didn't stop. Each one stepped forwards and grasped his cock, jerking it quickly back to readiness. It was torture. Most wanted to fuck. Two of them, F and J, wanted it up the arse. He hauled himself up to do it each time. Drained of energy.

By the time Z stepped forwards – a witch with long red hair – Alfie was lying back on the grass, barely able to move. Z grasped his cock.

'Oh no,' Alfie moaned, 'no, please, not again. Please.'

'Well,' said Z as she slipped his hard cock inside her and leant forwards to pinch his nipples, 'you're the werewolf who doesn't believe in Lure, doesn't believe in life mates, and, yet, everyone around you can see Iris is yours. Even like this, taking woman after woman like some kind of ultra virile fuck brute, you can only think of her. Can't you? It's only her.'

'So is that what this really is?' Alfie whispered. 'You're trying to show me how much she means to me by fucking me to death?'

'What do you think?' The redhead smiled and began to move faster on his cock. Alfie screamed, came again and passed out.

It was dark and quiet on the street when Iris parked up opposite the house off St Clement's. Blake, Pure, Pepper and Aurelia, sombre and silent in their red fatigues, dropped silently out of the back of the truck and lined up on the pavement.

The windows of the house were all dark, except for one, which had a little glow. As if the door of that room was open and there was a light on somewhere at the back of the house.

'What do you think, ma'am?' asked Pepper.

Iris squinted at the house, assessing. 'I think we should take a look round the back.'

Alfie opened his eyes. He was still in the park. It was night. The collar was lying on the ground beside him. As he picked it up and stowed it in his bag, the metal burnt his fingers.

He found his clothes first, a scalable part of the wall second and started walking home.

When he turned into the road he clocked the truck squatting on the other side of the road. Recognised it. But things didn't quite slot into place until he opened the front door.

He saw Pearl first. Half-naked Pearl, wrapped in a sheet and being dragged down the stairs by Pepper and Aurelia; behind her Iris and Pure had Zac at gunpoint. Blake was at the top of the stairs, covering it all with a gun in each hand.

Oh, he thought, they found us. And then he felt the wolf coming.

42

Iris was watching Pepper and Aurelia going down the stairs in front of her with Pearl. She'd had to practically pull her gun on Pure to get him to agree to taking Pearl in as a suspect lyc, even though that was his theory all along.

Pure and Iris were bringing the black guy – the same one from the pub – along behind. They were both coming quietly. Not saying much. Blake was covering everything from above. It seemed like a pretty simple operation.

She didn't really see what happened. She was behind Pure on the stairs. The front door flew open, then there was noise and then there was screaming. A gunshot. It was Pure screaming. He let go of Zac and vaulted over the banisters into the hallway below. Iris shouted after him and then she was flattened against the wall as an enormous animal thundered past her and up into the house. Out of the corner of her eye, she saw Blake get knocked to the ground as it passed him.

Iris leant against the wall, keeping her gun on the black guy and looked down the stairs. Pearl and Aurelia were both on the ground. Pure looked up at Iris from where he was crouched over Pearl. 'She's breathing,' he said.

But Iris was already looking at Aurelia. On the floor. Her chest covered in blood. Pepper was crouching in the dark hall, trying to close the wounds with her hands. She didn't look up at Iris. Didn't speak.

'Get up, Pure,' Iris said. 'Help Pepper get Aurelia into the truck.'

'Iris.' It was Blake. Iris looked round and he was at the top of the stairs, struggling to sit up.

'Are you OK?'

'I think so. Where's the hound? Has to be Alfie, right?'

'Upstairs, I think. Attic? But we need to get Aurelia back to the Institute. Best take the lycs too. Blake, can you manage her?' Iris indicated Pearl with a flick of her gun. 'Put her in the truck. Cuff her in case she comes round. I'll mark this guy. Then you can come back for him.'

Iris stood on the stairs and watched. When they came back for the black guy, Pepper was still white and shaking.

Blake stopped in the doorway on his way back out. He was looking at a canvas bag on the floor.

Iris recognised it. It was Alfie's bag. But she hadn't seen it for years. He used to carry his books in it. Had he been carrying it when he arrived home?

Blake picked the bag up and Iris came down the stairs towards him. 'What's in there?' she asked.

'Papers,' said Blake, tilting the bag. Inside was a sheaf of papers, some were clearly ancient, some looked like they'd come off a deskjet printer yesterday. At the top of the first sheet were the words: 'Prophecies and other information pertaining to the Ancient Beasts.' It also said, 'Clement's and Castle Coven' and 'Cate Ray'. Iris's mouth was very dry. She took them and leafed through, but – other than those headings – she couldn't understand a word.

'What language is this?'

'Not sure. From the character frequency I'd say transposed Latin. Need my books. I'll take them back with me,' he said taking the bag of papers from Iris.

'Alfie had papers about the Beast,' Iris said softly and mostly to herself.

'Yeah,' said Blake. 'Well, that'll give the two of you something to talk about. And you'd better take this with you too.' From inside the bag Blake pulled something else. The Silver Collar.

Iris looked at him. 'This needs finishing,' she said.

'I know, look, Pure's a basket case, Pepper's not much better. I need to drive. There are two lycs in the van and Aurelia's been . . .'

'Bitten.'

Blake nodded. He pulled a gun out of his pocket and held it out to her. 'Here. If you can't have me to back you up, at least take this.'

Iris reached for it. 'You're giving me your gun?'

Blake rolled his eyes. 'Don't make a big thing out of it, Iris. I've got four more.'

43

Iris walked along the upstairs landing and found the small reinforced door that opened to a flight of stairs up to the attic. She crept upwards with a gun tight in each hand.

Alfie was sitting on the bed – human and naked – with his head in his hands.

Iris walked across the room towards him, slowly. Keeping the guns on him the whole time. She felt quite calm. She stood right in front of him and pressed both guns against his forehead.

He reached up, took hold of the barrels firmly, one in each hand and moved them down, pressing them both against his heart. 'Better here,' he whispered. 'Neater.' He had blood all around his mouth. 'I ... Did I? I don't remember yet.'

'Yes.'

'Who?'

'Aurelia.'

'I guess we're even then,' Alfie deadpanned. He looked up at Iris. Big golden eyes. *My, my, what beautiful eyes you have.* 'For Misty.'

'What?' Iris kept the guns on his chest but drew back a little.

'It's OK. It's OK, Iris. I know it wasn't your fault. She was a monster, attacking.'

'I could have let Pepper or Aurelia tranq. her.'

'Why didn't *you* have any tranqs.? Because you had to take me down. And you knew you were the only person in that room capable of getting a clean headshot on her. You keep people safe.'

'I still did it. She's dead and I pulled the trigger.'

Alfie's face was stone. '*I* pulled the trigger. Years before you ever met her. I knew just what it could mean for her when I took her into my bed. Four years is a long life for a female werewolf. Without protection, they're vulnerable. Once I was gone, she was in big trouble and she knew it.'

'Once you were gone? Where were you going?'

Alfie glanced down at the guns Iris was holding to his chest.

Iris shook her head.

'You can't leave me like this. Unstable. Packless.'

Iris lowered both guns and took a step backwards.

As she moved away, Alfie launched himself off the bed at her in a tackle that probably should have ended with her on the floor and him on top of her. But she felt it coming and sprang to one side. Alfie landed sprawled on the floor. Iris dropped into a crouch and pointed both her guns at him. He rolled over onto his stomach. 'Nice dive.'

'You're an idiot, Alfie.'

'Don't waste time insulting me. I'll be on you again in a moment.'

'It's so obvious what you're trying to do?'

'I'm not pretending it isn't.'

Iris put both guns down on the floor, slowly and deliberately. 'I'm not going to kill you, Alfie.'

'For fuck's sake, Iris, why not? I ran away. I didn't save him.'

'I know,' said Iris quietly.

'And when you asked me to help you kill the thing that killed him I refused to help you.'

'I know.'

'And for some reason *you* are still stifled by guilt about it, Iris. Why?'

Iris sniffed. She ignored the question. 'I'm not going to kill you, Alfie, until you summon the Beast for me.'

Alfie looked at Iris. 'I can't. I . . .'

'Maybe. Maybe not now. But I know you will. One day. I know it. That's why I won't kill you.'

'It's never going to happen Iris. The thrall is just too strong. It's so bloody strong that Leon can't even get free of *me*. He's had to run away. You know what bad news that is, right? Pack splits, everyone dies.'

'Don't lie to me. You've been thinking about the Beast. That's why you had those papers in your bag.'

'What papers?'

'In your bag downstairs. With the collar. You got them to help you kill the Beast, didn't you?'

Alfie shook his head. 'I never saw any papers. Lilith must have put them in my bag. After I ... I passed out when I came.'

Iris frowned. The conversation had taken a strange turn suddenly. 'When you *came*? Came like orgasmed? How did you ... ?'

'Witches. I went to see them about the collar.'

'You had *sex* with *witches*. I didn't know witches had sex ever.'

Alfie looked up at Iris and raised his eyebrows. It was the first time Alfie had looked like himself since she'd walked into the room. 'Oh, they do. They really, really do.'

Iris paused and thought for a moment. 'Was Cate there? Oh my God, did you have sex with Cate? Cate has sex!'

'Who's Cate?'

'The witch who works for the Institute. Her name was on the papers.'

Alfie frowned for a moment. 'What does she look like?'

'Long red hair. Long skirts.'

'Actually there was a woman there with red hair. Yes. Cate. Their werewolf expert.'

'That'd be her. Did you have sex with her?'

'I kind of had sex with all of them. Actually Cate said this weird thing, she said she knew the Beast.' Alfie squinted up at Iris. 'When I mentioned the Beast she was all "Ew, he's so gross. I see him at the office ..."'

'All of them. How many were there?'

'Twenty-seven.'

'Twenty-seven!'

'Well, yes. They used magic to keep me, uh ... But, I'm

224

sorry, Iris. The papers about the Beast, whatever they are, are nothing to do with me.'

'Fine. Still not killing you.' *Not even over the sex with twenty-seven witches thing.*

'Why is that, Iris? Why, really?'

'I just told you.'

'It's not that though is it, Iris? It's nothing to do with the Beast. It's because you still love me. I've been able to smell it on you ever since I first came back. And now, God, Iris, you actually smell of *me* right now. I don't know how you've done it but . . .'

'Your shirt,' Iris said softly. 'I've been sleeping in your shirt.'

Alfie almost smiled. 'You're the one, Iris. It's always been you. Do you know about werewolves and life mates? I'm sure you do. It'll be in your books. Werewolves are meant to only fall in love once. With one person. For life. Not everyone believes it, but for the ones who do, well, you know who that person nearly always turns out be?'

Iris shrugged.

'Whoever you were in love with when you were bitten.' He smiled again. 'You think that's what's going on here? A werewolf can't just scent anyone across a city, you know.'

Iris raised her eyebrows.

'I know. I know you'd be the last person to believe in stuff like that. But that's not all. There's the collar. The fact that only you can work it. You. Isn't it time that you admitted that the reason you haven't killed me is that I still love you and you still love me?'

Iris shook her head gently. 'You know what, the truth is even stranger than that. It's nothing to do with whether I love you. I still trust you.'

Alfie laughed. A hollow laugh. 'Believe me, Iris, if there's one man you shouldn't trust it's me. Not only have I lied to you, tricked you and fought you, I don't even trust myself. I can't. Look at what just happened downstairs. I can't even trust my own body not to do abominable things.'

'All true,' said Iris softly. 'But I do trust you. I trust that you are doing everything you can not to be the monster that you could be. I know you look at the Beast and what it did and you see that evil infecting you. But you're not like that. You're a good man. In many ways you're the opposite of the Beast. That's why I trust you.'

Iris stood up and moved across the room. She went to kiss Alfie but he pulled away, shaking his head. 'You ... You don't ... You don't trust me. I'm not a good man, Iris. I'm not a man at all. I'm a werewolf. And you really shouldn't trust me. People who trust werewolves end up dead.'

'Well, I do. I trusted that werewolf that was snarling at me out at the parks and I trust you now. I trusted you when you had your hand round my neck. I trusted you enough to tell you about Misty when I was handcuffed to a chair. I trust you. I'll prove it.' Iris's voice was suddenly much sharper. Angry. 'Watch.'

'You might trust me, Iris. But I don't. I don't trust what's inside me.'

Iris bent down and pulled something out of her pack. 'You don't have to,' she said, turning around with the Silver Collar in her hands. 'You can trust this.' She fastened it around Alfie's neck and swallowed, her mouth was so dry it made her throat ache.

Then she turned away. She walked over and sat down on the foot of Alfie's bed. She picked up one of his manacles from the floor. It was big and heavy and the chain jangled. She pushed her foot through the cuff.

Alfie rolled his eyes. 'What are you doing? They won't fit ...'

He stopped speaking and Iris gasped as the manacles tightened to fit her smaller ankle perfectly. 'They're spelled, aren't they?'

'Don't do this, Iris. Maybe you do trust me, but you shouldn't.'

But she carried on. She slid herself onto the bed and fixed her other ankle into a cuff and lay back, squirming up the bed until she could reach one of the wrist cuffs. She slipped it on and then struggled with the other. All the cuffs tightened, the chains holding them to the bedpost tautened too, pulling her, stretching her until she couldn't move.

Alfie looked at her. 'If you think I'm going to . . .'

'You know you are.' Iris pulled against the restraints, feeling how firmly they held her. It was making her hot and wet and she knew he could smell it.

Alfie stood up. His tongue flipped over his lips as he looked at her. Predatory. Feral. He said, 'It didn't occur to you to take your clothes off first?' His breathing was shallow.

Iris pulled again at the chains that held her wrists. Suddenly, under Alfie's gaze, she felt vulnerable. Her breath started coming quicker. 'Can't a big bad wolf like you rip them off me?'

44

Pure pulled himself up straighter when he noticed how formally Pepper was holding herself. Dr Tobias smiled at them, but it was a sad smile.

'You both did very well. I can't imagine how difficult that must have been for you. But now we have two suspect lycs locked up and with full moon tomorrow we'll be able to assess their status and release them or deal with them.'

Pure's stomach turned to ice. 'What do you mean, deal with them?'

'Well, the male is probably surplus. The female, I think Blake will be interested in.'

Blake nodded, calmly.

'You mean you're not going to help them?' asked Pure.

'Help them?' Dr Tobias looked darkly amused. 'Help them how?'

'I don't know. But we have to help Pearl, she's a victim.'

Blake nodded again. 'Well, *Pure*,' Dr Tobias said, 'that is, I'm afraid, the real moral difficulty at the heart of what we do. The victims become the new perpetrators. Best to think, though, that by making these lycs safe we are protecting *future* victims.'

'But you can't, not Pearl.' Pure went for his gun, but he didn't even get his hand on it. Someone kicked him in the back of the thigh, knocking him to the floor on his stomach. He twisted to see Pepper was the one with her foot resting between his shoulder blades.

'Oh well done, Miss Pepper, thank you,' said Dr Tobias.

Pepper said, 'Those fuckers hurt Aurelia. If you want either of them dealt with, sir, just ask me.'

'Ah, yes,' said Dr Tobias. 'How is Aurelia? Are we soon to have two WXXs on the premises?'

'Too soon to tell if she's going to make it,' said Blake. 'She's locked in my lab right now.'

'We need to take her to hospital,' said Pure, struggling as Pepper ground her heel into him.

Dr Tobias exchanged glances with Blake. Pepper muttered something under her breath.

Pure said, 'What about Iris? What about that other wolf we saw?'

'Yes,' said Dr Tobias. 'I think Iris can be trusted to bring that one in alone. No point wasting resources.'

Blake said, 'Your call, doc. Now, if we're done here and you don't mind, I was going to take these papers to my office and translate them. They deal with some prophecies concerning the Beast.'

'The Beast?' said Dr Tobias. 'Well, that'll be an interesting read for Iris when she returns. Get me the translation as soon as possible, please, Blake.'

'I'm right on it, doc.'

Alfie – still very noticeably naked – practically leapt onto the bed. Iris braced herself for the impact of his big body as he landed astride her, but he was surprisingly controlled.

'They won't come back, will they?'

'Who?'

'Vix.'

'Vix? Oh, you mean the rest of the team? No, I think they're pretty sure I can handle you on my own.'

He lowered his face until it was so near to her she could have licked him on the nose. 'You always, always, have to have your own way, don't you?' he said, darkly.

Iris didn't reply, because Alfie dipped his head and kissed her, deeply but quickly. He pulled away short and sharp, leaving her gasping after his mouth, straining at the chains trying to recapture his lips. He said, 'I still know the truth, Iris.'

'Good for you,' Iris panted. 'Now, could you just kiss me again, please?'

Alfie smiled. 'Oh, I will, as soon as we've discussed the fact that the real reason you can't kill me is that you still love me.'

'We just did discuss it. It was the discussion that ended with me chaining myself to your bed. I'd've thought you'd remember...'

'You do, Iris. You love me. Do I have to *make* you say it?' Alfie dipped his head and placed his teeth threateningly on the part of her jawline that made the world turn inside out.

Iris struggled again, but there was simply nothing she could do as Alfie took his time biting the place on her jaw that drove her crazy. Usually she would've pulled away after a few seconds because the sensations were so intense, but what with the chains and one of his big hands holding her chin, there was nowhere to run. She was almost levitating by the time he finished dragging his teeth and his stubbled skin over that one sweet spot. He lifted his head to look at her, keeping up the tease with one fingernail so it was all she could do to understand what he was saying, let alone say anything back.

'Say it,' he whispered, 'tell me you love me. Admit it.'

Thankfully for her own sense of stubbornness, Iris was well beyond saying anything.

Alfie stopped tracing his nail over her jaw for a moment. 'I can put my mouth somewhere else,' he threatened, his tongue flicking between his lips.

Without the tease of his fingernails, Iris found her voice. 'Do your worst, werewolf.'

45

Blake's linguistic skills weren't anything like as rigorous as he liked to make out. At least half of the papers from Alfie's bag clearly represented a headache just trying to work out if they were in Arabic or Sanskrit. But he was reasonably sure of his knowledge of Latin in transposition for the rest of them, so he started there.

With that translation nearly complete, he picked up a cup of cold black coffee from the desk, working through the last phrases in his head. He froze with the cup less than an inch from his lips. *It couldn't be.*

He worked it through quickly again, then put down his cup and raced straight into Dr Tobias's spartan office without knocking.

Dr Tobias looked up. 'Blake?'

'The prophecy,' Blake panted. 'The one from Alfie's bag. It says that...' Unable to find the words, he spread the paperwork over Dr Tobias's desk. 'See?'

Dr Tobias read it over. Checked back to the original and swallowed. 'Oh,' he said in his usual soft tones, looking up at Blake. 'So it appears Alfie will be the one to kill me after all.'

Blake nodded again. 'What do you want me to do?'

The Beast looked at Blake. 'You better bring him in. Alive. Iris too.'

Blake turned, but he hadn't taken more than two steps across the carpet before the door burst open. Pepper rushed in. 'It's Pure,' she gasped. 'He's let Pearl and Zac out of the cells. They've gone.'

Blake looked back at the Beast, who said, 'Forget them, 'I just need Alfred and Iris now.'

* * *

Alfie's head was buried between Iris's legs. He'd ripped her combats off. Actually burst the seams open; they were ruined.

He was playing with her. He was letting his tongue drift over her, almost not touching her at all; sometimes he gave her nothing but his breath. Iris might be married to a professional torturer, but she had never felt anything like this. This was halfway to insanity.

Her body was strung tight in Alfie's chains. The stretch was just an edge too much. Just that extra edge that meant it was perfect. Meant that every squirm and every struggle, every movement she made, reminded her how helpless she was. She was so desperate for him. For anything. For more. She twisted her body in the chains, gasping when the metal scraped her skin, every part of her screaming for his touch.

Once or twice Alfie had slid one finger inside her, with a hand firm on her stomach so she couldn't even buck onto it. Just a tease. In and out. A suggestion of what could be around the corner if she just gave in to him.

She was almost past struggling, past begging, past even the desperate keening. She was only a fraction of a degree from the confession of love that she knew would win her his cock.

Alfie lifted his head and grinned at her. He had such a pretty face. A beautiful face. 'You know,' he said, 'you might be holding up well, but I'm not so resilient.'

Iris laughed a tiny bit, not much, she was too turned on. 'Feeling a little in need of release?'

'Oh God, Iris.' Alfie sat back a little and let a hand slip between his legs. Iris could just see the tip of his erection. She bit her lip. He caressed himself once or twice, arching, his head falling back. He was so close. 'Iris, I need to come. If I don't come inside you, it would be such a waste, but . . .'

'It would spoil your evil plan?'

'Yes. Damn you, why do you have to be so stubborn?'

'Why don't you forget about your silly mind games, admit I'm the winner and fuck me before you explode?'

'God, you are such a control freak, Iris.'

'Me. You're the ... Oh God.' Alfie started to drag a fingertip up her inner thigh in a way that made her start to rock her hips a little, even though there was only the faintest suggestion that he was ever going to run that finger over her clit or slide it inside her.

'I could just stick my dick your mouth, and come that way, you know,' he said, as he began to trace his fingertip between her legs.

Iris moaned. 'No, please ...'

'You were always so good at sucking cock, Iris.'

'Will you just shut up and fuck me.'

'OK, OK.' Alfie took his hand away and moved a little closer. 'Could you at least tell me nicely that you want me inside you? In fact, could you beg me for it? I kind of ... like that.' Alfie's voice was so cracked with desire he was barely audible.

'You want me to beg for your cock inside me?'

Alfie groaned.

'Pervert.' Iris laughed again. It was a short weak laugh. She bucked her hips. 'Do you have some doubts in that direction?'

Alfie laughed. 'How come,' he said, ducking down quickly and giving Iris's clit one last feather-light flicker with his tongue, 'how come you get to be the one chained up *and* the one who calls the shots?'

Iris could barely speak, 'Maybe ... maybe I'm just a natural alpha.'

Alfie stared at her for a moment, breathing hard.

Iris looked at him. 'OK,' she said. 'Fuck me, Alfie, please. I do want your cock. I want to feel you inside me, again. I've waited so long. Fuck me hard, Alfie, right now, while I'm chained to your bed.'

Alfie moaned and dived onto her. His mouth crashed into hers. He was kissing her in a way that would leave bruises. He fumbled with one hand in the angle between their bodies, struggling to guide his cock into her.

She gasped into his mouth. She was just a whisper from coming. He pulled out of the kiss and dragged his wolf tongue slowly across the edge of Iris's top lip. 'Iris.'

Everything exploded all at once.

46

As Blake burst into the attic room, the first thing he saw was Alfie on the bed. His great muscular back the size of a continent. His ridiculously hard and perfect arse. His mouth was crushed against Iris's; his fingers were curled tight in the bedclothes.

That split second would have been the ideal attack moment, but when he looked at Iris, Blake stalled. His mouth went dry. He thought he was ready for this, was prepared, but he was suddenly consumed with arousal, self-disgust, nausea, jealousy – the edges blurring into one another.

By the time he had a hold of himself, Alfie was off the bed and striding towards him – naked, magnificent and terrifying. He shoved Blake back against the wall – hard – with a big hand tight at his throat. With his other hand he found Blake's cock and kneaded it through his clothes. It wasn't a sexual thing – it was a nasty, dominating alpha-wolf thing. 'Like watching, do you?' Alfie snarled.

Blake choked, 'I'll watch her if I want. She's my wife.'

Alfie started. 'She's your what?'

Thankfully, it seemed like that one moment of confusion was all the diversion Pepper needed. Blake felt himself relax slightly as Alfie, confused for a second and with his back to the room, completely missed Pepper whisking past behind him and slipping across the room to press her gun against Iris's forehead, just a moment before Alfie turned around to look questioningly at Iris.

'*Ex*-wife,' Iris snapped.

'Not until we get divorced, baby. You think this might be grounds?' Blake stared past Alfie's shoulder at Iris on the bed. She was mostly naked but her shirt was incongruously still on, if gaping open. It wasn't until he wondered why she hadn't moved, hadn't even reacted, that he realised she was chained down. He found his gun still in his hand and jabbed it into Alfie's stomach.

Alfie snarled, 'That's not a fatal shot.'

Blake raised his gun and nestled the barrel underneath Alfie's chin. 'How about this? Fatal enough for you? You won't even be a pretty zombie; this'll take your face right off.'

Alfie lifted his head a fraction to relieve the pressure of the gun. 'Just leave Iris alone.'

'Afraid we can't do that. She's compromised.'

'I'm what?' Iris shouted from the bed.

'Oh, look at yourself, Iris, for goodness sake. How much more compromised is it possible to be?' Blake hooted. Then he switched down to a much colder gear and looked at Alfie. 'Take a step backwards, werewolf. Slowly.' Alfie held Blake's eye for a moment, then let go of Blake and did as he was told. 'Good. Another step. Now turn around. And kneel. Raise your hands.'

Alfie made each move stoically and slowly. Blake took each of Alfie's arms down behind his back and handcuffed him and then, keeping his gun trained on his kneeling prisoner, moved over to the bed. 'OK,' he said, calmly, 'where are the keys to these chains?'

Alfie's eyes were tight on his. 'In the drawer.'

Blake rummaged in the top drawer of the little cabinet by Alfie's bed. The keys were quickly obvious, stowed in a pink plastic box with a clear lid. Blake handed them to Pepper with a warning plastered over his face. He knew letting Iris free was a big risk. Finding her chained up was surely all their luck used up at once.

But Blake also had other concerns. Some things were just too fascinating to resist. He turned back to Alfie. 'What's this, werewolf?' he asked, showing Alfie the bundle of leather and metal in his hands.

'It's my muzzle,' Alfie said, his eyes calm and trained on Blake's.

'Oh, I see. It's what you had to use to control yourself before you stole that from me.' On the word 'that' Blake reached out and flicked a finger at Alfie's collar.

'Pretty much.'

'It suits you, actually. Nothing so nice as an alpha wolf who likes to wear a collar like a good doggie. The only thing that surprises me is that you wanted *her* chained up. How come you weren't the one in restraints? Aren't you the animal?'

'Her idea. She chained herself down, begged me to fuck her like that.'

'I am still here, you know.' Iris's voice was strident and Blake turned to see her sitting up on the bed, rubbing her wrists before doing up her shirt.

'You want me to shut him up, for you?' Blake said to her, holding up the muzzle.

Iris raised her eyebrows. 'What's this about, Blake? If this is some kind of delayed reaction to the separation . . .'

Blake had already figured out how the muzzle worked. He leant forwards. 'Open up now, puppy dog,' he said nastily.

Alfie didn't move. Blake shrugged and pointed his gun at Iris instead. Alfie opened his mouth.

As he strapped Alfie's face up, Blake looked at Iris. 'Yeah, not so much a delayed reaction to the separation as a perfectly normal reaction to you screwing werewolves. It's not very professional, is it? And in front of young Pepper.' Blake gave the muzzle one last tug and fixed the straps tightly behind Alfie's head. 'Oh, very nice.' But something inside Blake made him nervous. Alfie might be naked, on his knees, bound and gagged, but Blake still felt wary.

Well, he told himself, wary was good. Letting your guard down was where things always started to go wrong.

For example, Pepper was standing very close to Iris. Too close. In fact, Blake anticipated what Iris was going to do – almost like he saw a tiny flash of it – before it happened. But it was too late to shout a warning. Not looking, Iris lashed out with one arm, her fist hitting Pepper's forearm, disarming her as her gun went flying across the room. Iris dived for it. Meanwhile, Pepper, recovering fast, lunged for one of the other guns lying on the floor. The two women sat up at the same time, guns aimed at each other's heads.

'Iris,' said Blake, 'thrilling as that was, could you please put the gun down?'

Iris ignored him. 'Please, Pepper. Alfie's sire is the wolf that killed my brother. You know, Matthew. I've spent eleven years waiting for him to agree to summon his sire. And I still believe he will. One day, I'm going to kill the Beast. For Matthew. And if Blake thinks for a minute that I'm going to let him kill my only chance . . .'

'We're not going to kill him, ma'am,' Pepper said.

'What?' Iris blinked. 'You're not?'

'No, ma'am. Orders are to bring you both in for observation.'

Iris turned to Blake. 'What? For God's sake, Blake, what the hell is going on? If you think I'm going to let you bring Alfie in so you can torture him . . .'

'What is it with you, Iris?' Blake said. 'One minute it's bad Blake torturing our furry friends. The next it's, oh, but you can torture Alfie because I want him to do stuff for me. The next it's don't you dare torture my lovely were-wolf boyfriend. Talk about fickle. No wonder it was hell being married to you.'

Alfie grunted something into the muzzle.

Iris turned, gave Alfie a look and said, 'It was a rebound thing.' And right then Pepper shot her.

Blake watched Iris go down and then looked at Pepper, staring open mouthed at what she'd just done. 'Well,' he said slowly, kicking a screaming, struggling Alfie between the shoulder blades to force him to the ground and talking over the noise he was making, 'I think you'd better tell me right now, Pepper, that you knew all along that that was my tranq. gun.'

47

When Iris woke up she was in her office. She was lying on a sofa. Blake's sofa. Someone must have shifted it specially. A calm, mild voice was saying, 'Well, that'll have to be enough for now. Lock him in and leave him.' Iris opened her eyes. Dr Tobias was sitting at her desk. He was hanging up the phone with one hand and pointing her own gun at her with the other.

She realised why Alfie was so pissed off after she'd tranqued him before. She felt like her head was full of angry cotton wool. She tried to sit up, but found her wrists were tied behind her back. What with that and the wooziness, it took three attempts before she figured out how to get upright.

'Dr Tobias?'

'How are you feeling, Iris?'

'Um. I don't really know. Why have you got a gun on me?'

Dr Tobias smiled. 'Just a precaution. Blake thinks you might have been compromised. We had a security situation here yesterday. I just need to be sure who's with us and who's against us.'

Iris nodded, vaguely.

'I must admit I am a little concerned by your behaviour, Iris. I knew, when I took you on, that your interest in killing the Beast was somewhat consuming, but just lately I've been getting reports that you are letting your other work slide. Ever since your Alfie has been back in town you have been so fixated on getting him to summon his sire ... Well, you do realise that the Institute is not just here to settle your personal vendettas?'

'Of course I do. But I thought you always said that my past made me good at my job.'

Dr Tobias pursed his lips. 'Why did you remove Alfie's collar last month at full moon? You could easily have eradicated him.'

'He had a gun.'

'And yet you still did managed to tranq. him and lock him up. For what purpose?'

'So Blake could force him to summon his sire, I guess.'

Dr Tobias looked unconvinced. 'And then there are these papers Blake brought in. Did you look at them?'

'I couldn't understand them.'

'Ah yes. Well, Blake has translated them. Do you want to know what they said about the Beast?'

Iris nodded, but she wasn't really taking this in. Her head still felt twice the size it ought to be.

'According to this prophecy, the Beast will be killed by its own creation. By a one-eyed wolf with silver at his throat.'

Suddenly Iris's brain seemed to clear. 'Alfie?'

'So it would seem. With an Ancient Beast the thrall is so strong that his cub would never ... At any rate, it's never been documented. No one knows how many Ancient Beasts there are, but it is believed that none have ever been killed by their cubs. In fact the thrall seems to remain strong enough that even a Beast's cubs have such a strong hold over their own cubs ... Well, you know all this.'

Iris was barely listening. She felt a wisp of elation bubbling up inside her again. 'I always knew,' she whispered. 'Dr Tobias, I'm sorry. Maybe I have lost focus lately. But where is Alfie. He is OK?'

'Yes. Alfie. He's in the basement with Blake. You've been unconscious quite a long time. Did you give Blake any reason to be angry with you? It seemed like he'd given you quite a heavy dose of the juice.' Dr Tobias said all of this in the same distracted manner as he kept on sifting through the papers. Then he stopped, looked at Iris and seemed to suddenly snap back into the present. 'Actually,' he said, 'I think you should join Alfie. In the basement.'

'What?'

'Observation, you understand. It's full moon tonight and you've been alone with an unstable wolf. Anything could have happened.'

'What? You can check me for wounds.'

Dr Tobias shook his head. 'The basement, I think, would be best for everyone.'

Iris looked at Dr Tobias. Really looked at him. She felt like she might be seeing something in him that she had never noticed before. But she couldn't quite believe it. He gestured with the gun for her to get to her feet and she did so, awkwardly, still staring at him.

As he followed her out of the room and into the wide hallway, Dr Tobias said, 'The fact is, you're coming to the end of your useful working life, Iris. You've been fighting such a long time.'

'What?' Iris tried to look over her shoulder at Dr Tobias but he jabbed her in the small of the back with the gun and she had to keep moving towards the stairwell.

'Pepper is a perfectly adequate replacement,' he went on. 'She's so keen and dedicated. She's a soldier. We need to start training more people like her. People with less baggage. Not like you with your obsession with the Beast or poor Jude, who practically had a deathwish because of her mother. And, of course, that was why it went wrong with Pure. Baggage. The minute anyone has any kind of personal link with lycs they should be retired. Of course, I didn't have the resources to do that before . . .'

Iris stopped just in front of the door that led to the stairs. 'What did you say about Jude?' Dr Tobias tried to urge her to keep walking with his gun, but she ignored it and turned her head to look at him over her shoulder. 'Well?' Dr Tobias still didn't answer so Iris said, 'How do you know it was her mother? Jude told a different story every day about how the lycs had hurt her. But she never said it was her mother, except . . .'

Dr Tobias looked calmly at her. 'That was what she told me at interview. It was in her file. The Beast killed her mother.'

Iris's mind raced. Jude never said it was her mother. In fact, Iris could remember half-a-dozen occasions when she had said it was her brother, her father, her sister, but she'd only said 'mother' once. The night she bled to death in Iris's arms. Iris would have sworn that Jude wouldn't have casually mentioned her mother in Dr Tobias's first interview. Then again, hadn't Iris trusted Dr Tobias in those early years? She didn't trust him now though. But why?

Behind Dr Tobias, Iris saw a door open. He turned at the noise and Cate emerged from her office. She looked at the two of them. At Dr Tobias pointing a gun at Iris.

'Oh, hi,' she said, looking completely placid, as if this kind of encounter was perfectly normal, 'I'm just off for the day. It was a long one yesterday, having to come back in after a particularly draining coven meeting.' She smiled and walked passed them, inching around Iris to get to the stairs. 'Night, Iris, night, Malcolm,' she said as the door swung shut behind her.

Iris looked back over her shoulder at the door to Cate's office. Now closed and bearing the MAGICAL INTERFACING OPERATOR plaque. She remembered something. That odd thing Alfie had said he'd heard Cate say at the coven meeting. Something about seeing enough of the Beast at the office. She thought about the tiny wrinkling of Cate's nose as she had said Malcolm – presumably Dr Tobias's first name – and suddenly, she knew.

'I didn't need Alfie to summon you, did I? You were here all along?'

Dr Tobias smiled. 'I knew you'd figure it out, Iris. A good enough reason to shoot you right now. However, seeing as how you have been kind enough to bring me, not only my would-be traitorous cub, but also the full version of the prophecies about how he is going to kill me, I'll let you take a stroll downstairs. Come on.'

'You killed Matthew.'

'Yes.' Dr Tobias looked sad: strangely, distantly sad. 'Yes. We must all bear these things. All of us who suffer this curse. Just as Alfie bit Aurelia . . .'

'That's not the same. You were running loose on a full moon night. Alfie tries to keep people safe from what he can do.'

'He's a silly boy, that cub of mine. He ought to know you can't keep the wolf contained.' Dr Tobias jabbed with the gun again and Iris started to walk down the stairs. She felt dazed. She said, 'So you didn't know that Alfie was going to kill you?'

'You think I'd have let him live this long if I did? In fact, until I saw those papers I was pretty sure that Alfie was never going to find the power to betray me.'

'But I don't understand. If you're a werewolf why set up the Vix?'

'Oh, Iris, come on, think. You're better than this.' They were past the ground floor now, walking down the last flight of steps to the basement.

Iris turned around. 'You knew something. Just a bit of the prophecy maybe. That you could only be killed by another lyc. That a werewolf was slated to kill you. That's why you wanted to keep all lycs away. That's why you didn't care about capturing Alfie. You thought you were safe from him because of the thrall.'

'Keep walking down the stairs, Iris,' Dr Tobias said, calmly.

'No . . . I . . .' Blindly, not knowing what she was really doing, Iris launched herself at Dr Tobias, barrelling into him with her hands still tied behind her back. Her mind full of confused rage. It was a pretty doomed attack and her reactions were off – maybe the tranquilliser was still in her blood – and he caught her as she flung herself at him and shoved her backwards. She fell the rest of the way down the stairs, landing on the stone floor.

It was only half a flight, but she was winded enough that, when Dr Tobias grabbed her arm and yanked her towards one of the cages, she didn't really have any fight left. She was vaguely aware of Alfie rushing over, and then cowering away as Dr Tobias looked at him. He recovered, but he had given Dr Tobias enough time to force Iris inside the cage and get the door locked again.

While Iris was still face down on the floor she heard Alfie shouting, 'What are *you* doing here? Please. What have you done to Iris?' But Dr Tobias didn't reply.

48

Iris looked up at Alfie and tried to get up, struggling yet again because of her bound hands. 'Alfie, can you to untie me?'

Alfie nodded and crouched down next to her. When he was close she noticed that his face was bruised and at the corners of his mouth were chafe marks that must have come from the muzzle. He was wearing only his jeans and his ribs were bruised too. He also had some sooty marks all over the scar tissue on his shoulder. 'What happened?' Iris said, even though she sort of knew.

'Your husband happened. I guess he has some jealousy issues.'

'What did he do?'

'Nothing I can't handle. Really, I had more abuse from the cock-crazed witches.'

Iris shuffled around in her sitting position so her tied wrists were facing Alfie. 'Well, that's good. Uh, I guess. I'm sure Blake didn't mean to . . .'

Alfie paused his hands on her wrists. 'He didn't *mean* to! What, I'm sorry, are we still Blake fans?'

Iris shrugged. 'Oh, I don't know. Just, I'm sure he didn't mean . . .'

'To torture me?'

Iris looked back over her shoulder. 'Did he torture you? I thought you said . . .'

'I was being macho. I thought you got that?'

'Oh, well, er, no. Could you maybe give me some kind of signal when you're doing your bravado thing?'

Alfie said, suddenly as if he'd just remembered, 'That was the Beast.'

Iris inhaled then gave a long sigh. 'Yes, I know. Aka my

boss, Dr Tobias. God, I'm sorry Alfie. After all the grief I gave you for being loyal to the Beast, I was bloody well working for him. Keeping *him* safe from lycs.'

Alfie's hands were still on Iris's wrists. He slipped his arms right around her and rested his chin on her shoulder. 'Was that an apology?'

Iris chewed her bottom lip for a moment. 'I guess. Might as well be.'

'Well now I know we're both going to die, if you're *apologising*.'

Iris was looking up at the only window in the basement. It was one of those flat basement skylights that opened onto the pavement above. Through it she could see the sky – a darkening blue. 'Actually, Alfie, I think, right now at least, this little set-up is all about killing me.'

She glanced back at Alfie sitting behind her. He was looking up at the window too. 'Oh,' he said, 'I see.'

'It's full moon tonight, isn't it?'

'Yes. And looking at that sky I reckon tonight is pretty soon.'

Iris swallowed. 'What ... What's going to happen when you change?'

'You need to ask? You've seen lyc attacks.'

'Not you though. I've never seen you kill. How do you usually do it? Throat? Chest?'

'Um, I think my wolf tends to favour just ripping the head off. He's big enough to get his jaws right round the skull –'

'Oh OK, actually, I guess I shouldn't've asked.' Then she said slowly, 'Except, oh, except that you still have the collar on.'

Alfie's fingers flew to his throat. He hissed as he touched the collar and pulled them away again. 'OK, change of plan. My head is the one being ripped off.'

'But I can take the collar off you. Quick, untie me.'

Alfie looked at Iris and almost smiled as he shook his head.

* * *

Earlier that afternoon, Alfie had discovered that the Institute basement was much more difficult to escape from when you were chained to the back wall, standing taut, arms stretched by wrist cuffs and chains swooping up to the ceiling. The being tortured part wasn't exactly helping.

Silver nitrate solution – Blake had taken great pleasure in explaining exactly what he had in his brown glass bottle – was a new sensation. A very unpleasant one. It burnt, like silver, but it also dripped, ran down his back and his chest, leaving paths of stinging pain. He hadn't screamed yet. He had shaken quite a lot though – rattled the chains to Blake's amusement.

Blake reached between Alfie's legs and took hold of his cock, squeezing hard. He leant forwards and got in Alfie's face. 'You fuck my wife with this?'

'She wanted it. Begged me. Chained herself down so I could do it.'

'Really.' Blake let go of Alfie's cock so he could soak another pad of cotton wool in the liquid. 'I'm so glad you said that. So, do you want to know the hardest thing about torture?'

Alfie couldn't take his eyes off the liquid-soaked pad. He swallowed. 'The hardest thing? I don't know, getting to sleep at night, getting blood out of cashmere, your cock?'

'The hardest thing, werewolf, is not killing your victim accidentally. And that is what makes werewolves such perfect torture victims.' Blake placed the cotton-wool ball on Alfie's shoulder, right on his bite scar. This time Alfie did scream as the white-cold ball of pain made contact with his skin. Blake smiled and taped the cotton wool in place. The chemical was making his fingertips turn black. 'You are very hard to kill.'

Alfie was shaking, trying to stay in the moment; Blake moved closer. 'See that sign.' Blake nodded at the WOLVES ESCAPE notice taped to the wall outside the cage. 'I put that there. I know that's one of your lyc sayings. I like to have it there as a reminder. Because this is one time that you lycs have a harder time escaping than most. Can't escape into death. Not even if your torturer gets a bit clumsy.'

Alfie nodded, trying to keep his breathing even as the silver nitrate dripped liquid pain down his back.

'What's the worst thing about being a werewolf?' asked Blake.

Alfie just gasped.

'Well?' said Blake and then he stepped back and punched Alfie in the gut.

Alfie stumbled, held up by his chained wrists. He struggled to catch his breath. When he got his balance, Blake was still waiting for an answer.

'The loss of control.'

Blake laughed and ducked down to grab Alfie's muzzle which lay on the floor.

When you're a werewolf you have no choice about losing control. Whether you think the wolf is a completely different entity or some aspect of yourself coming to the fore. Usually, at full moon, Alfie didn't get to choose who lived and who died as a result of his actions.

Tonight he did have a choice. By keeping his collar on, he could choose not to kill Iris. That might seem like nothing to a human, but to a werewolf, it was an amazing feeling.

49

Iris was as far away from Alfie as she could get, right in the far corner of the cage, pressed against the back wall. He probably thought it was because she was scared of him changing. It wasn't though; it was because she didn't want him to notice that she was trying to get the ropes off her wrists.

She was also trying to talk him into letting her take the collar off him. Just in case the escapology failed.

'You might not kill me. What about before? Out at the University Parks? You didn't bite me then.'

Alfie wasn't looking at her. He was looking out at Blake's WOLVES ESCAPE notice, his face pressed against the bars of the cage. 'You were lucky. Besides,' Alfie said, 'the more I think about that night, the more I think the question isn't so much why the wolf didn't kill *you*, as why *you* didn't kill the wolf?'

'If this is more of your "you love me" talk ...'

'Oh, why not admit it, Iris? I'm going to be dead in ...' Alfie looked out at the oblong of darkening sky. 'What do you reckon? Half an hour?'

'I could tie you up. Untie me and we'll use the rope to tie you up.'

'Really, Iris, it's just bondage, bondage, bondage with you, do you ever thing of anything el–' He turned and looked over then. Iris looked back at him with a hard expression. 'The moon change is too strong. Rope'll just shred. Actually that thing you tried with the handcuffs the first time I came here probably wouldn't have worked if I had actually transformed. Do you know how much energy my body exudes when I change? How much heat I put out?'

'You know this is a trick don't you?' Iris said. 'Some mind game by Dr Tobias. By the Beast. We're both going to end up dead. He's just playing with us. Getting some kind of perverted kick.'

'All the more reason to shut up and not give him any fun.'

'All the more reason to try to beat him.'

'Well, we can't. If you take the collar off me and I kill you – which I will – they'll just shoot me. At least this way you stand a chance. They might just give you a mind wipe or something.'

'Sounds like the worst plan ever. If we take the collar off you might not kill me. You might just bite me.'

'Iris, it doesn't work like that. You don't become a werewolf because your sire thinks you look pretty and decides to keep you; you become a werewolf because you manage to get away. Because you run. Like I did. See this cage. Nowhere to run.'

The rope Iris had been working fell away from her wrists to the floor. Alfie didn't notice.

Alfie and Iris had scuffled a few times since he'd walked back into her life and he'd come out on top every time. He could best Iris in a fight, there was no arguing with that. However, she didn't need to win this fight, just get one good strike in.

She rushed him. He had his back to her again and, even though he started to turn as he heard her coming, she managed to jump up and career into him feet first. Not a very stylish move, but he went down. Smashing into the barred wall behind him and crumpling onto the floor. He was a big man and he went down hard. Winded and disorientated.

Iris leapt onto his chest and tugged at the collar; it came away in her hand like a tangled cobweb. Jumping up, she threw it overarm through the bars of the cage, as hard as she could, and watched it bounce twice on the stone floor of the basement. It was way out of reach.

Alfie sprang to his feet and whirled Iris around with

heavy hands on her shoulders. He sent her stumbling into the wall, holding her with one hand around her neck and the other tangled in her hair – hard enough to hurt. His anger was almost visible, coming off him in waves, but when she looked into his eyes, she almost regretted what she'd just done.

'How could you do that, Iris? I thought you cared about me. How could you make me kill you? How could you take that choice away from me?' he said, his voice aching. 'I'm the one who dies tonight, Iris. I'm the one who dies. I die. You live.'

'No. You live. You live and you summon the Beast and you kill him. Then it's over. If you die, it's never over for me. I'll never be free of it.'

'Free of what?'

'Of the guilt.'

'What guilt, Iris? What do you feel so guilty about? It wasn't your fault Matthew died. Or that I got bitten. What have you got to feel guilty about?'

Iris looked down at the ground. There was a long pause before she started to speak. 'You were only there because of me. Both of you were. Matthew didn't ask for you to do the photo shoot. It was my idea. I set the whole thing up so I could spend some time with you. Sort things out between us. He was going to tie you up.'

'Who was?'

'Matthew, for the shoot. He was going to tie you to a tree for me.'

Alfie frowned. 'Why? What were you going to do to me?'

'Make you apologise. For kissing that girl at that party. Except you sort of short-circuited everything by apologising earlier.' Iris looked away from him and then back. 'I was still going to get him to do it, though.'

'Were you really?'

'Oh God, Alfie. I know. It was silly and stupid. You don't think I haven't gone over a million times how damn stupid it was? Matthew died because of something I set up so I could get you back. I'm an idiot. A selfish idiot. That's why I need to kill the Beast for him. That's why I need *you* to kill the Beast for him.' A tear was running down Iris's cheek.

'Oh, Iris.' Alfie held her while she sobbed. 'Please, this isn't your fault. None of it is. Look, we know who's to blame for this and – I swear – whatever happens tonight, whatever happens to you, tomorrow I will kill him for you.'

Iris pushed back from Alfie's chest and looked up at him. 'Promise. What about thrall?'

Alfie said, 'Maybe there's something stronger than werewolf thrall.' And then he went quite pale and said, 'Oh.'

Iris couldn't see the moon through the window, but it was dark outside now, so it was fair to assume it was rising.

Alfie let go of Iris and backed away, his face full of horror. In a couple of steps he was as far away as he could get, pressed against the furthest corner of the cage. He screamed something. Iris stared at him. His head snapped back, clanging against the bars behind him.

He'd lost it. She could almost see the wolf trying to tear its way out of him.

He slid down the barred wall and rolled onto the floor, his body jerking and spasming like he was fitting.

Iris moved over to him and crouched down. When she touched him, his eyes snapped open. She could see him inside. His human self. She pressed her cheek against his chest. Whispered his name.

Alfie screamed again, bucked like he was trying to throw her off. Iris squeezed her eyes shut. She heard a noise like the earth exploding and the wolf underneath her sprang into the air, sending her flying across the cage. She landed on her back on the floor and it threw itself on top of her. Pinning her to the ground.

Her eyes were closed tight.

Iris waited with her eyes shut for ... something. Pain.

Sickening sounds. Oblivion. But none of them came. Nothing.

Iris opened her eyes.

The wolf was still there, still over her, but it wasn't looking at her. Its nose was aloft, sniffing the air.

'Come on daddy-wolf. Cub wants you.'

Iris heard the soft sound of the door of the cage swinging open. The wolf turned as she did. Blake was standing in the doorway. The wolf sprang suddenly, went straight for Blake, but then past him, through the cage door and up the stairs.

Iris sat up. 'Blake?'

'No time for chat, Iris, come on.'

Iris scrambled to her feet and followed Blake out of the cage and up the stairs. Up three flights until they got to the second floor where Blake's office and lab took up most of the square footage. 'Come on, Iris,' Blake shouted over his shoulder. 'We need to lock him in the lab.'

'Why is he going to the lab?'

'Because that's where Aurelia is.'

50

Later, with Alfie and Aurelia both secured in Blake's lab, Blake put the kettle on and then said quietly, 'I'm glad you're OK.'

'Yeah, no thanks to you, you bastard.'

'What? Am I wrong, but didn't I just save your life? Didn't I, in fact, save you from a hearty mauling by your lyc boyfriend?'

'It hardly counts as saving my life if you put my life in danger in the first place.'

Blake raised his palms. 'Hang on, hang on. I didn't know Tobias was going to go nuts did I? I just thought he'd finally decided to see sense and have Fido brought in by someone who could handle the job. I knew he might do some nasty things to the lyc. Hell, I was even hoping I'd get to do the nasty things. In fact, I *did* get to do a few nasty things. But I never thought he'd take you out.'

Iris looked at Blake. 'Why torture Alfie, Blake? What was that even about?'

'Gathering information. We knew from the prophecy he was going to summon the Beast, but I didn't know how he could. So I was trying to find out. Hey, maybe even me torturing him is part of how the prophecy comes true.'

Iris rolled her eyes. 'That is *so* unconvincing.'

'You think? I kind of liked it.'

Iris stepped forwards and closed the gap between her and Blake. Blake was taller than her, but not by much. She looked up at him. 'I'll tell you what then, Blake, as you saved my life I'm going to give you a break. I'm not going to ask.'

'About Alfie?'

'No. I'm not going to ask how long you've known Dr Tobias is the Beast.'

Blake paled. 'Iris, I . . .'

'No really. I don't want to know. I really don't. But I won't forget this, Blake. You owe me.'

Blake stuck out his bottom lip. 'But can't we pay off that debt with me saving your life?'

Iris gave Blake a look.

'OK fine. You might not believe this but I do know when to shut up. I owe you. I won't forget. Call it in whenever you like.' Blake yawned and rolled his head back on his shoulders. 'What do you want to do now?'

Iris shrugged. 'For once, on full moon, I don't want to do a sweep. It'd be the first time in eleven years, but it feels kind of tainted – now I know all I was doing was keeping the Beast safe from lycs. And there'd be no point going out to find the Beast now because he'll be in his wolf form with that impervious pelt, and anyway we know that in the morning Alfie will summon him anyway.'

'He will? Are you sure, Iris? I know what the prophecy said but there's still the question of how he can.'

'I think Dr Tobias trying to get him to kill me helped quite a lot.'

Blake chuckled. 'So what then? What do we do until morning?'

'I don't know. What do most married couples do in the evening? There must be a TV here somewhere.'

In the morning, after a lot of television had been watched and far too much of Blake's vile excuse for coffee had been drunk, Iris and Blake found Alfie and Aurelia sleeping in the lab in their human forms.

'What have they been doing all night?' Iris said, looking at Alfie curled up around Aurelia's startling naked beauty and trying desperately not to interpret this sight like a human.

'I don't know,' said Blake. 'No one really knows what

this ritual is all about. The sacred bond between sire and cub, or some such lyc crap.'

'You don't think they . . . ?'

'What? Have sex? I'm pretty sure that isn't part of the deal. I'm sure if Alfie had ever had sex with the Beast he would have mentioned it.'

Iris yawned and stretched. 'Yeah, I guess.' She turned away from the lab doorway and wandered back into Blake's office. The witches' prophecy documents, which they had retrieved from Iris's office, were scattered all over the floor. 'So,' she said, 'if the Beast knows that it's Alfie who kills him does that mean if Alfie summons him he won't come?'

'I don't think he has a choice really. If Alfie summons he'll have to come. But he'll know about the prophecy so he'll be super charged. On guard.'

'Really? What will he do?'

'He's Alfie's sire. And he's crazy powerful. He can make it pretty bad for Alfie if he wants to.'

Iris swallowed. 'How bad?'

'Well,' said a soft voice from the lab doorway behind them. 'I'm pretty sure I won't be thinking twice about what your husband did to me after a mind-fuck session with my own daddy wolf.'

51

Sunday 25 November 2007

In the University Parks, Alfie stood steady against the wind. He took off his shirt and put it on the ground. 'Iris,' he said, turning to where she was standing next to Blake, 'can you take the collar off me.'

'So it's true,' Blake said, 'about summoning and metal.'

Alfie didn't reply.

Iris stepped forwards and removed the collar. As she did so, she noticed Blake raising his gun and pointing it at Alfie. Iris bit her lip. She should have brought tranqs., but she didn't think. She didn't think that Alfie would take off the collar, so all she brought was fire power. Everything she could hit the Beast with if she needed to.

Alfie's skin was so warm under her fingertips. He said, 'Can I have your blade, Iris?'

Iris pulled her silver blade from her back pocket and placed it in Alfie's hand.

What Alfie did next was strange and confusing. He cut himself with Iris's blade, let the blood fall on the ground, moved strangely, made some sounds that might even be words, but no kind of words that she'd never heard before. And then Dr Tobias appeared. Just walked out from behind one of the trees nearby.

'Alfred. So soon,' Dr Tobias said as he drew near. Iris could hear Alfie's breathing, ragged and anxious. 'And you've brought company.'

'Sire,' said Alfie, in a deferent voice Iris had never heard him use before, never would have dreamt he had. As he said it, his legs sort of wobbled and then he fell to his knees on the ground. Iris thought he was hurt and took a step towards him, but he looked at her over his shoulder with an expression that stopped her in her tracks.

He didn't say anything else. There was no complaint about him trying to kill both of them, no drama about Dr Tobias and the Beast being the same person, and no, absolutely no, attempt to attack. It was just Alfie, quiet on his knees on the wet ground with his head bowed. Iris knew then that this wasn't what was meant to happen.

Dr Tobias reached down and lifted Alfie's chin.

Alfie pulled his head away and dropped his gaze. He couldn't even look at him.

'You're not ready, cub,' said Dr Tobias, almost sadly. 'It's a mistake. You'll never be ready.'

Iris swallowed. Her stomach turned over. She pulled her silver gun from her pocket. 'Maybe not, but I am.'

Dr Tobias took a step back away from her in shock.

'Iris,' hissed Blake, 'you can't. The prophecy. Only a werewolf can. His own creation.'

'We'll see. I'm not really sure I believe in that prophetic crap. Not very logical. I'm far more interested in seeing if silver will kill him now he hasn't got that bullet-repelling pelt.'

Dr Tobias stared calmly at Iris for a moment. Then he said, 'Iris, you don't want to do this. You're standing here next to my cub. He's still loyal to me, in my thrall, do you think he'd let you live if you killed me.'

'Well, we could find out.'

'And you do realise that if I told Alfred to kill you, right now, he'd do it? In his human form. Tear you apart. Do you want to put him through that?'

Alfie looked over his shoulder at Iris. 'Get out of here, Iris,' he said, 'please.'

Behind Iris, Blake said, calmly, 'Well, I can solve this little problem quite simply.' Iris heard an explosive bang. Behind her Blake had fired a gun. Alfie dropped to the ground.

Iris whirled around to look at Blake feeling like her heart was going to stop. 'Oh, God, Blake, I –' Blake was smiling, faintly amused by Iris's distress, '– you brought tranqs.'

'Yeah, baby.' Blake winked. 'I do love my tranqs.'

With Alfie out cold the Beast looked a little rattled. Iris turned and got him back in her sights.

The Beast said, 'And how about you, Blake, are you going to stand here and let this woman try to shoot me? Do you have no loyalty?'

Blake said, 'Generally, no. But even if it came down to a choice between you and her, well, I am way more scared of her than I am of you. Even if you are the Ancient Beast.'

'Thinking with your dick for a change.' Dr Tobias turned to Iris. 'So I guess it just comes back to you, Iris. Are you *actually* going to kill me? Me. The man who made you. The man who found a confused, bereaved young woman and trained her, made her into the most accomplished werewolf assassin in the world.'

'I'm not the most accomplished –'

'Made you into the Vix.'

'You didn't make me into any –'

'I made you Iris Instasi-Fox. I saved you. I made you. I chose you.'

Behind her Blake shouted, 'Shoot him, Iris. Do it now. He's just trying to confuse you.'

But Dr Tobias was talking over him. 'Clever young woman. Physical. Single-minded. Excellent at biology. The best they'd seen in years your tutor told me. Just what I needed for my team. I had Blake here. I had that crazy bitch Jude. I needed one more. You. All *you* needed was motivation. A boyfriend dead in a werewolf's jaws seemed perfect. Or as it turned out, a twin brother. Blood kin. Even better.'

Iris's voice was weak. 'You killed Matthew so I would...'

Dr Tobias nodded. 'Ancient Beasts aren't mindless like your common or garden hounds.' He kicked the unconscious Alfie lying at his feet. 'But you knew that, didn't you? You always spoke to me as if I was human, even though you ignored the others, just blew them away.' He smiled an admiring smile. 'But *Ancient Beasts* can be targeted, specific. I meant to kill Alfie that night, but Matthew – when I realised who he was – was an unexpected bonus. Especially as this one –' another kick at Alfie '– can really run fast when he can hear the sounds of someone else being torn apart.'

Iris was shaking. Her whole body was falling. Collapsing like a tower of building blocks. But just before the gun dropped out of her hand, someone took her wrist, supported it, held it firm. An arm snaked around her waist. Something solid beside her. Real. Iris turned her head and Matthew was standing right next to her. More than a hallucination this time, as real and solid as he'd ever been. His hand was cool and tight over hers. His finger on the trigger of her silver gun.

They both squeezed.

52

Back at the office Alfie spent a long time sleeping off his tranqs. and then a while walking around the car park with Aurelia, talking. Iris went to see Blake.

He was sitting on his sofa – now moved back into his own office – next to Pepper.

He looked up. 'Hey,' he said.

'Hey. Are you OK?' Iris asked, walking into the room.

'Yeah. I'm fine. I do feel like a bit of a jealous wanky idiot.'

'You *are* a jealous wanky idiot.'

'Yeah, so really, I was just being true to myself.'

'Have you figured out how come I killed the Beast? Was the prophecy wrong?'

'Not exactly,' said a voice behind Iris. She turned around. Cate was standing just inside the doorway. She practically skipped into the room, looking happier than Iris had ever seen her. 'The prophecy was not only right, but has now been fulfilled. Which is always for the best. Things get in an awful mess otherwise.' She actually sounded perky. Perky Cate – this was new.

Blake screwed up his brow. 'It has. I don't see how . . .'

Cate settled herself at Blake's desk, commanding the room instantly and unnervingly and perkily. 'You know I was very dubious about this whole idea of Lilith's. I mean prophecies usually just sort themselves out, no need to start sticking them in people's bags and setting off whole self-fulfilling chains of events. But she has this theory, you know. Give people a prophecy and whatever they do as a result of reading it will be whatever needs to be done to make it come true. Whether that's what they want or not. The theory of Prophetic Irony she calls it. She's writing a paper. I'm not really sure if I believe it, but when I said so we got into a big argument about causality and she is the High Witch of more than seventeen covens, and I like my skin covering my body, so . . .'

'It was Lilith then?' Alfie walked into the room with Aurelia half a step behind him.

Cate nodded, her eyes flickering over Alfie for just a second too long. 'Yeah.'

Iris said, 'But I'm not a werewolf. How come I killed the Beast? It should have been Alfie – the one-eyed wolf with silver at his throat.'

Alfie said, 'It's wrong. The prophecy is wrong. There was no way I could have killed him. I could barely look at him.'

Cate said, 'Oh no, prophecies don't do wrong. They just do misinterpreted. It didn't mean Alfie at all. His eye is healed and he wasn't even wearing the collar.'

'Then who?' Alfie said.

'Iris, of course. The prophecy is clearly talking about Iris. I thought you would have worked that out. That's why we gave you various copies. If you look at the original version, say, here, you'll see that "the one-eyed wolf", here, is "the Iris wolf", here.'

'Woah! What!' Blake practically vaulted across the room. When he looked at the documents Cate was showing him he actually slapped his hand to his forehead. 'Oh. My. God.'

Iris looked at him. 'You didn't translate all the versions?'

Blake shifted. 'I was in a hurry. And then when I read it . . .'

'And the silver?' said Iris. 'Oh.' Her fingers went to her throat, where, on a piece of black cord she was wearing the ring Alfie had given her. His grandmother's ring.

'Damn,' said Blake shaking his head. 'I am so dumb.'

Iris was still staring at the documents. She couldn't understand them but she couldn't quite get over the fact that they told her future. 'It all fits. "His own creation." I am Dr Tobias's creation. He said as much. But what about the "wolf" part in the "one-eyed wolf". If that is "Iris wolf", well, I'm still not a wolf.'

Cate sniffed. Blake looked up from where he was reading, smirked and caught Alfie's eye. Iris noticed all this, but didn't get the joke. 'What?'

'Well,' said Cate, 'um, you might not like this, not very, ahem, politically correct, but you have to remember that this was written a long time ago. They saw things differently then. Which is why...'

Alfie walked over to Iris, still standing by Cate at the desk. He put his big arms around her from behind. 'You're a wolf's woman,' said Alfie. 'That makes you a wolf. In pack terms.'

'I'm not a ... What? No! That is not true.'

'It is,' said Alfie. 'If you're a wolf's woman you have to be part of the pack. And that means you have to be, nominally, a wolf. Think of it as an honorary status.'

Iris rolled her eyes.

Cate said, 'Actually there is a bit more you should know about. This is only the older versions. The ones Blake didn't translate...'

'I would have got to them,' Blake muttered.

'I'll just read it verbatim. "For the kingdom is home to many beasts. The warrior wolf will kill them all."'

'Right,' Iris said, 'and I'm the "warrior wolf". So I'm going to bag me a whole heap of Ancient Beasts. Does it actually say how many?' She was laughing as she said it.

Blake's face was serious. 'Really, Iris, prophecies might be vague and they might be tenuous but they are not wrong. Like Cate says, you are clearly the person who is going to wipe out the Ancient Beasts.'

Iris was still laughing. 'OK, OK. I'm in a prophecy. I have some kind of destiny calling. So does that mean I don't have to worry about looking both ways when I cross the road any more?'

Cate sighed. 'And this is just what I told Lilith was the problem with telling people what prophecies say about them. Don't go around thinking you're invulnerable, Iris, that never ends well. Next thing you'll all want to know your dates of death and goodness knows what else.'

Cate started to gather up the papers. Blake was hovering round her, probably asking about his date of death. Alfie pulled Iris closer and said softly, 'Look, there's something you're going to need to know about the way I get the day after full moon.'

Iris nodded. 'Fatigue, thirst and hunger, isn't it? *Hard* on the body.'

Alfie's breath was heavy in Iris's ear. 'You could say that. *Hunger* is actually always the most pressing need.'

'Hunger, eh? So what are you saying? That I'm going to have to be a good little wolf's woman and start learning how to cook steak extra rare.'

'Well, I wouldn't actually object to that but ... Actually Iris, this is far too urgent to banter about. Your place or mine? And before you make that decision can I remind you that my place is the one with the chains on the bed.'

To be continued

The Institute of Paraphysiology
A glossary of selected terms, jargon and classifications

Last updated 19 October 2007 Blake Tabernacle, Senior Paraphysiologist

* – indicates known lycan terms

Alpha – The leader of a group of werewolves

Ancient Beast – Powerful lycan believed to be one of the original werewolves

Cub – A werewolf infected by a particular wolf

Cub mater – A werewolf that attempts to turn humans into werewolves to gain sexual authority over them

Flip – To change from human to wolf, usually unexpectedly

Hound – Field term for a werewolf in wolf form

Line* – The werewolf hierarchy system

Lock down – The controversial werewolf practice of trapping itself inside a cage, cell or room before full moon, to prevent it injuring others

Lone wolf – A strong packless werewolf, usually an Ancient Beast

Lyc – A slang term for a werewolf. Taken from the formal classification system Lyc-W1XX, Lyc-W2XX, Lyc-W1XY, Lyc-W2XY

Lycan – A werewolf

Pack – A group of werewolves, who live and hunt together, usually linked by sire–cub bonds

Red – An Institute-trained werewolf hunter

Sire – The wolf that infected a particular werewolf

Sniffers* – Humans turned on by lycanthropy

Stray – A young packless werewolf, usual a sire reject

Thrall* – The power a werewolf sire has over his cub

Vix* – Werewolf hunters

W1 – A werewolf in wolf form

W2 – A werewolf in human form

Weredog* – A werewolf that tries to do what humans want

Wolf close to the skin* – A werewolf with the ability to change into a wolf from minor or non-moon light stimulus

WW – A werewolf

WXX – A female werewolf

WXY – A male werewolf

Acknowledgements and Author's Note

Many thanks to my fellow Black Lace authors Portia da Costa and Madelynne Ellis who made some vital early suggestions that helped transform Alfie into the magnificent creation that graces the pages of this book. My thanks also to Helen Raven for some further timely inspirations. To Alice for a conversation about Oxford University and fur. To Ewan, Isabel and Sue who rearranged their schedules around me and gave me the time to write this book. To Liz who makes my website look all proper. To everyone and anyone associated with Lust Bites – especially all those who offered to pop round and feed my werewolves. To Black Lace editor Adam Nevill for his Lure. And to Kristina Lloyd for her special lighting effects.

And many, many thanks to my team of brave volunteer draft readers, Ewan, Isabel, Lizzy, Portia, Madelynne, Liz, Myf, Jana, Myst and Aldabra.

I have taken some tiny liberties with the geography of Oxford for which I must apologise to the residents.

Iris and Alfie's story continues in Book Two of the Silver Werewolves Trilogy: The Silver Crown.

Read an exclusive preview here.

The Silver Crown

Mathilde Madden

Far, far away, on the most southwestern tip of the British Isles was a small wooden cabin. It was a simple place. One room. Perfectly situated just off a dirt track on the edge of some woodland. The cabin's previous owner, a middle-aged man, had died the full moon before last. Now, in this solitary spot, a werewolf lived alone.

The werewolf was very happy. Finally free. He found work where he could. Manual labour mostly on the farms and conservation centres. He'd be raping the earth with pesticides one week and saving the planet the next. This was the kind of thing that amused him. And if work was hard to come by he knew the land. He trapped rabbits and game birds. Once he broke into a farm and stole a goat, but that was really far more trouble than it was worth.

He never got lonely. If you are a werewolf there is always the company of women.

This particular night, the werewolf had brought home a woman called Sabrina. He had found her in the pub in the nearest village, looking totally out of place amongst the tangled, tousled surfers' girlfriends and lithe, hardy farmers' wives.

Sabrina was one of the most beautiful women the werewolf had ever seen, with perfectly curved hips under her dark-indigo jeans and a tight pink sweater that even the werewolf could tell was very, very expensive. She had golden skin that spoke of warm places and soft breezes and a dark cloud of wavy hair. Her white teeth glittered too. One of her front teeth glittered more than the others. It was silver. A silver tooth. When the werewolf looked at it – when he imagined it scraping across his skin – he got scared and hard.

He'd already asked her back in the pub if it was real

silver. She'd laughed. 'No, I don't think so. Some kind of special alloy, I think.' And when she said that, the way she'd looked at him, it was almost like she'd known.

The werewolf's cabin was all wooden floors and warm rugs. There was a stove for heating but it wasn't much of a match for the January cold. It had been a hard winter. The werewolf pulled Sabrina into his bed, covering her with soft blankets and his own paranormal-warmth before he started to strip her.

Her body was amazing. Firm and toned, shaped like his fantasies. He used his tongue everywhere. Werewolves love to use their tongues. Every inch of skin got anointed as he revealed it: her stomach as he pushed up her sweater, her legs as he drew down her jeans, her breasts, her hips, her back. He dropped onto the floor in front of her and kissed the tops of her elegantly arched feet. He worshipped her. He was an arrogant creature usually, cocksure and confident, but Sabrina unnerved him just a little. Too beautiful. Too beautiful for him.

She smiled down at him and normally a smile from a girl like Sabrina would make him preen inside, but she still had him on edge. There was something about her. He was scared. Like this must be some kind of trick. Like there had to be a catch. Like she would suddenly stop and laugh at him for thinking he could land a woman like her.

She slipped off the bed to the floor, onto the rug next to him. They were both naked. He thought she really ought to be too cold, but somehow she didn't seem to notice. He gave off a lot of heat. Werewolves do. Maybe he was giving off enough to keep her warm too.

She pushed him flat onto his back and got on top of him, her whole body pressing itself the length of him. She put her mouth to his. They kissed closed mouthed for a little, and then slowly she worked her tongue between his lips. He opened his mouth like he belonged to her.

Some werewolves have a particular affinity for metal. All werewolves can sense mercury and silver. But he could do more than that. When he ran his tongue over her tooth he only had to graze it twice with the tip before he muttered, 'Chromium alloy,' and Sabrina laughed darkly into his mouth.

She moved down his body, used her chromium alloy tooth to pluck his nipples to hardness and then let her hot mouth cover his cock. He writhed on the floor.

The chromium alloy didn't hurt him. It tingled but it was not an unpleasant feeling, even when it was nipping at the head of his cock. It was nothing like silver or mercury. Those could sting. He'd been with a girl once who had every one of her back teeth filled. That mercury amalgam against his cock had left him sore with the memory of her for weeks.

Sabrina's mouth was hot and damp and spiked with sensation. He bucked his hips and she pulled back. She sat up and sucked on her bottom lip as if savouring the taste of him. Then she smiled that unnerving smile again, hitched forwards and slipped herself onto his needy twitching cock. He looked up at her: curves and dark hair and chromium tooth. She was like something from a fairy story. She was like the reward that good werewolves got.

When the werewolf woke up the next morning and saw her puffy cloud of dark hair on the pillow, he almost felt sad. Sad that he was going to have to say goodbye to her. Sad that he never did more than one night with anyone. It was better that way. Now that he didn't have a pack he preferred to keep his ties as loose as possible.

He blew lightly in Sabrina's ear and she opened her eyes. 'Hi, tiger,' she said, smiling.

The werewolf nodded. 'Hey, baby. Listen, I've got to work today. Sorry.'

'That's OK,' Sabrina said. She climbed over him and out of the bed, picked up her jeans and started shimmying into them. Then she grabbed her sweater and pulled it over her head as she walked across the cabin to the chair by the door and picked up her handbag. The werewolf had a small mirror on the wall by the front door. Sabrina turned to it and started rooting in the bag.

'So,' said the werewolf, looking at her reflection. 'I guess I'll see you around.'

Sabrina caught his eye in the mirror and smiled. She turned slowly, drawing something from her bag at the same time. 'Oh you won't be seeing me, baby. You won't be seeing anyone.'

The werewolf ran his tongue over his suddenly dry lips. 'What?'

Sabrina was pointing a gun at him. She winked. 'That's right, Leon. Silver bullets.'

Leon pushed back his shoulders. 'Oh, what? You're a Vix? What's going on? Vix don't come this far west. They staking out new territory?' He sniffed. 'And using new tactics?'

'Tell you what,' said Sabrina, 'when you're holding the gun you can ask the questions.'

Leon let his eyes slide down her body and up again. He couldn't decide whether the fact she was so eerily beautiful made this easier or harder.

It certainly made something harder. He slid his legs out from under the bedclothes and stood up naked in front of her, his erection bobbing against his scarred belly.

'Stay where you are.'

Leon stopped still. 'I just have one more question.'

'What?'

'Why is it that you pointing that gun at me is making me so horny, sweetheart?'

'Really? It's making you horny? Well you'll love this, then.' Sabrina laughed. She tipped the nose of the gun and fired straight into Leon's shin.

Almost before he heard the shot Leon crashed onto the floorboards, crying out. He grabbed his wounded leg, squeezing the wound tight, trying to push out the pain. He looked up at Sabrina with tears in his eyes. 'What did you do that for you, crazy bitch?'

'What? Didn't that make you horny? *Sweetheart*?'

'Of course it fucking didn't.'

'Well isn't that a shame.' Sabrina walked across the cabin, until she was close enough to bend over and press the gun against Leon's chest. 'But now perhaps you understand why it's important not to piss me off.'

Leon looked up at her. He had only been this scared of one other person his whole life. 'What do you want?' he choked.

'I want your sire, Leon. I want Alfie Friday.'

LOOK OUT FOR THE ALL-NEW BLACK LACE BOOKS – AVAILABLE NOW!

All books priced £7.99 in the UK. Please note publication dates apply to the UK only. For other territories, please contact your retailer.

THE CAPTIVATION
Natasha Rostova
ISBN 978 0 352 33234 9

In 1917, war-torn Russia is teetering on the brink of revolution. A Russian princess, Katya Leskova, and her family are forced to leave their estate when a mob threatens their lives. Katya ends up in the encampment of a rebel Cossack army; the men have not seen a woman for months and their libidos are out of control.

When the Cossack captain discovers Katya's privileged background he has no intention of letting her leave the camp. Against the turbulent background of a country in turmoil, Katya and the captain become involved in an erotic struggle to prove their power over each other.

Coming in November 2007

SPLIT
Kristina Lloyd
ISBN 978 0 352 34154 9

A visit to Heddlestone, a remote village in the Yorkshire moors, changes librarian Kate Carter's life. The place has an eerie yet erotic charge and when Kate is later offered a job in its puppet museum, she flees London and her boyfriend in order to take it.

Jake, the strange and beautiful curator and puppeteer, draws her into his secluded sensual world, and before long she's sharing his bed, going deeper into new and at times frightening explorations of love and lust. But Kate is also seduced by Eddie, Jake's brother, and his wild Ukrainian wife, and she becomes tangled in a second dark relationship. Split between the two men, Kate moves closer to uncovering the truth behind the secrets of Heddlestone, ever sensing danger but not knowing whether the greatest threat comes from ghosts or reality.

WILD KINGDOM
Deanna Ashford
ISBN 978 0 352 33549 4

Salacious cruelties abound as war rages in the mythical kingdom of Kabra. Prince Tarn is struggling to drive out the invading army while his bethrothed – the beautiful Rianna – has fled the fighting with the mysterious Baroness Crissana.

But the baroness is a fearsome and depraved woman, and once they're out of the danger zone she takes Rianna prisoner. Her plan is to present her as a plaything to her warlord half-brother, Ragnor. In order to rescue his sweetheart, Prince Tarn needs to join forces with his old enemy, Sarin, whose capacity for perverse delights knows no civilised bounds.

THE SILVER CROWN
Mathilde Madden
ISBN 978 0 352 34157 0

Every full moon, Iris kills werewolves. It's what she's good at. What she's trained for. She's never imagined doing anything else . . . until she falls in love with one. And being a professional werewolf hunter and dating a werewolf poses a serious conflict of interests. To add to her problems, a group of witches decides she is the chosen one – destined to save humanity from the wolves at the door – while her new boss, Blake, who just happens to be her ex-husband, is hell-bent on sabotaging her new reltionship. All Iris wants is to snuggle up with her alpha wolf and be left alone. He might turn into a monster once a month, but in a lot of ways Iris does too.

MINX
Megan Blythe
ISBN 978 0 352 33638 5

Miss Amy Pringle is pert, spoilt and spirited when she arrives at Lancaster Hall to pursue her engagement to Lord Fitzroy, eldest son of the Earl and heir to a fortune. The Earl is not impressed with this young upstart and sets out to break her spirit through a series of painful and humiliating ordeals.

The trouble for him is that she enjoys every one of his 'punishments' and creates havoc at the Hall, provoking and infuriating the stuffy Earl at every opportunity while indulging in all manner of naughtiness below the stairs. The young Lord remains aloof, however, and, in order to win his affections, Amy sets about seducing his well-endowed but dim brother, Bubb. When she is discovered in bed with Bubb and one of the servant girls, how will father and son react?

Black Lace Booklist

Information is correct at time of printing. To avoid disappointment, check availability before ordering. Go to www.black-lace-books.com. All books are priced £7.99 unless another price is given.

BLACK LACE BOOKS WITH A CONTEMPORARY SETTING

☐ ALWAYS THE BRIDEGROOM Tesni Morgan	ISBN 978 0 352 33855 6	£6.99
☐ THE ANGELS' SHARE Maya Hess	ISBN 978 0 352 34043 6	
☐ ARIA APPASSIONATA Julie Hastings	ISBN 978 0 352 33056 7	£6.99
☐ ASKING FOR TROUBLE Kristina Lloyd	ISBN 978 0 352 33362 9	
☐ BLACK LIPSTICK KISSES Monica Belle	ISBN 978 0 352 33885 3	£6.99
☐ THE BLUE GUIDE Carrie Williams	ISBN 978 0 352 34131 0	
☐ BONDED Fleur Reynolds	ISBN 978 0 352 33192 2	£6.99
☐ THE BOSS Monica Belle	ISBN 978 0 352 34088 7	
☐ BOUND IN BLUE Monica Belle	ISBN 978 0 352 34012 2	
☐ CAMPAIGN HEAT Gabrielle Marcola	ISBN 978 0 352 33941 6	
☐ CAT SCRATCH FEVER Sophie Mouette	ISBN 978 0 352 34021 4	
☐ CIRCUS EXCITE Nikki Magennis	ISBN 978 0 352 34033 7	
☐ CLUB CRÈME Primula Bond	ISBN 978 0 352 33907 2	£6.99
☐ COMING ROUND THE MOUNTAIN Tabitha Flyte	ISBN 978 0 352 33873 0	£6.99
☐ CONFESSIONAL Judith Roycroft	ISBN 978 0 352 33421 3	
☐ CONTINUUM Portia Da Costa	ISBN 978 0 352 33120 5	
☐ COOKING UP A STORM Emma Holly	ISBN 978 0 352 34114 3	
☐ DANGEROUS CONSEQUENCES Pamela Rochford	ISBN 978 0 352 33185 4	
☐ DARK DESIGNS Madelynne Ellis	ISBN 978 0 352 34075 7	
☐ THE DEVIL INSIDE Portia Da Costa	ISBN 978 0 352 32993 6	
☐ EDEN'S FLESH Robyn Russell	ISBN 978 0 352 33923 2	£6.99
☐ ENTERTAINING MR STONE Portia Da Costa	ISBN 978 0 352 34029 0	
☐ EQUAL OPPORTUNITIES Mathilde Madden	ISBN 978 0 352 34070 2	
☐ FEMININE WILES Karina Moore	ISBN 978 0 352 33874 7	
☐ FIRE AND ICE Laura Hamilton	ISBN 978 0 352 33486 2	

☐ WILD CARD Madeline Moore   ISBN 978 0 352 34038 2
☐ WING OF MADNESS Mae Nixon   ISBN 978 0 352 34099 3

BLACK LACE BOOKS WITH AN HISTORICAL SETTING

☐ THE AMULET Lisette Allen   ISBN 978 0 352 33019 2   £6.99
☐ THE BARBARIAN GEISHA Charlotte Royal   ISBN 978 0 352 33267 7
☐ BARBARIAN PRIZE Deanna Ashford   ISBN 978 0 352 34017 7
☐ DANCE OF OBSESSION Olivia Christie   ISBN 978 0 352 33101 4
☐ DARKER THAN LOVE Kristina Lloyd   ISBN 978 0 352 33279 0
☐ ELENA'S DESTINY Lisette Allen   ISBN 978 0 352 33218 9
☐ FRENCH MANNERS Olivia Christie   ISBN 978 0 352 33214 1
☐ LORD WRAXALL'S FANCY Anna Lieff Saxby   ISBN 978 0 352 33080 2
☐ NICOLE'S REVENGE Lisette Allen   ISBN 978 0 352 32984 4
☐ THE SENSES BEJEWELLED Cleo Cordell   ISBN 978 0 352 32904 2   £6.99
☐ THE SOCIETY OF SIN Sian Lacey Taylder   ISBN 978 0 352 34080 1
☐ UNDRESSING THE DEVIL Angel Strand   ISBN 978 0 352 33938 6
☐ WHITE ROSE ENSNARED Juliet Hastings   ISBN 978 0 352 33052 9   £6.99

BLACK LACE BOOKS WITH A PARANORMAL THEME

☐ BRIGHT FIRE Maya Hess   ISBN 978 0 352 34104 4
☐ BURNING BRIGHT Janine Ashbless   ISBN 978 0 352 34085 6
☐ CRUEL ENCHANTMENT Janine Ashbless   ISBN 978 0 352 33483 1
☐ DIVINE TORMENT Janine Ashbless   ISBN 978 0 352 33719 1
☐ FLOOD Anna Clare   ISBN 978 0 352 34094 8
☐ GOTHIC BLUE Portia Da Costa   ISBN 978 0 352 33075 8
☐ THE PRIDE Edie Bingham   ISBN 978 0 352 33997 3
☐ THE TEN VISIONS Olivia Knight   ISBN 978 0 352 34119 8

BLACK LACE ANTHOLOGIES

☐ BLACK LACE QUICKIES 1 Various   ISBN 978 0 352 34126 6   £2.99
☐ BLACK LACE QUICKIES 2 Various   ISBN 978 0 352 34127 3   £2.99
☐ BLACK LACE QUICKIES 3 Various   ISBN 978 0 352 34128 0   £2.99
☐ BLACK LACE QUICKIES 4 Various   ISBN 978 0 352 34129 7   £2.99
☐ BLACK LACE QUICKIES 5 Various   ISBN 978 0 352 34130 3   £2.99
☐ BLACK LACE QUICKIES 6 Various   ISBN 978 0 352 34133 4   £2.99
☐ MORE WICKED WORDS Various   ISBN 978 0 352 33487 9   £6.99

To find out the latest information about Black Lace titles, check out the website: www.black-lace-books.com or send for a booklist with complete synopses by writing to:

Black Lace Booklist, Virgin Books Ltd
Thames Wharf Studios
Rainville Road
London W6 9HA

Please include an SAE of decent size. Please note only British stamps are valid.

Our privacy policy
We will not disclose information you supply us to any other parties. We will not disclose any information which identifies you personally to any person without your express consent.

From time to time we may send out information about Black Lace books and special offers. Please tick here if you do <u>not</u> wish to receive Black Lace information. ❏

Please send me the books I have ticked above.

Name ....

Address ....

....

....

....

Post Code ....

Send to: Virgin Books Cash Sales, Thames Wharf Studios, Rainville Road, London W6 9HA.

US customers: for prices and details of how to order books for delivery by mail, call 888-330-8477.

Please enclose a cheque or postal order, made payable to Virgin Books Ltd, to the value of the books you have ordered plus postage and packing costs as follows:

UK and BFPO – £1.00 for the first book, 50p for each subsequent book.

Overseas (including Republic of Ireland) – £2.00 for the first book, £1.00 for each subsequent book.

If you would prefer to pay by VISA, ACCESS/MASTERCARD, DINERS CLUB, AMEX or SWITCH, please write your card number and expiry date here:

....

Signature ....

Please allow up to 28 days for delivery.